"Harper St. George never misses! *The Stranger I Wed* delivers everything I love about historical romance—a marriage of convenience that erupts into a red-hot passion; two characters who grow to love and respect each other; and a thoughtful discussion of political and social issues that are still relevant to this day. In one word, *The Stranger I Wed* is magic!"

—*USA Today* bestselling author Liana De la Rosa

"A sexy, emotional, romantic tale . . . Harper St. George is a must-buy for me!"

—*USA Today* bestselling author Terri Brisbin
on *The Heiress Gets a Duke*

"*The Stranger I Wed* by Harper St. George is a delicious start to a new series, with all of my favorite things—a marriage of convenience, scandalous family secrets, and feisty American heroines who bring too-handsome aristocrats to their knees. A fantastic, fast-paced read by one of the best historical writers around!"   —*USA Today* bestselling author Joanna Shupe

"Wit, seduction, and passion blend seamlessly to create this deeply emotional romance. St. George weaves an intriguing plot with complex characters to provide the perfect sensual escape. There's nothing I didn't love about *The Heiress Gets a Duke*, especially its lush, captivating glimpse into history."

—*USA Today* bestselling author Anabelle Bryant

"With sizzling chemistry, brilliant banter, and an unapologetically strong, feminist heroine, Harper St. George sets the pages ablaze!"

—*USA Today* bestselling author Christi Caldwell
on *The Lady Tempts an Heir*

"Fun, tender, and definitely sexy, *The Heiress Gets a Duke* is already at the top of my list for the best books of the year. Don't sleep on this refreshing and feminist romance."
—*BookPage* (starred review)

"Harper St. George just gets better and better with every book, penning the kind of page-turning stories that you will want to read again as soon as you finish each one."
—Lyssa Kay Adams, author of the Bromance Book Club series

"A rich, compelling, and beautifully written romance. St. George brings us the story of Violet Crenshaw, an American heiress with distinctly modern ideas about love and marriage."
—Elizabeth Everett, author of *The Love Remedy*, on *The Devil and the Heiress*

"Luscious historical romance."   —PopSugar

"Rich with period detail, *The Heiress Gets a Duke* brings to life the Gilded Age's dollar princesses in this smart, sexy, and oh-so-satisfying story."
—Laurie Benson, award-winning author of the Sommersby Brides series

"You'll sigh, you'll cry, and you'll grin yourself silly as this independent and cynical heiress finally gets her duke."
—Virginia Heath, author of *Never Wager with a Wallflower*, on *The Heiress Gets a Duke*

ELIZA AND THE DUKE

HARPER ST. GEORGE

BERKLEY ROMANCE
NEW YORK

BERKLEY ROMANCE
Published by Berkley
An imprint of Penguin Random House LLC
1745 Broadway, New York, NY 10019
penguinrandomhouse.com

Book design by George Towne

Library of Congress Cataloging-in-Publication Data

Names: St. George, Harper, author.
Title: Eliza and the Duke / Harper St. George.
Description: First edition. | New York: Berkley Romance, 2025. |
Series: The Doves of New York ; 2
Identifiers: LCCN 2024034573 (print) | LCCN 2024034574 (ebook) |
ISBN 9780593441022 (trade paperback) | ISBN 9780593441039 (ebook)
Subjects: LCGFT: Romance fiction. | Novels.
Classification: LCC PS3619.T236 E45 2025 (print) |
LCC PS3619.T236 (ebook) | DDC 813/.6—dc23/eng/20240809
LC record available at https://lccn.loc.gov/2024034573
LC ebook record available at https://lccn.loc.gov/2024034574

First Edition: June 2025

Printed in the United States of America
1st Printing

The authorized representative in the EU for product safety and compliance is
Penguin Random House Ireland, Morrison Chambers, 32 Nassau Street,
Dublin D02 YH68, Ireland, https://eu-contact.penguin.ie.

*To Laurie Benson for helping me
bring my heiresses to life.*

You are the best.

You pierce my soul. I am half agony, half hope. Tell me not that I am too late, that such precious feelings are gone for ever. I offer myself to you again with a heart even more your own than when you almost broke it . . .

FROM *Persuasion* BY JANE AUSTEN

ONE

Bloomsbury, London
Late Spring 1878

A YOUNG WOMAN IN SEARCH OF A HUSBAND SHOULD not go wandering the halls of Montague Club. This was particularly true if the young woman in question was only pretending to be a gently bred American heiress. Any hint of scandal could not easily be absorbed by a centuries-long family lineage that didn't exist.

Eliza Dove knew that. She knew it in her bones. The problem was that, sometimes, once an idea took hold, she had trouble reining it in. Her bad angel always seemed to be more persuasive than her good angel.

This is how she found herself searching for the nearly imperceptible crease where the hidden door that would lead her to the club met the wall. The door was covered in wallpaper and made to look like part of the corridor. She wouldn't have noticed it at all except she'd seen a man in livery pass through it only moments ago. Her fingertips slid over the wall, fingernails trailing over the scarlet-and-gold wallpaper in search of the break in texture. She found it right at the edge of a section of molding, exactly where she thought it would be. There had to be a way to open it.

Aha! Her thumb brushed against a gilded latch that was disguised in a section of gold pattern on the wallpaper. She very gently gave it a tug and the door swung toward her. Victory pumped through her veins, along with a fair amount of wine from dinner. She paused to make certain no one saw her and to give fate a moment to catch up and intervene. No one happened by, and the twinge of guilt that made itself known was so puny it might not have existed at all.

Camille, the Dowager Duchess of Hereford, was Eliza's sponsor for the Season. The widow was engaged to one of the proprietors of Montague Club, Mr. Jacob Thorne, who just happened to live in an elegant home attached to the establishment. The couple had invited Eliza, her sister Jenny, and their mother over for dinner. Eliza had only seen the secret entrance because everyone was enjoying dessert in Mr. Thorne's salon when Eliza had excused herself to use the facilities and went exploring on her way back to the group. She probably hadn't been meant to see the servant using the entrance, but now that she had, there was no way she was passing up an opportunity to get a glimpse at a real gaming club.

What could it hurt to take a peek, especially if no one saw her?

She hurried through the doorway, making certain that the door shut behind her, and found herself in a service corridor. The narrow hallway was rather plain and unadorned except for gas sconces that dimly lit the space. Her excitement dampened, though it made sense that the corridor would exist if Mr. Thorne utilized the club's servants for his own household.

Luckily, there were doors on the opposite wall, which she was certain would lead her into the club. Now that she had come this far, she couldn't turn back without seeing something. The doors on this side had visible handles and were not camouflaged into the wall, since they needed to be seen and easily accessible for the servants who would likely have their hands full. Pressing her ear against the first door she came upon, she listened for noise. There were voices, but it sounded like revelry coming from deeper in the club. She slowly opened the door and peeked inside to find a very wide and extravagant hall.

It was like stepping into another world. The walls were white with opulent gilded molding broken up by swaths of scarlet wallpaper. The molding continued all the way to the recessed ceiling where each section was inlaid with gold. Fine paintings of landscapes lined the wall in either direction.

Like the infamous White's, London's oldest gentleman's club, Montague was notorious for its card tables, smoking rooms, and extensive collection of priceless wines and whiskies. Unlike White's, Montague allowed women into its membership. Eliza had hoped to step into a gaming room or, at the very least, a lounge with men and women draped about in various stages of discussion, debate, or debauchery. Any one of them would have satiated her curiosity.

But all wasn't lost. While one direction led to a window that no doubt overlooked the street, the other way led to sounds of merriment. Male voices rose in excitement, likely at a gaming table. Other voices could be heard singing out of tune, but no one seemed to mind. They kept right on singing. She could see a railing not twenty feet away from her. She'd only take a quick look and then run right back to Mr. Thorne's residence.

The secret door behind her had been made to look like the wall with panels of white wood obscuring the entrance. She made note of the location of the hidden latch and set off toward the railing. As long as she kept to herself and generally out of sight, no one would notice her. She only wanted to observe.

Eliza soon found herself in a gallery of sorts. It encircled the room below it, which was one of the gaming rooms. A quick look over the balustrade revealed the gaiety below. A crowd of mostly men, but a few women, gathered around tables playing various games. The table with the loudest spectators had a wooden wheel set into it. The wheel seemed to be divided up into many compartments with painted numbers in alternating colors of red and white. A man wearing an elegant evening suit spun the wheel. The small white marble made a feather-soft *whirrrrrr*, zipping around the circle of numbered compartments, and then the wheel slowed, stopped, and the ball-of-chance landed with a *clink-clink-clunk* in number twenty-two. Another cheer went up from several of the men while the others exclaimed in dismay.

She watched for two more spins, silently wagering on where the marble would land, but the stubborn wheel thwarted her every time. Finally, one of the patrons glanced up and caught her watching. He murmured to his friend next to him, who also looked up at her. She might be impulsive at times, but she was no fool. When one of them stood as if he meant to come upstairs, it was her signal to go.

She sprinted to the secret door and hurried inside. When she pulled it closed, she was shaking with laughter at her own audacity. That might have been the most reckless thing she had done since she and her family had arrived in London.

Determined to make her way back to the residence without getting caught, Eliza turned to dart through the door that would take her back to the dinner party but ran into a solid wall of muscle instead. The impact nearly knocked the breath from her. The man grunted but didn't move.

"Pardon me," she said, and backed up against the club door to create space between them. The corridor was very narrow, not large enough for two people to stand abreast easily.

The man didn't say anything. In fact, he seemed to be leaning against the wall awkwardly, using it for support. He was dressed entirely in black with his hat low over his forehead, his jaw tight, his chin unshaven, his arms wrapped around his middle as if holding in pain.

"Are you injured?" she asked, but he didn't respond.

Where had he come from? He leaned heavily against the door that would take her back to Mr. Thorne's residence, but she didn't think he had come from there. She had no clue where the service corridor might lead or how he had come to be in it or why he stood blocking her path. He wasn't dressed like a servant. His coat was finespun wool, and his boots had a sheen that made them appear to be of the highest quality.

"Do you need—?"

Before she could finish, he moved, a sound like a groan rumbling deep in his chest. His steps took him down the corridor away from her, though he continued to lean on the wall. His hat fell to the floor behind him, and she picked it up.

"Your hat!"

He paused again, but she didn't think it was because he had heard her. He rested his head back against the wall, breathing shallowly. When she took the few steps needed to reach him, he didn't acknowledge her in any way. The light from a nearby sconce bathed his face. He was young, likely in his twenties; older than her but younger than Mr. Thorne. A thick shock of dark hair fell over his forehead. Pale skin was pulled tight over a face that was too coarse to be conventionally handsome but too interesting to be common. His eyes were closed in obvious pain.

"You are injured," she said.

His eyes glittered when he opened them, but he didn't seem to see her. They were glazed in a look she had seen once before. Years ago in New York, her mother had had a male friend over to visit. He'd spent the evening drinking and smoking a pipe that had left a sweet smell in the air. By the time he had left, his eyes had been glazed like marbles and he had regarded her without focusing on her face. This man's eyes had the same look, but whether it was from intoxication or pain or some mixture of both, Eliza couldn't tell.

The injury seemed to originate from his midsection, so she dropped his hat and gently attempted to open his coat. He allowed her ministrations by easing the grip of his arms, and she parted the wool and gasped aloud. He was shirtless. His chest was broad and solid with well-developed muscles. That alone might have been enough to surprise her under normal circumstances, but it was the gore that made her catch her breath. Streaks of blood crisscrossed his chest and stomach. There were knicks in his skin, but she couldn't tell if those were the source of all the blood. Some of it had dried to blotches of black, but there were patches of crimson smears near his shoulders. His ribs were mottled with what would likely become bruises as the night wore on.

"You need a physician," she whispered. The club must have someone on staff who could be called upon to handle medical issues. If not, then a doctor could be sent for.

The man only grunted in acknowledgment of her words and pushed forward. It seemed it took all of his concentration to stay mostly upright as he continued down the hall. She made to put an arm around him to assist him.

"No." It was the first word he'd said and was spoken in a low and gravelly tone that gave her pause.

"I can help you," she insisted.

"No."

Standing upright again, she looked at him with growing annoyance. "Who are you?"

"Who'm I?" He might have laughed. She wasn't sure how to interpret the chortle that barely made it out of his chest before he swallowed it. "I'm the Duke, milady."

A duke?

He didn't give her a chance to respond as he continued down the hall, his shoulder pressed to the wall to keep himself upright. This time an arm trailed behind him, exposing his scraped knuckles.

What had he been up to tonight, and what did he mean by calling himself that? He wasn't a duke. Although his accent was decidedly English, it lacked the crisp drawl she had come to associate with the aristocracy. The word *duke* wasn't spoken with the *dj* sound that so many of them seemed to use, and the words *who* and *am* had slid into one.

Light seeped in beneath the secret door that led to Mr. Thorne's residence. Her good angel urged her to *open, open, open* that door. It would lead her to safety and to a life where a very well-qualified nobleman would marry her at the end of summer to gain her inheritance.

Her hand hesitated on the latch. Safe was almost always boring.

Sensing weakness, her bad angel rose to the task of leading Eliza astray and urging her to follow the strange man. He was already halfway down the corridor and a million miles away from the monotonous life that had been laid out for her. It would take her five minutes to find out who he was and where he was going. His destination couldn't be that far. If she was quick, no one would be the wiser and her boring life would be waiting for her.

She followed him.

TWO

ELIZA CREPT AFTER THE INJURED MAN FEELING A little like Alice following the White Rabbit down the rabbit hole. The narrow passage took a sharp turn, and the man walked toward the very last door. He obviously meant to go inside that one, but before he could, he stumbled and would have fallen if she hadn't rushed to catch him.

"I have you," she murmured as he groaned in pain.

His arm looped around her shoulder, this time eager to accept her help. Bloody fingers with their busted knuckles gripped at her body like a lifeline. She faintly wondered if they would leave stains that she wouldn't be able to explain, but the thought was whisked away as he nearly fell forward again. It took all of her strength and concentration to keep them upright. Even then, they managed to bump up against the door.

It opened immediately, as if the inhabitant inside the room had been waiting for him. A man stared down at them with an expression of wild incomprehension. The thick, ruddy skin of his face crumpled as his brows drew together and his eyes darted back and forth between her and the invalid. Eliza couldn't blame him for his momentary confusion. She knew her own expression must mirror it back at him. Her heart fluttered like a caught rodent's. Was he friend or foe?

Someone had to say something. "Do you know this man?" she asked the stranger in the doorway.

To his credit, he didn't hesitate to take ownership of him. "Course I do, ma'am." To the invalid leaning heavily on her he said, "Simon, you bloody twat, get in 'ere!" A powerful hand accompanied the gruff voice and yanked him inside, relieving her of the burden.

Simon. His name was Simon. For some reason it was very important that she knew his name.

The door would have closed behind them if Eliza hadn't rushed forward to catch it. There was no way she was leaving without solving at least a little of this mystery. With a glance at the deserted corridor, she promised herself that she would stay only a minute and closed the door behind her.

The room was a lounge of sorts. It was a fairly large space, at least as large as Mr. Thorne's dining room. The walls were a rich brown, and that color was echoed in the rugs that were shot with threads of crimson and gold. Oil paintings of hunting scenes dotted the walls all the way to the ceiling, except for one wall that was almost entirely covered in chalkboards with white scribbling and tick marks all over them.

Closed double doors were directly across from her. They would no doubt lead to the club. She noted the key was turned, which would lock them in. Good, no one would wander in and find her here. Several groups of small tables and upholstered chairs were set around the room. An intricately carved mahogany bar loaded with various liquors occupied an entire corner. A scarlet sofa faced the hearth, and this is where the room's occupant deposited Simon.

Simon groaned in pain. Her heart twisted for him. Whoever the man was that had helped him inside didn't seem to be the least bit gentle.

"D-do you know what's happened to him?" she asked.

Simon's friend—she was fairly certain he was friend and not foe, at least to Simon—grunted but he didn't answer her. He tore open Simon's coat and clucked his tongue at the welts of rapidly forming bruises. "Simon, me boy, how much?"

Simon opened his eyes. They were blue, and they reminded her of the sea, deep and fathomless. To her amazement, he grinned. He had a gold eyetooth and it winked at her in the gaslight. "A hundred quid."

The man exclaimed, jumped back, and landed a blow to Simon's shoulder, but then he laughed so she took this to mean he was happy. Simon groaned again from the shock of the blow but his smile broadened. She was terribly confused.

His friend began patting Simon down, as if looking for a hidden pocket in his coat. "Where is it?"

"Me ones and twos. Where else?" Simon answered.

Seeming to understand this, the man switched his focus to Simon's boots. Simon lay there in a daze staring at the ceiling as his friend quickly and none-too-gently unlaced his boot.

"Simon," she said, finally addressing the invalid himself, and taking a few steps closer. His dark hair, longer than was fashionable, had broken free of its pomade and now fell back over the arm of the sofa leaving his face exposed. There was a cut over his cheekbone, beneath his eye, and another over his brow, and the flesh was swelling, promising a black eye come morning. His bottom lip was split, as well. He'd clearly been in a fight. "What happened to you?"

He jerked at the sound of her voice and turned his head until his eyes met hers. His pupils were dilated, making the irises a slim swirl of indigo and midnight, and he seemed to have trouble focusing on her.

"Milady," he said.

She didn't bother to correct him. "Who did this to you?"

"Mum your dubber, mate." Simon's friend paused long enough to speak, give her a warning glare, and then went back to unlacing Simon's boot. He'd already rid him of the right, and now he was on to the left one.

Eliza had never heard that phrase before, but she knew the man had warned Simon about giving her any information, or perhaps he had warned him against talking to her altogether.

"What is your name, sir?" she asked the man unlacing Simon's boot.

She caught him glance at her from the corner of his eye. She didn't think he was going to answer, but then he said, "Dunn."

"Should we send for the police, Mr. Dunn? This man looks a fright."

Mr. Dunn was already shaking his head. "No, no police."

He pulled off Simon's boot and held it aloft, upside down. A roll of bills fell out and dropped to the floor. A hundred pounds, she'd guess. His eyes widened in glee before he scooped the bills up and thumbed through them.

Growing irritated, she said, "A physician, then. He needs medical care."

"No, we'll get 'im fixed up."

Mr. Dunn was proving himself to be of little help.

"Simon, do you need me to send for a doctor?" His gaze had already drifted unfocused to the ceiling again, so she reached out to touch his chin and gain his attention. The stubble on his jaw scraped the pads of her fingers in a way that was not completely unpleasant.

"Don't bother yourself, milady. I'll be better after a sleep."

His coat had fallen open to reveal the terrible trauma he had endured. "At the very least you need to bind your ribs." She knew next to nothing about medical care, but it seemed logical.

He moved to sit upright and let out a groan. "'Tis not that bad." Upright probably wasn't the best way to describe how he leaned to the left. "I won the quid and 'tis all that matters."

"You won? Did you fight for money?"

"The only reason to fight there is." He wasn't smiling anymore, but he had the aura of someone who was very pleased with himself.

"This . . ." She indicated the mess of his body. The bruised, likely broken, ribs. The swollen face. The lacerations that were too numerous to count. "This is for money? One hundred pounds?" She couldn't conceive of that amount being worth the damage. Not that she had grown up with money. She and her mother and sisters had scraped by with very little extra, but this wasn't worth it.

"Drink." Mr. Dunn pressed a flask of what she felt certain was full of alcohol into Simon's hand, and he dutifully drank down a healthy portion. To her, Mr. Dunn said, "Shouldn't you be going, miss?" He pointedly looked down at her dinner gown. "Someone must be missing you."

He was right. She had been here for far too long as it was, but she had learned shockingly little and her curiosity was running rampant. "But . . ."

"Go on with ye, milady," Simon said. "I'll be well."

He did seem a bit better. His gaze seemed to be focused on

her again, and he wasn't staring at the ceiling. "Are you certain?" she asked because she simply couldn't leave yet.

His answer was to sing. *"She's as sweet as a rosebud, and lily flow'r chang'd into one. And who would not love such a beauty, like an Angel dropp'd from above."* It sounded like a jaunty music hall tune. Even inebriated, his voice wasn't half-bad. He paused in his singing to ask, "Are ye my guardian angel? Wot's yer name?"

She shouldn't tell him, but something out of her control made her say it. "Eliza."

He smiled up at her. The joy and admiration in his face at such an inopportune time and situation brought her up short. There was a charisma about him that made her breath catch.

"There ye go." Mr. Dunn interjected himself between them and wrenched Simon's coat off his shoulder. Simon helped him as he was able and together they got it off him. "If yer going to stay, ye might as well help." Mr. Dunn nodded toward a bolt of cotton on the floor next to the sofa that she had missed seeing.

She walked over to pick it up, and Mr. Dunn directed her in how to get it started. Together they wrapped it around him with Mr. Dunn pulling it tight and Eliza skirting it around Simon's ribs with him balanced between them. Simon wobbled as they worked and continued to sing under his breath, *"If ever I cease to love,"* over and over again with an endless list of ridiculous consequences. *"If ever I cease to love may cows lay eggs, may I be frozen to death with heat,* or *may we all turn into cats and dogs."*

When they were done, Mr. Dunn said, "Have to get the coat back on him so no one's the wiser when we walk to his room."

She didn't see how it was possible that no one would notice

his swollen face but didn't mention it. "In there?" She pointed toward the double doors. "He lives in the club?"

Mr. Dunn didn't answer her as he struggled to pull the coat back on him and button it. Eliza let her gaze roam the room again, looking for some clue to who Simon was. He must be employed by the club. She searched the blackboard filled with writing that she had noticed earlier, but she didn't see the name Simon written there. She did, however, see the name Mainwaring, her fiancé. She looked closer and realized his name was part of a large chart.

A vertical list of names was written, including Mainwaring and the men he traveled with to the Continent. Horizontally, there was a list of women's names: Maria Antoinetta, Lucia, Paolina, Giulia; the list went on with multiple tick marks beneath them, which corresponded to the men. Mainwaring had tick marks next to his name beneath three women.

"What is this list?" She turned back to the men. They were now standing by the sofa and Mr. Dunn was supporting Simon as they headed toward the door. At her question, they paused.

"The blokes in It'ly," Simon said.

"A tour o' coffeehouses," Mr. Dunn elaborated.

"Coffeehouses? Why would that be noteworthy?" It didn't make sense. Why were the coffeehouses in Italy given women's names?

Unease swirled through her stomach. Wouldn't there be only one reason those men's names would be associated with women? A white-hot heat made her face flame. She and Mainwaring were meant to marry when he returned at the end of the summer.

Simon sighed. "Wagers on how many courtesans the young

lads will conquer on their trip. I'm winnin' . . . so far." He smiled broadly.

Winning? Betrayal and anger and humiliation warred for dominance. She and Mainwaring were by no means a love match, but she found it difficult to swallow that he would philander his way through Europe before their wedding. It was unseemly. Is this what marriage to him meant? She had assumed they would live a quiet life of comfort together. There would be no great passion, but she had deemed that an acceptable trade for stability. She had assumed she would be due a modicum of respect as his fiancée.

Perhaps this was all wrong. How did they even know the men were visiting these women? "How do you know? They haven't returned yet." And weren't due back for a couple months.

"They wire their progress. The numbers are accurate because we always check with the houses. Why? Do you want to place a bet?" Mr. Dunn inquired, eyes alight at the prospect of adding to the pot.

They wired their progress! "No, and I can't believe you would, either." Her voice sounded sharper than she intended. The tone of a scorned woman.

He shrugged, completely uncaring or unaware that she was going through a crisis.

"I should go," she said. She couldn't risk someone seeing her when they opened the door to the club, though the prospect of being caught made a glimmer of hope perk up inside her. If she was caught, then she wouldn't have to go forward with this marriage. It would serve him right. It would serve everyone right for arranging the marriage to begin with. That thought was accompanied by a wave of guilt. Her sisters didn't deserve the scandal that would fall on the heels of her being caught in a gaming hell.

Mr. Dunn nodded and waited for her to reach the door to the corridor. "Goodbye, Mr. Dunn. Simon."

Mr. Dunn ignored her, but Simon looked back. "Goodbye, Angel."

With that word echoing in her head, she left the rabbit hole behind and hurried back to her life. Her perfectly boring life.

THREE

SIMON'S FORMER LIFE WASN'T READY TO LET HIM GO. He knew that because it came after him frequently. In that life, he had been a punisher. James Brody, the man who ran Whitechapel, had paid him to bend people to his will. Often those people were far from innocent, but their guilt wasn't something Simon had been allowed to question. For a long time it hadn't even occurred to him to question it. Brody had been like a father to him, the only one he'd ever had. Questioning him had been akin to questioning God. Except, in many ways, Brody was higher than God. God had left him and Mary to die on the street. Brody had fed and sheltered them.

His body still aching from last week's fight, he gingerly made his way through Whitechapel's warren of alleyways. Memories of the phantom woman he'd encountered in the club's corridor pushed at the edges of his mind. That's how he thought of her . . . a ghost or an angel, because he remembered so little about her. She might not have been real, except he'd asked Dunn about her and the man had indeed confirmed her existence. Simon had no idea who she was, and Dunn couldn't remember if she'd given her name. She had dark hair and pale skin and she fit nicely under his arm. Trying to pin her down more made her dissipate like vapor, which was as it should be. His life was too complicated for a woman who smelled like roses and felt like heaven in his arms.

The pub with a wooden sign of a faded red rooster and a lamp hanging from a hook at the bottom loomed ahead. A hollow opened up inside him, pushing all thoughts of the elusive woman aside. That bloody rooster used to signal home for him. It meant security and acceptance. Now it meant the opposite. Every time he went in, a small part of him wondered if he'd ever come out again.

The lantern gave off an oily light that only barely managed to penetrate the thick and humid night. The air here was cloying in a way it wasn't in Bloomsbury where Montague Club was located. Simon hadn't noticed the difference until he'd been away from this part of the city for a few weeks. The moment he'd returned, he'd felt the air heavy around his legs and wrists, seeping into his pores as if identifying him as one of its own and attempting to reclaim him.

Inside, the pub was dimly lit by lanterns and a low fire in the stone hearth. A long rectangular bar joined the two rooms that made up the main area of the pub. Simon recognized the man working behind it and nodded a greeting. Smith raised his chin and indicated the door at the far end of the room. Brody was waiting for him.

A bruiser he recognized as one of Brody's personal men sat near the door. No one was getting through there without his say-so. He nodded, and Simon took a deep breath and stepped through the passageway. The door opened to a narrow and uneven hallway. It had a distinct downward grade that led under the street and to the cellar of the building there.

Brody liked to brag that the room had served as a dungeon a few hundred years ago, but it was now an office of sorts where the man conducted his business out of sight. The ceiling was low and the walls felt like they closed in around him, though it did feel strangely like coming home. If home was a dungeon where vipers waited to tear their fangs into your flesh.

"Cavell." Brody sat at a desk scattered with papers.

A long table was set off to the right. Men usually sat there divvying up opium, whisky, or vodka . . . whatever vice Brody was selling at the time. Tonight it was empty.

Simon's gaze automatically went to the other corner behind the desk. He and his sister, Mary, had spent many nights there as children, huddled under a shared blanket, trying to sleep on the stone floor. His stomach churned uncomfortably at the memory.

"Brody," he said, and forced his attention back to the man.

Brody wore a bespoke suit that fit him well, and his hair was greased back. His hairline had receded some from when Simon had first met him. His usual cigar was clamped between his teeth. He might have been handsome in another life, in another place. He might have been a decent person. Here there wasn't time or space for such niceties. Beauty withered and died before it ever had a chance to bloom.

"I expected ye hours ago, lad."

"Came as soon as I could," Simon answered.

Simon made the trip to Brody's hideout on the first of every month to make good on his debt. Lately, a suspicion had begun to creep in that maybe he'd never be able to pay it off.

"That's right. Yer a bleeding working man now."

Brody's eyes held a challenge that Simon refused to accept. It was a point of contention between them that Simon had chosen to walk away. The fact that he would rather work a shift for *bleedin' blue bloods* than stay with Brody had very nearly got him killed in the early days. They had since come to a stalemate about it, but it was tenuous at best, and it was the reason Simon was here with money. Brody reasoned that Simon owed him bucketfuls to repay him for taking him and Mary in off the street. If Simon wasn't going to pay him back by fighting for him, then he'd take his payment in cash.

Reaching into a hidden pocket inside his coat, Simon pulled out a roll of banknotes and tossed them onto the desk. "A little more than a hundred quid." All of his winnings from the fight and the extra he'd been able to add in from his pay. He kept only what he needed to clothe himself to Montague's high standards as the club's manager. A small portion went to the care of Mary's daughter and the rest went to Brody. He nodded toward the roll and waited as Brody untied the twine and counted the rumpled bills.

"Good." Brody pulled out the ledger he used for recording personal debts and made the proper notations with a pencil. Lines of payments on Simon's sheet stared back at him. Money that Brody gobbled up like a greedy piglet.

Every time he saw the notations they made him angry. He had already paid thousands of pounds on a debt that was bollocks. Simon had no choice but to pay it, however, because Brody kept Daisy a hostage to his greed. Daisy, Simon's niece, who had done nothing other than be born to the wrong mother. When Mary died, Simon had already been detaching himself from Whitechapel. Brody had wasted no time in using the girl to his advantage to attempt to lure Simon back.

"How much is left on my debt?"

Brody arched a brow. "Some." He closed the ledger and sat back in his chair. He had no intention of answering the question.

The bloody bastard was too arrogant for his own good. He could drag this out for years, and there was little Simon could do about it if he wanted Daisy.

"Then I'll bid you good night," he said, unwilling to play the groveling victim for Brody. He knew from experience it never got results.

"Wait. Ye look to be healed enough from the last brawl. How 'bout ye sign up for another?" Brody's eyes glittered from across the desk. He was a predator who came alive at the scent of blood.

As a matter of fact, Simon wasn't healed from the last fight. It had only been a week ago. His ribs were wrapped and bruised. His face still showed signs of the brawl. He needed at least another fortnight to recover, but he knew that showing weakness to Brody would be a mistake.

"Thorne is away and I'm in charge of the club. Now isn't the best time."

"Heard he's in Paris. Sounds like the perfect time to go out. Yer guv'nor won't be the wiser and ye'll be at least a hundred quid richer . . . well, a hundred quid plus the gambling take closer to paying yer debt and the little girl's freedom."

Pain darted through his chest. Brody knew she was his weakness. She should not be a part of Brody's games, but she was the only hold the man had over him and they both knew it. The quicker he got her away from Brody's clutches, the better.

"I want double."

"Double would be 'alf of my take." He did not look pleased.

"I deserve more than half your take." Simon did the work in this arrangement, after all.

Sensing he might have gone too far, Brody raised a hand, palm up, for peace. "Ye want more? I'm working on something bigger."

"Bigger? How big?"

"Big enough that the winnings will more than cover your debt."

Simon's heart pounded at the base of his throat. "And you'll let me have Daisy?"

Brody nodded. "If all goes to plan."

"When? What's the plan?"

"I'll let ye know when the time's right. All's not been settled yet, but it will be soon."

"But I'll need to—"

"Not yet, Cavell." His voice had gone hard, as it often did when he was pushed too far. "I'll send word when I'm ready to talk more." He sat back down at his desk and Simon was dismissed.

Simon's hand fisted at his side as he made his way back through the corridor. Mary had died not long after Daisy was born, from a fever that had been relentless as it ravaged her body. Daisy's father was a miscreant, so she only had Simon. His entire life was dedicated to getting her out of this pit and away from Brody.

His distasteful task complete, he made his way back through the streets of Whitechapel to his suite at Montague Club. Only Dunn knew about his arrangement to fight for Brody. Since the owners of the club thought little of Brody and had in fact tangled unfavorably with him over the years, Simon had thought it best not to share his continued association with the underworld boss. He was able to explain his injuries by claiming they were from the private fighting lessons he offered to a few of the club's members. The more heinous injuries, like bruised ribs and black eyes, he told them came from being jumped by men in Whitechapel, which often wasn't a lie because it happened from time to time.

As he walked, his thoughts wandered back to the phantom woman. He'd never had a woman of his very own before. There had been girls aplenty. They had seduced him in his youth in the hopes of getting closer to Brody. Now they bedded him for the thrill of shagging a brawler. None of them had been his. He could still feel the impression of her at his side and see the concern in her eyes—even if he couldn't recall their color—when she'd looked up at him. If he ever did have one woman at his side it would be someone like her. Someone soft and kind who smelled of roses. Thoughts of her accompanied him the entire way back home.

He meant to go directly to his room when he returned, but one of the club's footmen met him when he arrived and informed him that Lords Leigh and Devonworth were waiting for him in a private drawing room. The Earl of Leigh owned the club along with his half brother, Jacob Thorne, who was in Paris at the moment. They shared a father, with Thorne being the illegitimate one. The Earl of Devonworth was a friend of the brothers. He'd called on Simon for help recently when his wife, one of the many American heiresses invading London lately, had been threatened by one of Brody's men. It was a problem he thought they had solved, but he wondered if that is what had them both here.

"My lords," Simon greeted them as he walked into the room, schooling his voice into a vague imitation of their posh accents. He'd been working the club for so long that the switch came naturally to him now.

The men were sat in oxblood leather chairs near the window, though it was quickly apparent that Devonworth was anything but relaxed. He sat forward with his elbows on his knees and his hands clasped together, a furrow on his brow.

"Cavell." Leigh smiled in greeting. He was around thirty years old with dark hair and gray eyes. He took up his cane—today's selection appeared to feature a silver wolf's head as the palm grip—and rose to his feet. Unlike several gentlemen who carried canes as a fashionable accessory, Leigh used his to aid his walking due to an old injury. He stepped toward Simon with a slight limp and said, "Devonworth tells me that you were quite heroic when it came to saving his wife from ruffians."

Brody's man had retaliated against Devonworth for a perceived slight by threatening his new bride in the park. Simon had . . . intervened. "It was nothing," Simon said.

"You saved Cora's life." Devonworth came to his feet. He was several years younger than Leigh and blond. He was known for having a penchant for solemnity, and his eyes were dead serious now. "Thank you, Cavell. I'll never be able to repay you." He looked like a man who had been utterly wrung out.

"I only did what had to be done." Devonworth had confronted the bastard. Simon had only come up from behind with a revolver. The man had all but crumbled after that.

"Nevertheless," Leigh put in, "it was commendable bravery."

Devonworth nodded in agreement. "I know that I have no right to it, but I've come to ask for another favor."

"What sort of favor?" Simon asked.

Devonworth took in a breath through his nose and waited, as if whatever he had to say would be a great burden. "Without going into the particulars, I've come across some rather delicate information on a political rival. He knows that I have this information and has made threats. Given what has so recently befallen Cora, well . . . I'd like to make certain that she and her family are protected."

"You want me to protect your wife?"

"Not precisely. I've arranged to conduct much of my work from home in the near future, and I can oversee my men while I'm there. I'd like you to watch out for her sisters and her mother. The Dowager Duchess of Hereford has graciously sponsored their entrance to Society and they are residing in her Mayfair residence, so I can't watch out for them as I'd like. I've offered to have them stay with Cora and me, but they prefer their own space. Would you manage their protection?"

Playing nursemaid to a group of spoiled Americans was the last thing Simon wanted to do, especially since Brody had promised him a fight on the horizon. "Thank you for thinking of me, but I'm not certain I'll have time with my duties here at the club."

"That's why he spoke to me first," Leigh said. "We'll be at loose ends without you, but we can survive for a bit."

"How long do you expect to need my help?" Simon asked Devonworth.

"A fortnight at most. Cora believes I'm being overly cautious, and I myself suspect the threat is hollow, but I'd not be able to live with myself if something happened to them."

"What of my training?" Simon asked Leigh. In addition to fighting for Brody, Simon participated in exhibition bare-knuckle brawls here at the club. He fought men from other clubs in a very gentlemanly display of violence that rarely ended with more than the odd bloody knuckle. The upside was that it paid very well.

"If you hire some men you trust, you should be able to slip away and use the club's facilities for an hour or two a day," Devonworth said.

"All right, then. I suppose I can't say no to that." The extra money would only help.

"Excellent." Devonworth's brow relaxed for the first time. "Good. I'd like you to start first thing tomorrow."

FOUR

"I CANNOT BELIEVE THAT DEVONWORTH IS SADDLING us with a protector."

Eliza tromped across the receiving room of Camille's home for the tenth time that morning to peer out the window that overlooked the street. She was waiting for her brother-in-law's carriage to appear at any moment. He had sent word that he would be bringing over the man who would be in charge of their security for the next couple of weeks. This would have been fine, except a man whose sole responsibility was to watch over them would most definitely hinder her plan to sneak back into Montague Club.

"Hmm," her sister Jenny muttered noncommittally from where she sat at the writing desk situated between the two windows. Nearly the entire flat surface was covered with porcelain miniatures of cherubs and angels, leaving Jenny precious little space to pen her letter. Honestly, she didn't know how Camille lived here. The whole house felt overbearing.

Without looking up from the paper, Jenny added, "Assigning someone to protect us does seem to be a bit of an over-reaction."

"A bit? A strange man will have access to our home at all hours of the day and night. Devonworth even implied that other men will be watching from outside. Strangers will be given leave to look into our windows, to come into our bed-rooms at will. Why, we'll have to lock our doors every night before we sleep."

Jenny paused her writing and pinned Eliza with her stare. "Devonworth is overreacting, but *that* is histrionics."

"It isn't!" Eliza shot back, even though she secretly agreed. Probably. She hadn't been thinking straight the past week. Ever since she'd run across that brawler named Simon, she'd been trying to figure out a way to get back into the club. The problem was that Mr. Thorne had gone to Paris where he was opening a new club, and Camille had gone with him. They were her only ties to the club. She couldn't very well show up and demand entry without ruining her reputation, which would mean the end of her marriage plans. She didn't particularly *want* to marry Lord Mainwaring, but she did want to collect her inheritance from Mr. Hathaway, and the two were a package deal.

Mr. Hathaway had made it very clear that she and her sisters would collect the money only if they married men he proclaimed suitable. Men like Devonworth who had a title and a long, respectable lineage. Lord Mainwaring had that and he'd offered for her and Mr. Hathaway had accepted. There was her future settled, except now she was questioning everything.

"Oh, I hate Mr. Hathaway." Eliza stomped her foot like a child.

Perhaps it was a harsh stance. The man *was* their father, not that many outside of their small family knew that. To the world he was their godfather, a kindly friend of the late Jeremiah Dove who had stepped in to help the Doves after the death of their patriarch. No one knew that their mother Fanny had been Mr. Hathaway's mistress.

When Mr. Hathaway's mother died last year, she had left the sisters a substantial, guilt-induced inheritance, but it came with a catch. It would only be doled out to each of them upon their marriage to a suitable man. Since Mr. Hathaway had wanted them as far away from New York and his *real* family as possible, suitable had come to mean a titled husband whom he could use to further his ambitions in Europe.

"Eliza, what's wrong?" Jenny sighed and set her pen back in the little stand. Then she pushed her chair back and rose with a look of resolve on her pretty face. "You've been acting distracted and odd all week. What does Mr. Hathaway have to do with anything?"

It was the only prompt Eliza needed. She needed to talk to someone about what had happened at Montague Club. "You have to swear on your life that you won't repeat to anyone what I'm about to tell you."

Jenny smiled at her. "Do I want my life to be on the hook for yet another secret? Let's see . . ." She looked up and to the right, appearing to catalog them all in her head. "Would this be on par with the night you sneaked out to go to that dance hall or is it more like the secret about you and Olek?"

Eliza could barely keep herself from shaking her sister. This was serious and Jenny was treating it like this was one of Eliza's indiscretions back home. Granted, those secrets had felt very serious at the time as well, but this was different. This was *now*.

"Let's say it's a combination of the two. The stakes aren't quite as high as the Olek one." She didn't fancy herself in love with this Simon fellow as she had with Olek, but what she was about to propose was much more dangerous than looking through the windows of a dancing hall. "But it does involve sneaking into somewhere." She lowered her voice on that admission and glanced around needlessly; they were alone, after all. Fanny was still upstairs asleep, and Camille's servants didn't know what to think of Americans so generally gave them a wide berth unless summoned, the same way they treated Camille.

"Oh, all right, you know I can't resist. I swear not to tell anyone, but it had better be good." Jenny's smile became conspiratorial as they settled themselves on a nearby settee.

"It's about that night we dined with Mr. Thorne."

Eliza explained everything that had happened after she'd disappeared into the wall. Well, almost everything. She left out the part about Simon calling himself the Duke. It seemed important to keep that part to herself, as if she was keeping a secret for him. She did tell her about that damned blackboard with Mainwaring's name, though it smarted a little to say it.

"Ugh!" Jenny scoffed. "That is the most disgusting thing I have ever heard. The nerve of that cad. What a little nincompoop." She went on with a string of insults for him, and that's when Eliza realized she was focusing on the wrong part of the story.

"Yes, yes, he is all of those things," Eliza said, hoping to hurry things along.

Jenny stopped mid-insult and frowned. "But?"

"The man that I followed . . ." How could she describe him? Seeing him had sparked something to life inside her. She'd spent these past months in England resigning herself to her future as a lady and she'd ignored everything she'd previously liked about herself. She was curious and she enjoyed learning new things. She wanted to know more about the secret fight he'd come from that night. She wanted to attend a secret fight. Ever since they'd come to London, however, she'd been forced to put on this persona of a mild-mannered wallflower.

The corners of Jenny's lips quirked upward and she nodded as if to say, *Now I see.* "This man piqued your interest, did he?"

"A little." She stopped short of admitting that she thought she might have seen him again a few days ago at Cora's home. A man had been accompanying Devonworth to his study, and he'd looked suspiciously like Simon. Unlike Simon, this man had been dressed finely and his hair had been styled differently. Eliza had seen him for only a moment, but she was almost certain it had been him. Her need to go back to Montague Club had been almost feverish ever since.

"Let me put this together, then," Jenny said. "You are hoping to sneak back into that club and you're upset because Devonworth's hired men will almost certainly keep you from doing that?"

"Precisely."

"Well, I hate to be the bearer of unwelcome tidings, but Devonworth is set in his plan, and you shouldn't be running back to that place anyway. You'll ruin your chances at a respectable marriage." Jenny paused and her eyes widened. "Unless you've decided that you don't want to marry Lord Mainwaring?"

"It's two hundred fifty thousand dollars, Jenny. I can't give up my rightful inheritance because my husband who I barely know anyway is off . . . having an adventure." She wanted to. God, how she wanted to, but it would be stupid.

Jenny had already decided that she would rather forfeit her

inheritance than marry a nobleman who wouldn't allow her to sing. She had spent the last several years in Paris living with a widowed friend of Fanny's learning the art of opera. She had been born with a beautiful voice, and it had only been refined and polished under Mrs. Wilson's tutelage. Her goal was to have a starring role in an opera soon, which was why she didn't want to marry. Not many aristocratic husbands would allow her to continue in that sort of career, or any career, actually.

Singing was her dream and the only thing she wanted to do with her life. Once Eliza was safely wed, Jenny would make her operatic debut in Paris. The odds of a suitable man marrying her after that would be greatly diminished, which meant that Eliza could not give up her own chance to secure her future. Jenny and their mother might need to rely on her fortune one day.

"I have to think of our future stability."

"Then why go back there?" Jenny asked.

"Now that I know that my future husband is enjoying his last summer of freedom, is it too much to ask that I have my own? I want to go out and see things before I'm stuck in some drafty manor house in the country with a lap blanket and a man with venereal disease."

Jenny laughed but then immediately sobered, contrite, when she saw that her sister wasn't joining in. Before she could say anything, the clip-clop of horseshoes on the cobblestones outside drew their attention to the window. Devonworth dashed out of the carriage as soon as it pulled to a stop, his blond hair bouncing with his step and his face set in a grim expression.

Eliza rose and Jenny followed suit.

"Perhaps this is a good thing," Jenny said in a gentle voice.

"It will save you from yourself. You should not go back to Montague Club."

Eliza's heart sank. If the one sister who generally condoned her every impulsive thought believed returning to Montague Club to track down the brawler would be a bad idea, then perhaps Eliza should accept that it was a bad idea. The door knocker sounded and Sampson, Camille's butler, shuffled from the back of the house and across the front hall to open the door.

Eliza took in a calming breath. Perhaps fate was saving her from herself. Lord Mainwaring could do as he liked and she simply didn't have that luxury. She would resume the role of a gently brought up young woman whose only dream in life was to marry well and rear children. Who cared that she wished to attend college? Lord Mainwaring certainly didn't. She'd mentioned the idea of women in higher education to him once and the corner of his mouth had turned up in what could only be described as a sneer.

This was for the best. It would clip her wings before she could do any real damage.

The butler greeted the men, and there was a fair bit of a clamor as they handed off their outerwear. Devonworth's voice came to them in the drawing room, clear and crisp, accustomed to being heard above the din of Parliament. Another voice answered him, a low baritone that vibrated through the walls, vibrated *inside* her. A quick glance to Jenny confirmed that it hadn't had a similar effect on her sister. She pushed it from her mind and tried to make out the words he spoke, but she couldn't.

It didn't matter. This man would be her jailer whether he knew it or not.

She despised him already.

Devonworth stepped into the room and offered them a cursory smile. "Jenny. Eliza." He kissed them both on the cheek in turn. He still treated them formally—he was a blue-blooded aristocrat, after all—but the kisses were his one concession to familiarity. "Cora told me that you're none too pleased with this arrangement. Thank you for humoring me."

Jenny muttered a polite reply, but Eliza stayed silent. She couldn't very well go on about how she hated this idea without raising suspicion, so she didn't say anything. Her brother-in-law took a step back and turned to the man he'd brought with him. She nearly gasped when she saw him. Unfashionably long dark hair tamed with pomade, deep blue eyes that scoped out the room as if an assailant might very well be lurking in a corner, and a nose that had been broken at least once.

It was Simon. He wore a three-piece suit similar in style to Devonworth's own suit, but there was no mistaking it was him. He still sported a bruise on his cheekbone, though it had faded to a greenish yellow. He was the man she'd seen in the service corridor at Montague Club *and* the man she'd glimpsed at Cora's house assisting Devonworth.

"This is Mr. Simon Cavell," Devonworth finished the introduction.

Simon Cavell. Simon.

Eliza couldn't stop the smile that spread across her face. Fate had brought him to her. It wasn't trying to rein her in, nor did it want to clip her wings. Fate had delivered Simon to her all but tied up with a bow.

"Good morning, Mr. Cavell." Eliza's smile did not dim as she held out her hand to him.

Cavell glanced from her to Devonworth and back again, undoubtedly confused by her warmth after being told she was cold to the whole idea of him. Left with no alternative, he took her hand. His fingers were strong beneath hers. He did not bring her hand to his lips as a gentleman might have done. Instead, one dark brow rose as he met her gaze head-on, a questioning intensity simmering in his eyes.

"Miss Eliza," he said.

"Mr. Cavell," Jenny cut in and offered her own hand.

He hesitated only a moment before letting go of Eliza to take her sister's hand, finally breaking their stare. "Good morning, Miss Dove," he said.

Devonworth was either too relieved that they weren't fighting him on this or too concerned about the minuscule threat of danger to notice. Introductions made, he sat them all down and briefly went through how their lives would change, which was to say that he didn't intend for them to. He explained that they would go about their day and Mr. Cavell would be there lurking in the shadows somewhere. When he wasn't there, his associate Mr. Cox, who also worked at Montague Club and was now outside taking in the perimeter of the house, would work in his place. While in the house, the Doves would hardly know the men existed after this little introduction. They only needed to give Mr. Cavell their schedule for the next day every evening when he came to lock the doors and windows down for the night.

Finally, Devonworth said, "If you'll excuse us, I'll take Cavell on a tour of the house. We won't be long."

"Of course," Eliza said, and watched them walk away.

Mr. Cavell glanced over his shoulder once, his brow furrowed as if he was trying to figure her out, as he followed Devonworth.

She couldn't wait to get him alone.

FIVE

WHO WAS ELIZA DOVE? SIMON RACKED HIS BRAIN, but he couldn't remember having any sort of interaction with the woman. He was almost certain he had seen her at Devonworth's residence a few days ago, but he'd barely acknowledged her then and they hadn't spoken. There was no reason she should be looking at him with such familiarity. A strange sort of triumph had come over her face when he'd walked into the drawing room. He almost got the feeling that she'd been waiting on him. Him, specifically, not some unknown bloke who would act as her protector. *Him.*

But why?

As he followed Devonworth through the depths of the house to all the various entrances, he did his best to pay attention as a niggling concern wormed its way through the back of his mind. She couldn't be the phantom woman. He couldn't imagine a situation in which she would have found herself in the club. Everyone knew that Lady Devonworth and her sisters had come to London to find husbands.

The newspapers hadn't been kind to the Americans since their arrival a few months earlier. There had been a particularly crude cartoon in one of them that showed the sisters standing with bags of cash behind them and a line of lords before them, except instead of human heads the men had been drawn with horse heads, preening like prized stallions so that the women would pick them. Eliza Dove would not have risked her reputation and a possible marriage to come into the club. She could not be that woman.

Thankfully, when they returned to the front entrance almost an hour later, there was no sign of her in the drawing room. An attractive woman who appeared to be in her forties stepped out, instead. She was dressed in a fashionable morning dress of olive green with her shining brown hair pulled up to artfully drape across her shoulder.

"Devonworth, the girls mentioned you were here." She sailed over and leaned up to kiss Devonworth's cheek. "This must be Mr. Cavell."

Devonworth made the introductions and Mrs. Dove held out her hand for him. "I've heard of you," she said in a way that might have been rude coming from anyone else. Her directness, however, was accompanied by a glint of good humor in her eye that softened her words. "They say you're quite the prizefighter."

It all clicked into place. Eliza must have heard about his reputation as a fighter. Montague Club had formed an informal league with several other clubs. Every few months or so they would arrange an exhibition bare-knuckle brawl for club members. Simon had quickly become a crowd favorite because he actually knew how to fight, unlike most of the gentleman participants who played at brawling. Several upper-class women, bored wives, had sought him out in the past year, hoping to see if his stamina in the ring translated to the bedroom. He'd been quite happy to show them that it did. She must have heard about his reputation and been keen to meet him.

That shouldn't have disappointed him, but it did. He was accustomed to people only being interested in the idea of him, without caring about who he really was. Why should one slip of a girl be any different?

He took Mrs. Dove's hand. "Undefeated, ma'am."

She nodded, suitably impressed. "Good, then I'll not worry about my girls. They'll be in your capable hands."

"I'll do my best to stay out of sight," he said.

"Don't do that. The place could use a livelier atmosphere, don't you think?"

It was rather stuffy and formal in here. Every tabletop was cluttered with bric-a-brac and curios, and the furniture was old and wouldn't hold up to Montague Club standards. As the Hereford dower house, it likely hadn't been updated in the past century.

Mrs. Dove was very clearly a woman who appreciated familiarity, so he said, "You liven it up all on your own, Mrs. Dove." He was accustomed to such talk with the few women who frequented the club.

She smiled at him in a way that lit up her entire face. She was quite beautiful. Glancing to her son-in-law, she said, "Oh, I do enjoy him, Devonworth."

Devonworth gave a long-suffering sigh. "Please, Fanny, don't interfere—"

"I wouldn't dream of interfering with his very important work." The tone she used implied she didn't think his work here was very important at all. "In fact, I am on my way out. Would you be available to drop me off at a friend's house for luncheon?"

"Of course," Devonworth agreed. "We were finishing here. Cavell, is there anything else?"

Simon assured him that things were well in hand and ushered them out the door. Then he turned to take the servants' stairs to the kitchen downstairs where he had a meeting set up to go over things with the staff. He'd need to meet them all and make certain that he understood their schedules and that they understood that under no circumstances would strangers be allowed inside the house.

He made it as far as the butler's pantry next to the dining room. The door to the stairwell was closed, and before he could open it, a voice stopped him cold.

"Hello again, Mr. Cavell."

He turned to see Eliza Dove, one arm raised to lean against the doorway. She wore the same rose-colored morning dress she'd had on earlier. It was pretty on her. She was pretty regardless, but it brought out a rosy tone in her cheeks and a golden glow in her skin. "Miss Eliza."

"You sound different." She smiled at him, that same knowing smile from earlier, and let her arm fall to her side, as if she'd only been leaning that way for some great effect that escaped him.

Different than when he'd met her an hour ago? "In what way do you mean?"

She took a few steps into the small space, which put her close enough that he could reach out and touch her. It was an interior room with counters and cupboards that ran the length of two walls. The other two walls held the door that led out and the door that led to the stairs. If she got it into her head to kiss him, then there would be nowhere for him to go. The idea of kissing her in itself wasn't repulsive, but he rather felt that it would be in bad form while he was working.

"I mean that on the evening we met, you sounded less formal and polished."

Had he met her at a fight, then? He could hardly believe that a debutante would attend a Montague Club fight. Besides, the last one had been months and months ago. By all accounts, the Doves had only arrived in England a few months back. She couldn't mean one of the fights Brody arranged. Those were always in far less fashionable areas.

"Forgive me, but I believe you've confused me for someone else," he said, and turned toward the door to the servants' stairs.

"You don't remember me, do you?"

The affectation was gone from her voice and she sounded genuinely amused now. She put her hand on his arm. Her fingers were long and gracefully formed. She wasn't wearing gloves, and there was nary a callus to be found on her fingers. But what struck him was the rose scent that wafted over him.

That scent was familiar. It was one of the few things that had stayed with him from that night a week ago. Rose water. Many women used it. Yet, even as he reminded himself of that, he looked back at her much as he imagined a deer that had been run to ground might gape at the hunter responsible, with fear and rounded eyes.

Sensing his alarm, she sobered and released him, holding her fingers spread wide as if to show him she wasn't a threat.

"We've never met." He stated it firmly so that she would understand the topic wasn't up for debate.

"But we have." She trampled all over the statement. "Last week. I met you in the service corridor at Montague Club and helped you get to your friend Mr. Du—"

He moved so fast that even he didn't know what he was doing until he held her pressed with her back against the stairwell door. He held her upper arms in a firm grip. Her brown eyes widened, but she seemed more intrigued than afraid.

"Promise me that you won't mention what happened that night to anyone." He kept his voice low.

The corner of her mouth twitched upward but she didn't smile. "Perhaps I want to tell."

"Then you'll give yourself away. I'll tell your parents about how you were sneaking around where you don't belong. I can say that a footman saw you."

"You clearly haven't met my mother." She had the nerve to smirk at him. Damn her. "She would quite enjoy my tale of that night. In fact, perhaps I'll go tell her."

She made to go around him and he pressed her back into place before him, one hand on her arm while the other shifted to her hip to hold her there. His fingers molded themselves to the curve of her body, and he tried to ignore how he quite liked the feel of her in his hands. She was firm but soft, small but strong. He could break her with his bare hands if he had a mind to, but hurting women had never been part of his job description, not even with Brody. Her sweet scent tugged at him, and his mind began to toy with thoughts of far more pleasant things he could do with her. She caught the change in him and her eyes widened. The antagonism between them shifted to something charged and needy. It was subtle but enough to make his breath waver. He reeled in those unruly thoughts and forced himself to focus on the very real danger at hand.

From what little he'd gleaned about Mrs. Dove from their brief interaction, he was afraid she was right. The woman had seemed unconventional. "Your father, then," he said. "No father of heiresses would condone one of them cavorting in a gentleman's club."

"Well, then it's a good thing I don't have one of those."

What sort of heiress didn't have a father? She was so damned full of herself that he wanted to shake her. Or kiss her. She had a perfectly bow-shaped mouth with a full lower lip, and he'd had too many fantasies about the phantom woman.

The triumphant look had returned to her eyes. He leaned down, part of him wanting to bask in the heat of that look, part of him still holding on to a shred of the intimidating bruiser he was meant to be. "Your fiancé, then?" he whispered near her temple. The fine hairs there tickled his mouth. "I'm nearly certain you have one of those." The sisters had all come here to procure one. He couldn't imagine one of the young lords passing over such a delectable piece.

The reminder of a fiancé made her stiffen, and goose bumps broke out on her arms.

"I don't believe you'll tell anyone," she said.

Gold flecks in her eyes caught the light and twinkled up at him. "Why wouldn't I?"

"Because there's a reason you don't want anyone to know that you were in that corridor with me. You tell my secret, Mr. Cavell, I'll tell yours." Leaning forward so that the tips of their noses almost touched, she whispered, "Or should I address you as the Duke?"

Fucking hell.

He hadn't realized he'd revealed so much that night. Something about his expression must have made her think she'd gone too far. She pushed at his shoulder but he didn't budge. He couldn't. He was paralyzed by her admission. Before he could get his bearings, she stomped hard on his instep. She was wearing heeled shoes, so a dart of pain shot through his foot and threw him off-balance. Using that to her advantage, she elbowed his stomach and made her way past him and out of the pantry. She was gone before he got over his shock that she'd used violence against him.

He made it to the pantry door before he caught hold of himself. There was no point in going after her. He couldn't chase her without bringing attention to them. She need only scream to bring the entire household down around them. His only hope was that she'd wait before she told anyone. He'd have to come up with something to offer her, some incentive that would make her keep her mouth shut.

Grumbling at his own poor luck, he stormed back across the room to the stairwell and trudged down for his meeting with the servants.

SIX

THE STREET WAS QUIET AND SLEEPY WHEN THE CAR-
riage pulled up to Camille's residence where Eliza and
her family were staying. Cozy streetlamps flickered in the inky
darkness and reflected off the cobblestones, still shiny and wet
from the late-afternoon rain. They were returning from a
soiree hosted by the Duke and Duchess of Rothschild. August,
the duchess, had been very helpful with ensuring the Doves' successful launch into Society. As an American heiress herself, she
knew how vicious the ton could be to outsiders.

Eliza tried her very best to be grateful for the opportunity
presented to her, but it was difficult when she knew that marriage to Lord Mainwaring waited for her on the other side of
this particular opportunity. That dread of the future had to be
why she was so preoccupied with Simon Cavell. He'd occupied
her every thought since their confrontation yesterday, even
though she hadn't seen him again. Mr. Cox had accompanied
them to the soiree.

He offered her his hand now to assist her out of the carriage.

She met his gaze as she stepped out, but he only held it briefly before releasing her to help Fanny and Jenny.

"Where is Mr. Cavell?" she asked with a petulance in her voice that even she found annoying. Simon was around here somewhere. He'd gone into hiding because of her, but she was determined to find him.

"Out, I reckon." Mr. Cox's voice was as unperturbed as if she'd asked about the weather.

As she stood waiting for her mother and sister, she searched out the dark corners of the houses and stoops across the road. Would he be hiding there? The only thing she could pick out was the shadow of a cat as it leaped from the ground to a window ledge. He could be on the roof, she supposed. But she couldn't make out anyone up there when she looked. She sighed inwardly and turned to follow her family inside, but a pinprick of orange light in the darkness across the narrow street caught her eye. It came from the park in the center of the square.

A cigarette? Did Simon smoke? Perhaps a trace of tobacco *had* lingered in the air when he'd cornered her in the pantry. She had relived that moment a thousand times since yesterday. His hand on her hip and his body only inches from her, so warm and so very solid. She should have felt threatened—any sane woman would have—but *she'd* wanted to kiss him.

Was he in that park right now watching her? A thrill of excitement zipped through her. Trying to behave as if she hadn't seen the light, she hurried inside. She didn't want to tip him off that she was coming to find him.

Eliza called out a quick good night after handing off her cloak to the waiting footman and then walked as normally as she could upstairs to her bedroom. A maid had drawn the curtains for her and lit the small bedside lamp. Eliza hurried across the room and peeked out the curtains. The window was cracked to let in the cool breeze. The orange glow was still there, and this time she could make out a dark form next to a tree. There was no way to know for sure, but something told her it was him.

"Good evening, Miss Eliza." The lady's maid she shared with her mother and sister strolled into the room.

Damn. There was no good reason to send her away without raising suspicion. Releasing the curtain, she allowed the woman to help her out of her gown, but only down to her chemise and then she shooed her out. She drew her thin dressing gown around her and hurried back to the window. The orange light had disappeared, and the shadowy form along with it.

Eliza paced her room for the next half hour as she waited for her mother and sister to go to bed. It wouldn't do for them to see her sneaking around. She didn't want to explain that she had a mild obsession with the man tasked with keeping them safe. It would be embarrassing. She even tried to talk herself out of it. Her good angel tactfully put forth all the reasons she should go to bed, while her bad angel obliterated those arguments with the only one that mattered: he can give you the adventure you want.

Put that way, she had no choice.

Once she was certain everyone had retired, she slipped into a cloak and ankle boots and opened her bedroom door. A single sconce flickered in the hallway, casting a yellow light over the brown and dated wallpaper. Nothing else stirred.

As quiet as a mouse, she pulled her door closed behind her and made her way to the stairs. There were two squeaks in the floorboards, but nothing to rouse curiosity. Still, her heart was beating in her ears by the time she made it to the turn that led to the stairs. The light didn't quite reach here, and anyone could be waiting to find her out. She'd have a devil of a time explaining the strange ensemble she wore.

A figure separated itself from the darkness. She would have run right into him had he not reached out a firm hand and grabbed her waist. The other covered her mouth, stifling her surprised screech. The blue of his eyes had been turned a dark gray by the shadows, but Simon stared down at her, imploring her to keep quiet. She nodded and he lowered his hand fractionally. He gestured toward her room.

She shook her head no.

He rolled his eyes and lifted her by the waist, taking her there whether she wanted to go or not. If a servant caught them in her room together, her reputation would be shredded. On the other hand, there was no room in the house where their having a midnight discussion would be considered proper. At least her bedroom afforded them privacy.

Once inside, he gently set her down and turned the key in the lock behind them. This probably should have startled her, and it might have with anyone else, but it didn't. Not with him. But she reevaluated her stance and took a step backward when he turned toward her, because his eyes were flames.

"Where were you going?" His voice was low and so deep that he was almost growling the words.

"To find you."

He nodded once. "You haven't told anyone about me."

"I wanted to give you a chance to make a deal with me first."

"A chance to make a deal?" The corner of his mouth ticked in annoyance. "Need I remind you that *you* ran away from *me*?"

"Well, you cornered me in the pantry against the wall. What did you expect?"

"You weren't afraid of me."

It was true, but she didn't know how he knew that. She'd left him because she'd been overwhelmed by how he'd made her feel. Alive and free and wanted.

"That hardly matters. We need to finish our discussion and quickly before someone catches you in here." She needlessly pulled the edges of her cloak tight across her torso to make sure it was properly closed. Having him here was making her absurdly aware of her lack of a corset.

"I'm listening." His lips formed a hard line and his eyes narrowed on her. He didn't seem inclined to negotiate with her.

"I gather that you don't want anyone to know of your other identity." She still had no idea who the Duke was. "I won't say anything, but only if you do something for me."

He gave her a once-over, from her breasts all the way down to her flat boots and up again, and his eyes grew wary. "What do you want?"

She'd have been insulted if she—no, she *was* insulted. She wasn't offering him anything remotely related to her body, but it wouldn't have killed him to pretend an interest. Straightening her shoulders, she said, "As you surmised, I am getting married at the end of the summer. Lord Mainwaring. I believe you're acquainted with him."

His eyes widened, and she saw the final piece of that night at Montague Club click into place for him. "Mainwaring." He gave a soundless laugh and there was a brief flash of pity in his eyes before he added, "The blackboard. I remember now."

She didn't appreciate his pity. "I want to have an adventure, and I think I deserve one." The rest of it was difficult to say, because she fully expected him to laugh at her. "I want a night . . . with you."

He didn't laugh. He didn't move. He stared at her until it became awkward. Just when she was about to decide he hadn't heard her, he asked, "That's what you want? A night with a brawler?"

She read about prizefights sometimes in the backs of the seedier newspapers. She had even picked up a penny dreadful about a gang of brawlers. They fought for money and were brutal in their violence. The fights were almost always illegal. He wasn't an illustrated character who traveled in a gang, but he was part of that world that she knew very little about. She wanted to see those areas of the city that he saw. That world that he sometimes inhabited.

She was thinking of the best way to explain this when he said, "Kiss me, then."

That wasn't at all what she had expected him to say. A warning, a flat-out refusal, or maybe even an order to swear a blood oath—any of those would have been less surprising. All she could manage was an inarticulate "What?"

"Kiss me. Go on." There wasn't the slightest bit of passion in his voice. His command was a gauntlet thrown down between them.

By their very nature, the words had her looking at his mouth. His lips were surprisingly well-formed. Though not full by any means, his bottom lip looked pillowy and soft. The wound from last week hadn't been as severe as she had feared because it had already healed. His lips were a pretty shade of pink with a white scar bisecting the left side of his top one.

Kissing him wouldn't be a hardship. But it was wrong and unnecessary to the conversation at hand, she reminded herself. It felt as if she'd been drawn toward him, like he had some sort of magnetic power to pull her in. She tightened her grip on her cloak and took a step backward.

His mouth twisted into a smirk. "That's wot I reckoned."

That accent again. The words rumbled together, unhurried and gravelly, reverberating under her skin.

"Why would I kiss you?" She simply wanted a tiny peek into his world. Kissing had nothing to do with it.

"If you can't even do that, how will you find the courage to go through with it?"

Courage? This was a test of her *courage*? Oh, she would not let him go on thinking she was a coward. Growing up with two older sisters who had often seemed bent on overprotection, this was one point of contention for her. She always had to prove her bravery when it was called into question. Also, she sensed that he wouldn't agree to her bargain unless she passed this ridiculous test.

She inched closer until she had eliminated almost all the space between them. The heat from his body warmed her front and his scent wafted over her. There was a faint hint of lemon mixed with the sweetness of tobacco and mint. She had kissed a man before . . . well, Olek. They had both been sixteen and spent a summer half-convinced they were in love. She raised up on her toes and lightly rested her palms against his chest to keep her balance. He was solid muscle beneath her hands. This man was no boy. A fact that intimidated her, but instead of letting it stop her, she charged ahead.

He didn't budge as she leaned forward and pressed her mouth to his. His lips were firmer than she'd thought, or perhaps he was simply very disappointed in her. Kisses were supposed to be passionate, and this one was distinctly not. It was probably because her lips were closed. She parted them, tilting her head slightly to fit them to his, but he didn't answer her movement in any way.

She wasn't doing this right. What an inopportune time to

have forgotten how to kiss. His entire body had gone stiff, and she was in danger of sliding off, so she gripped his broad shoulders to keep herself in place. When she pulled back briefly to catch her breath, his eyes were more hooded than usual and held the distinct air of disapproval.

Oh, God, he'd laugh at her later tonight when he was alone. Determined to try again and prove that she could do it properly, she quickly put her mouth back on his. One of his hands found the back of her head. He meant to pull her away. She held his shoulders tighter and flattened herself against his chest. It was a stark reminder of her lack of a corset because her nipples responded to the friction and some light flicked on inside her. It spilled heat that pooled low in her belly. She gasped silently and her tongue found the seam of his lips.

He jerked away, but only slightly to give a breath of space between their mouths. His palm cradled the back of her head and his fingers tightened in her hair. His other hand roamed down her spine. There had never been a time when she wanted a kiss more. She pressed her fingers into the unyielding muscle of his shoulders, silently urging him to continue. With the same urgency she felt, he came back to her, turning his head a bit so their mouths fit together nicely. This time his lips were soft as they moved over hers and she melted into him. The textured slide of his tongue against hers created an electric friction that hummed its way through her veins and buzzed in her body.

All at once, she wasn't kissing him. *He* was kissing *her* and she loved it. His hand roamed farther down to settle on her bottom. He squeezed and pulled her forward into his solid strength and that part of him that very clearly wanted her. It was rigid and thick where it nudged against her stomach. She ached to touch him, and that need drew her back to her senses.

"Stop," she whispered, suddenly aware that they were in

her bedroom right next to her bed. It frightened her that she didn't actually want to stop what they were doing.

He didn't let her go, but his grip on her head loosened and the one on her bottom eased up to her lower back. His mouth relinquished hers. They were both breathing heavily. "Change your mind?" he asked.

"No." She shook her head and fought for breath. "You said a kiss. That was more than one."

He chuckled and his hand slid from her hair, his fingertips tracing the side of her face as they slid down to toy with the edge of her cloak where it lay across her breasts. "You want far more than a kiss, though," he whispered.

Was it that obvious? She was fairly certain she was already blushing, but she still noted the influx of heat to her face. "Regardless, I did as you asked."

"You did." He pushed an errant strand of hair off her face. "You're a very good girl, Eliza."

She shouldn't like his praise as much as she did. It lit her up inside with radiant heat. "Shouldn't we get going?" She took a step backward and he let her go.

"You're right. I can't bed you here." He indicated the bed. "Not with your family near."

Bed her? The nerve of him! "I did enjoy our kissing, I'll admit that," she said in a very firm whisper. "However, we cannot do more. I hardly know you and if this . . ." She waved her free hand between them, her gaze catching on the impressive bulge in his trousers. She swallowed audibly, surprised that the sight of it wasn't as abhorrent as it should have been. Two heartbeats passed before she dragged her gaze up to his. "If this is a condition of our night, then I'm afraid I cannot agree."

"What the devil are you on about? This was the deal. A night with me. You wanted me to bed you, yes?"

She gasped. "*I did not want that*. I wanted a night with you. A night *out* with you in London, the parts of it that no one thinks I should see. I meant the dance halls and the gambling parlors of Whitechapel or Covent Garden, not . . . not . . . not to be . . . bedded."

He stared at her. "But you kissed me."

"You made me kiss you." She probably said that too loud. Taking her voice back down to a whisper, she said, "I thought it was an odd condition of the deal, a challenge of sorts to see if I'd pass."

He laughed, one of his hands coming up to stifle the sound, and backed silently toward the door, putting much needed space between them. She was slightly too humiliated to find humor in the situation.

"What you want is out of the question," he said when he finally stopped laughing.

"A night out in London is out of the question, but a night in my bed isn't?"

He shrugged. "Yes. One can be done in private, and the other by its very nature must be public. We cannot be seen in public together because it would cause too much trouble for me, and you as well, I presume."

That was true. "Fine. Not Covent Garden, then. Whitechapel. No one who knows me would go there. Even if I did run across some gentleman, I very much doubt he would notice me out of context." She had met hundreds of people at balls and soirees in the past couple of months and hardly any of them more than once or twice. The Dove name might be notorious but her face wasn't. Outside of the proper venue and a ball gown, she'd be virtually anonymous. The likelihood of a gentleman identifying her was slim. It was a bet she was willing to make.

He was shaking his head before she had even finished the word. "No. It's dangerous there."

"There would be little danger to me with you at my side."

"No, Miss Dove. It's not something I'm willing to risk." He had made it to the door and was on the verge of fleeing.

Desperation pushed her forward. "There isn't a risk, though. Not really. Women go there all the time."

He eyed her dubiously. "Women not of your class."

"What do you know of my class? I'm not what you think, just as I'm beginning to suspect that you aren't what I think. There's more to you beneath that gruff exterior, Mr. Cavell."

"It's not going to happen. I will not take you out and I will not bed you, either. You've lost your chance." She opened her mouth to retort that she'd never asked him to bed her, but he hurried on. "I'm leaving this room and we will not speak of this again."

"I cannot agree to that." She followed him toward the door. "If you want my silence—"

He rounded on her, his legs eating up the distance between them, and she closed her mouth abruptly. His eyes were alight with aggravation that made her think she might have pushed him too far. What did she really know about him? Though she did feel safe with him, there was no real reason that she should feel safe.

Coming to a stop not a foot away from her, he said, "I'll think about it. The danger . . . the planning . . . it will take time." His jaw firmed in resolve. "That's the most I can offer you."

She knew better than to push him further. "Thank you."

He exhaled in what might have been relief. She almost felt sorry for him. He clearly had a secret to keep and it was important to him. He gave her a brisk nod and left. The bedroom door didn't make so much as a thud when it closed behind him.

SEVEN

THE PAST WEEK HAD BEEN TORTURE FOR SIMON. HE tried to stay out of sight, and for the most part he succeeded, but he was charged with the Doves' security and that meant he was always near them. Near her. He heard her, saw her, and even smelled her delicate scent when he was forced to get close to her.

The first time he saw her after the incident in her bedroom, he'd accompanied Eliza and her mother on a shopping excursion to Bond Street. His task was to shadow them and stand outside each shop while they browsed; they didn't buy very much. He hadn't been certain of her intentions then—he still wasn't—so he'd felt anxious as he waited. She'd opened the door of the millinery shop, and the bell had jangled as she'd stepped out onto the pavement. Her eyes had flashed to his, the secret they both knew shining within them, and her mouth had twisted into an intriguing little smile before she'd turned away to head to the next shop. He'd avoided looking at her the rest of the day, afraid it would tempt her into spilling their secret.

He had encountered her so closely only once after that. He'd made the mistake of crossing the front hall as she came down the stairs. They weren't alone, as her mother and sister were trailing behind her. She was far enough ahead of them, however, that she was able to whisper to him, "My offer still stands," as she passed him by on her way to the drawing room. Her smile had been teasing and unconsciously seductive. The pull of her perfume had had him moving toward her before he'd managed to stop himself. He wished that she *would* request a night with him.

All he had to do was close his eyes and the memory of her lithe body against his had him pondering things that were better left unimagined. Things like how thick her hair would feel wrapped around his wrist, the sounds she would make underneath him, or how long her rose water scent would last on his sheets. Not that she would ever be in his bed. The thought was preposterous. He lived at the club, an employee; she lived here in one of the most fashionable neighborhoods in London.

"Don't tell me Sir Barnaby has written to ask for your hand in marriage yet again?" Eliza's voice drew him back to the present.

He'd finished his nightly meeting downstairs with the butler, where he'd been briefed on all the planned comings and goings of the staff the next day. He was walking to the parlor at the back of the house to get the family's schedule for tomorrow from Mrs. Dove. She usually relayed the information to him after the family arrived home from their evening excursion, but they were having a rare night at home tonight.

"The third time, the poor dear." This came from Jenny,

and then a flutter of paper as the letter in question was presumably discarded. Her tone was not as forgiving as her words implied. "He won't take no for an answer."

Simon peeked inside the room to see Eliza sitting on the sofa wearing a blue dress with a high satin collar. There was a gap in the front that displayed just enough of her soft neck to draw his eyes. He nearly groaned in frustration at how taken he was with her and forced himself to notice her sister on the opposite sofa. Mrs. Dove was nowhere in the room. He quietly eased back and pressed his shoulders to the wall outside the parlor door and told himself he was waiting for Mrs. Dove to join her daughters. She was probably upstairs refreshing herself before dinner.

It was sound logic that he would wait, but he also knew that he simply enjoyed hearing Eliza's voice. Truth be told, he liked her. As far as he could tell, she hadn't confessed his identity or what had happened in her room to anyone. She could have, and he respected that she hadn't.

Eliza laughed at something her sister had said. There was a lightness to it that he found refreshing. It suggested that she hadn't been touched by hardship or loss. It floated around the room with an amused, unbothered air and a sweetness that called to him. "Have you considered telling him that you have no interest because he asked for Cora's hand first?"

"Yes, I did mention that to him," Jenny said. "He wrote back that he was mistaken. He'd been blinded by my beauty and too overcome by it to ask me, so he asked her instead. He dearly regrets his error."

"I'm sure he does."

They both giggled, and he found himself smiling against his will. He didn't want to like Eliza or her family. She had the power to ruin everything he had worked for. One word from her, and Leigh and Thorne could send him away from Montague Club for prizefighting for Brody behind their backs. He'd have nowhere safe to bring Daisy once he finally got her. But he couldn't help it. She was kind and good and he liked existing near her.

"If you jilt Lord Mainwaring, I'm certain Sir Barnaby would offer for you," Jenny teased her sister.

"Ugh. I wouldn't be so certain. Sir Barnaby's a timid one. He might fold under the sort of scandal a jilting would bring," Eliza said, her good humor gone.

Simon hated the thought of her with Mainwaring. That prick did not deserve her. His head dropped back against the wall with a thud of dejection. He stiffened, but it was too late. The sound had already been noted. Eliza appeared at the parlor's threshold before he could take two steps down the hall.

"Well, good evening, Mr. Cavell. What brings you lurking about the hallway?" Her sly smile captivated him.

"Miss Eliza." He inclined his head in greeting. "I was hoping to speak with Mrs. Dove about the schedule for tomorrow. I'll return later." He turned to go, but she rushed forward and put a hand on his arm.

"There's no need for that. I can give it to you."

Her fingers were long and tapered with perfectly oval fingernails that had been buffed to a shine. He had to tear his gaze away from her hand, which had fallen to rest on his forearm.

"I don't mind returning," he said.

"But that's silly. I can tell you now." She smiled up at him and still hadn't released his arm.

He couldn't think of a good reason to put her off. Saying that he needed to put space between them seemed unwise. Instead, he inclined his head.

She finally let him go and took his place at the wall, leaning back a little to look up at him. Her rose scent teased him, and he almost stepped forward to get closer.

"Tomorrow will be a full day, and you'll likely need Mr. Cox's assistance," she began. "Jenny and I have a luncheon with the London Suffrage Society, but Mama is going to meet a friend for tea at Claridge's. She'll go there after dropping us off. After that, we're all going to the British Museum." She paused and her eyes became devilish slits. "We should have time to stop by Montague Club should you—"

"Eliza," he said in a low warning tone. He didn't realize that he'd used her first name until her eyes deepened and her smile widened. He was becoming entirely too familiar with her.

"I didn't mean that I would go in, only that you might need to go there."

"Thank you for your consideration, but I won't need to go there."

"Are you certain? I've heard there's a big exhibition brawl there next week and that you're the main attraction. You must need to—"

"Where did you hear that about the brawl?" he asked.

"I saw Violet, Lord Leigh's wife, yesterday when Mr. Cox was escorting me." At his distressed look, she rolled her eyes. "Don't worry. I kept your secret," she whispered.

Devonworth believed that he'd have things well in hand by the end of the week, so Simon wouldn't be here much longer. The bloke who had made the initial threat seemed to have reconsidered things. Simon couldn't wait for this to be over so that he wouldn't have to see her every day, almost as much as he dreaded not seeing her every day.

"Eliza." He glanced around to make certain they were still

alone. "Do not mention that here. The very fact that there's a secret to keep would be suspect."

"I've offered you a very fair negotiation."

He was starting to reconsider how much he liked her. She could be annoying. "You have not and you know it. I cannot take you out." He infused his whispered words with every bit of indignation he could muster.

"From what I can see, Mr. Cavell, you could do what you want." Her eyes dropped to his shoulders and then his chest, sizing him up.

The way she looked at him, as if she truly believed that, gave him pause. It made him want it to be true. If it were, he'd reach out and touch her soft skin, tip her head to the side and take her lips with his.

He was saved from answering by Mrs. Dove. "Mr. Cavell, good evening." She had somehow come down the stairs without him hearing and now approached them. "I found it, Eliza." She waved sheet music over her head. "I knew I had packed it. Jenny, darling, sing this for us. I'll accompany you on the pianoforte."

Jenny hurried out to retrieve the music and then walked back into the room as she read it over.

Mrs. Dove turned back to them. "You're going to love this song," she said to Eliza. "It's very sanguine and with a fast meter." To Simon, she said, "Come join us, won't you, Mr. Cavell?"

"Thank you, madam, but I cannot."

Her face fell. "Why not? Do you sing? We could use a nice baritone."

He wanted to. He imagined being in that room with them, watching Eliza and singing with her family, and something about it felt warm and good. He'd never spent a night like that, like someone who was part of a real family.

"It wouldn't be proper." Though as he said it, he suspected the woman didn't give a fig about propriety. "I was on my way out," he rushed to add. "Mr. Cox is staying overnight. I must get back to Montague Club." His gaze jerked to Eliza at the mention of the club.

She merely smiled back, her dark eyes knowing and playful.

Mrs. Dove continued to entice him to stay, but he managed to pull himself away. He'd get their precise schedule in the morning. He'd meant what he said about having other things to do tonight, though Montague Club would have to wait a bit.

He didn't have time to change his clothes as he made his way across town to the alleys of Whitechapel. He liked to dress in more nondescript clothing when he came here and not the finer fabrics he wore at the club and in Mayfair, but it couldn't be helped. Daisy would be waiting for him and wouldn't want to sleep until she saw him. The cab dropped him off at Commercial Street, and he made his way through the rabbit warren of alleys, keeping his head down and ignoring the shapes that moved in the dusk shadows.

It wasn't long before he came to the brothel that had become familiar to him these past several years. His sister, Mary, had been let go from her position at the factory once she had been unable to hide her advanced pregnancy and had taken up residence here at the behest of her friend who worked in one of the upstairs rooms. After her death, Simon had negotiated with the owner to allow Daisy to stay in the attic. Mrs. Jeffries charged him exorbitant rent, but he slept every night knowing his niece was protected.

He knocked on the door and waited, his gaze scanning the street out of habit. A man's form moved in the shadow of the building across the narrow street, one of Brody's men that he kept in the area to make certain that Simon didn't take Daisy away.

"Good evening, Mr. Cavell." Mrs. Jeffries opened the door. She was also being paid to sound the alarm should he make the unwise decision to abscond with Daisy. She'd told him as much when he'd first made the arrangement with her. "You're later than usual today."

"Couldn't be helped."

Her brow arched in quiet judgment, but she stood back to allow him to enter.

He took the stairs to the attic two at a time. When he reached the small attic room and knocked, Henrietta opened it within seconds. Her eyes filled with relief. "Mr. Cavell, I'm glad you're here."

Daisy fretted in the background. "Heni!" she called from the bed they shared and sat up. Her face lit with happiness when she saw him. "Papa!"

Simon rushed into the room and reached his niece about the time she stood and was launching herself into his arms. He caught her and swung her around once, much to her delight, before he pulled her close. She nuzzled into his neck, her hair tickling his nose. He breathed in her sweet scent and felt an unexpected ache build in his chest. She should be in a home like the Doves were, with music and laughter surrounding her, not here in this dark attic space. Henrietta took her out daily to get air, but there were no gardens for her to play in.

"I missed you, love," he said.

Daisy pulled back and looked up at him, her white baby teeth shining up at him in a smile.

"Where have you been?" Her brow creased almost as quickly as her smile had appeared.

"You really must try to come in the morning," Henrietta admonished him gently, her eyes a little bit skittish as she looked from him to Daisy. She was only around fifteen years old and had been Daisy's caretaker for the last year. She'd come to the brothel to work around the same time Daisy's previous caretaker had decided she wanted to marry and had readily agreed to the position. "It's what she's accustomed to. She worries all day when she doesn't see you, sir."

"I know, Heni." He'd taken to Daisy's nickname for the girl. "I'm sorry. This job should only last for a few more days and then I'll be back every morning as usual. Here." He reached into his pocket and withdrew one of the oranges he'd pilfered from the Doves' kitchen and handed it to Heni. The other one he gave to Daisy. "One for each of you."

They both grinned and he was forgiven. As Daisy tucked into the skin of her orange, trying her best to remove it, he kissed the top of her head and prayed that the final fight Brody had planned would be the last one, as he'd promised. If it wasn't, he'd have to try to sneak Daisy out somehow and go on the run with her. That would be dangerous because Brody would try to chase them down, but Simon would have no choice.

EIGHT

BLOOMSBURY WAS AN AREA OF THE CITY THAT HAD become known for its intellectualism and progressivism. It was home to the British Museum, writers, several colleges, and, perhaps most notably, Montague Club. At that fateful dinner several weeks ago when she'd met Simon, Mr. Thorne had told them that the club was the first in the city to allow both men and women members. He had spoken at length about how the club had begun as a home to second and third sons and all manner of lower nobility who found White's and Brooks's too absorbed in the minutiae of tradition. Professionals and scholars of all bent also sought out the club. He'd made it sound like a haven of forward-thinking individuals, which is why Eliza had been so desperate to see the inside.

And yet again she was pushing the bounds of propriety to be here. She pressed her forehead against the side window of the cab to peer out at the club as Jenny handed their fare up to the driver. Montague Club was an expansive building that spanned the length of half a city block and was several floors tall. Its white marble facade seemed illuminated beneath the full moon overhead and the gas streetlamps flickering in the mild evening air. A line of carriages disappeared down the street and around the corner as people arrived for the exhibition fight. A wide red carpet had been laid out at the main entrance to welcome spectators. The club only hosted these fights a couple of times a year and they always drew a crowd.

"It looks like a palace, doesn't it?" Eliza asked. Doormen in double-breasted livery stood on either side of the massive front doors. Torches lighted the way from the carriages.

"Yes." Jenny hurried from the carriage and Eliza roused herself to follow her sister. The cab took off and they were left there on the pavement. "A palace complete with guards. How will we get in?" Jenny asked.

The club was opened to nonmembers tonight, but only to those who had been able to acquire a ticket. Cora had refused to purchase tickets for them, proclaiming that a brawl was no place for unmarried women. She was right, and looming over them was the fact that Eliza didn't have Mainwaring's permission. Though there was a betrothal contract in place, he could call the whole thing off and it would be Eliza's reputation that suffered for it. It was why they had dressed in black veils.

"We'll wait for an opportunity," she said, watching the people make their way inside in small groups of two and four.

It had been about a week since she'd last spoken with Simon. A few days after their conversation in the hall, Devonworth had deemed them not to be at risk anymore. He still had his own men escort them in public, but Simon had been able to return to his work at Montague without a proper goodbye or giving her an answer. They had managed to sneak out tonight after Jenny had pleaded a headache and Eliza had insisted on staying home to watch over her sister. Fanny had gone out to the previously planned dinner without them.

Simon was participating in the brawl tonight, and there was no way she would miss him.

"Let's look for a large group—There!" Jenny discreetly pointed toward a group of young men walking down the sidewalk. They were well-dressed but slightly unkempt, likely students, and they were clearly intent on the club. "We'll fall in behind them."

Eliza shook her head. "That won't work. It looks as if they're checking tickets." One of the doormen appeared as stoic as a palace guard as he inspected a piece of card stock that an older man and woman presented to him. Only after examining it thoroughly did he step aside to welcome them. "Besides, I'd wager that Lord Leigh is inside greeting guests. We can't go in the front and chance him catching us."

They would also have to avoid the Duke of Rothschild along with his wife, Leigh's wife, and Cora and Devonworth. Wives of titled men didn't suffer under the same constraints as young debutantes hoping to marry well. It wasn't fair, but it was true, and there might be others they would need to avoid. But as long as they stayed toward the back of the crowd with their veils, she didn't think they would have to worry.

"Come on," she said. "We'll try a service entrance."

Together they hurried across the road, dodging the cab that came from the opposite direction and had slowed to gawk at the spectacle of the arrivals. They had each worn a nondescript black cloak and hat with veil, but that didn't stop pedestrians they passed from looking at them in curiosity.

Around back, they spotted a servants' entrance. A wrought iron railing was set into the sidewalk surrounding a narrow set of stairs that led to the lower level. Hopefully, the door would be unlocked.

"Eliza, I don't know about this." Jenny's voice wobbled a bit when they approached the stairwell.

The door was cracked open; clanging and clattering came from inside, the sounds of pots and pans in the kitchen, she'd guess. "You can't back out now." She grabbed Jenny's hand and pulled her toward the steps. "We won't get in trouble. We'll stay hidden."

Jenny nodded but worry clouded her eyes. They carefully made their way down the steps and inside the building. The kitchen was on the left and it bustled with activity. Shouts in several different languages accompanied the clanging of metal pots, so no one noticed them as they slipped by. The corridor made a turn, putting them in the path of a maid who hurried toward them with a tray at her side. She passed them without a second glance on her way to the kitchen. Another turn put them at the foot of a set of stairs that led up one floor to another service corridor. This one was much busier with servants scurrying around, and the walls were thin enough they could hear the club's guests through it. Eliza tried a door and it opened.

The elegant hallway was packed with people who chatted and laughed as they made their way deeper into the club. Men made up the majority of the crowd, but there were a fair few women dressed in finery. They wore satins and silks with sparkling embellishments and detailed embroidery. The men wore dark suits with silk ties, some with waistcoats, and some made of coarse wool. She imagined they were a mix of professionals, nobility, and students.

Eliza hadn't dared wear anything too extravagant because she had thought it would be better to blend in and she hadn't wanted to risk soiling it. The precious few gowns they had been able to afford were to be saved for Society events. She pulled her cloak around her to hide the plainness of her dress.

"Come," she said to Jenny. "It looks as if everyone is going this way."

Jenny nodded and they worked their way into the flow of the crowd. Last time Eliza had been in Montague Club, she'd been upstairs. This part of the club had dark paneled walls, gleaming parquet floors, and gaslight sconces lining the wide hall. When they passed a footman positioned in an alcove with a tray of champagne, Jenny took two glasses for them, giggling like a schoolgirl as she handed Eliza hers.

"Merde," Jenny muttered and stopped short.

"What?" Eliza looked to her sister and then followed Jenny's gaze across the crowd.

Two doors had been opened ahead, and from the glimpse she had through the shoulders and heads in front of her, it looked like a ballroom. A giant crystal chandelier glittered with the light of hundreds of candles. That wouldn't have jarred her sister. Eliza looked harder, her gaze darting over the crowd flooding into the ballroom, until it caught on a blond head. A shot of trepidation quivered in her stomach. The man turned his head to speak to his companion and she got a clear view of his profile. It was unmistakably Devonworth. He had the profile of a classical statue.

"It's fine," Eiza said, though she wasn't entirely certain it was. "We knew he was attending. We must simply avoid him."

Jenny shook her head as if she didn't think their chances of that were good.

"Is Cora with him?" Eliza asked.

"I think . . ." Jenny moved from the left to the right to see around the man in front of her. "Yes, I see red hair. She must be here."

Damn. "Okay, we'll watch which direction they go and turn the other way." Nothing was going to stop her from getting to Simon tonight.

Jenny nodded and grabbed her arm. When it was their turn to enter the already crowded ballroom, they fled to the opposite side of the large room. It was lit up with two massive chandeliers and gold sconces along the wall. The ceilings were vast and inlaid with intricate carvings and designs. The floors were shining parquet wood and the walls white and gold. This end of the room had bars of various lengths affixed to the wall at different heights. She had heard people whispering that the ballroom had become the club's gymnasium, as if this were scandalous, but it might very well be true. Montague Club was noted for its exercise apparatuses along with its bare-knuckle brawling club.

A large square ring took up the center of the room. Double rows of black silken ropes around fifteen feet long enclosed it. The whole thing was on a raised dais so that the spectators could have a better view of what was to come. Excitement chased the trepidation away. She lifted up her veil and Jenny followed suit. It was too crowded for their brother-in-law and Cora to notice them anyway.

"Let's go over here." Jenny indicated a space a few yards away that was a little more open and where they wouldn't have to look over the shoulders of the men in front of them.

Eliza agreed and they headed in that direction, but they got there at the same time as a group of young men. Eliza placed them for university students from their disheveled hair and the fine but worn look of their coats.

"What have we here?" One of them smirked. "I didn't know the club provided this sort of entertainment." He reached out to touch Jenny's cheek, but her sister pulled away.

"Keep your hands to yourself, sir," she said, none too kindly.

The friend to his left laughed. "You're a lively one and an American." Damn, they'd meant to keep from talking to anyone so they didn't draw attention to themselves. "How about you?" Then he reached out and placed his hand on Eliza's shoulder, but she managed to shrug away from his advance. "What's wrong? Don't you want to make friends?"

"We came to watch the brawl, not make friends," she said.

The third student had used their inattention to walk around behind the sisters. He put a hand indecently low on each of their backs at the bend of their waists. Squeezing, he effectively blocked them in. "Nice ladies don't come to brawls alone not hoping to make friends." His voice was so close that Eliza could feel his breath tickle her earlobe and smell the stale liquor he'd drunk earlier.

"They're not alone," the clipped and cultured tones of a familiar voice said.

The men glanced to the newcomer as Lord David Felding strode up to them. He was dressed impeccably in a dark suit with a maroon brocade waistcoat. His dark hair was swept back with pomade, and he exuded a smooth confidence that gave his expression a slightly haughty cast. He was one of Devonworth's dearest friends, so they had encountered him at numerous events over the course of the Season. As the brother of the Duke of Strathmore, he'd been born to privilege, and every bit of that shone in his expression.

The student who'd spoken first didn't seem inclined to give up his find, so he chose not to believe him. "Leave off—"

Before he could finish the sentence, Lord David's hand moved faster than a striking snake and grabbed him around the throat just under his jaw. The boy made a choking sound but didn't otherwise move. Lord David had lifted him so that he was poised on his toes, rendering him immobile.

Without turning his gaze from the leader of the group, Lord David said, "Let go of my wife."

The one who held them immediately dropped his hands and moved back from them.

"I don't want to see you again tonight." With those words of warning, he released the leader. The students fled into the crowd like discarded fish that had been tossed back into the sea.

Lord David gazed at them, his eyes roaming over Jenny in a visual inspection as if checking for some hidden injury. "That should be all we'll hear from them tonight."

"Thank you, my lord," Eliza said.

Jenny made a concerted effort to keep her face toward the fight ring, but Eliza knew her sister well enough to know that it was a struggle. She practically vibrated with energy. "Your *wife*?" she said, her tone textured with a mixture of pique and amusement.

He didn't talk for a moment, but the silence spoke to a deep well of complicated feelings. Cora and Eliza often joked about how the man, a known rake, seemed entirely too preoccupied with their Jenny. So consumed in fact that he often didn't seem to know what to do with himself in her presence. Finally, he said, "I didn't . . . It . . ." Rarely one to be tongue-tied, he huffed out a breath. "It was convenient they believe that."

Seeming to have recovered, Jenny glanced over and blinked her eyes at him. "Or your wish that it be true."

He looked toward the ring, but his lips turned up in a smile. "I assure you that's not the case. I thought we'd already estab-lished that I'm not in the market for a wife."

"Ah yes. You're in the market for something else entirely." Jenny's tone had become slightly mocking.

Lord David turned his head to look at her sister and, though Eliza wasn't in his direct line of sight, the heat of his gaze nearly singed her. "That's right. Something I've been told isn't for sale."

"You don't possess the right currency," Jenny said.

His gaze sharpened, catching that tiny opening. "What currency do you mean?" he asked as if he'd comb all the sands of the earth to find it once he knew what it was. Eliza imagined that he'd never been in such a position before, wanting someone who didn't want him back, though Eliza knew for a fact that wasn't true. Jenny wanted him, she just didn't want to be tossed aside by him after their fling was over, so she abstained.

Before Jenny could issue a retort, Eliza cleared her throat rather obnoxiously to remind them that she was there. She couldn't listen to any more of this. They both glanced at her in mild annoyance. Jenny returned to her senses first and took several steps forward to distance herself from him.

"How did you find us?" Eliza asked him.

"Luck," he said. "I happened to be in the crowd behind you and saw you when you lifted your veils."

He moved to stand behind Jenny, far enough away that he wasn't touching her, but close enough to keep her protected should the need arise again. His attention was not on the ring. Eliza rolled her eyes. The ground could swallow her whole and Lord David wouldn't notice unless it took Jenny along with her.

"Aren't you going to tell us to leave, that we have no business being here?" Eliza asked.

The corner of his mouth tipped up and he finally spared her a glance. "Why would I do that? As far as I'm concerned, Society and their rules can go hang."

He had propositioned Jenny, a debutante, so Eliza wasn't entirely shocked by his attitude.

Before she could reply, the lights along the wall dimmed and an expectant hush rumbled through the crowd. The fight was about to start.

NINE

A DOZEN MEN WALKED STOICALLY OUT OF A DOOR that led to a corridor. They wore nondescript black suits. "Back now, back!" the middle-aged man in charge called out. The crowd roared as it accommodated them and created a narrow path. The men lined up six on each side of the path, close enough they could touch each other if they reached out their arms, presumably so that none of the spectators could come between them.

Soon three men walked out of the corridor and down the path. The man in the lead wore a plain white shirt buttoned to his collar. His hair was somewhere between blond and brown with dark muttonchops that extended down to his jaw. He could have been anywhere between the ages of twenty-five to forty-five. It was impossible to tell. He walked with comical pomposity, his nose in the air and his step measured and formal. A mixture of cheers and boos greeted him when the crowd got a good look at him.

"Do they not like him?" Eliza leaned over to ask Lord David.

He gave a brisk shake of his head. "That's Mr. Rodney Carstone, a member of Gummidge's, a rival club across town. He's been claiming to any who would listen that he could beat Cavell. Some of his club has come, but it sounds like most are ours."

Indeed the jeers now far outweighed the cheers as Mr. Carstone climbed into the ring and walked from corner to corner with his chest puffed out, his expression smug. He didn't strut around for long before the cheers started up in earnest as Simon walked through the door. The crowd surged toward him as one, unsettling her footing. She might have stumbled had Lord David not been standing next to her. He reached forward and took hold of Jenny, who held on to his forearm to steady herself. She called a thank-you to Lord David, but a raucous cheer filled the room, swallowing up the words.

Simon bounced on the balls of his feet, his gaze straight ahead as he made his way to the ring. His hair was pulled back similar to the style he'd worn on the night they met. It was tied in a queue at the crown of his head. The effect was startling in how it emphasized the planes and angles of his cheeks and jaws. He seemed dangerous and single-minded in his pursuit of victory. His glittering eyes only enhanced the effect. She had kissed this man twice. The memory did very pleasant and joyful things to her insides.

Lord Leigh was in his entourage, which surprised her. She'd never seen him less than formally dressed, but he was now. He wore trousers and shirtsleeves with a black silk waistcoat, but no coat or tie.

Simon climbed the dais and stepped through the satin ropes. His breeches were the color of parchment and he wore a white shirt. Unlike his opponent, his was open at the neck, and she caught a glimpse of dark chest hair. His sleeves were rolled up to reveal his forearms and, she imagined, to not hamper his reach. Lord Leigh stood outside the ropes, intent on whispering last-minute instructions to Simon. She might have tried harder to figure out what he said if she'd been less preoccupied with the state of Simon's chest. A very small part of her regretted that she hadn't let the night in her bedroom play out as it might have had she not corrected his assumption.

Mr. Carstone had stopped his preening before the audience and turned his attention to Simon. He paced from side to side on his end of the ring, watching Simon as he did so. Eliza had never seen a bare-knuckle brawl before, or any brawl really, save for one or two between neighborhood children when she was growing up. But by looking at the two of them, she really didn't see how Mr. Carstone would have been foolish enough to challenge Simon. He had the fit but slight physique of a gentleman who spent his leisure time in genteel pursuits. Simon wasn't a terribly large man, either, but his chest was solid and she had felt the power restrained in his arms. Mr. Carstone didn't stand a chance.

An older man stepped to the center of the ring. He was bald with a thick neck and frame that made him appear as if he'd lived most of his life brawling. He motioned to both men and they stepped over to join him. He introduced them both, yelling out their names to the same cheers and jeers as earlier. Then he started speaking only to them. She had no idea what he was saying to them—the rules of the fight, perhaps? This was followed by the men shaking hands as well as they could, considering both men's hands were wrapped with some sort of batting that left only their fingers free. They each retreated to their side. Lord Leigh was on the floor now, but she could see the top of his head, as if he stood upon a stool, and he was talking to Simon, who nodded. A bell rang and the match started.

The men paced in a circle, the hands of a clock careful to face each other. Simon indicated with his hands that Mr. Carstone should come to him, but the man didn't move forward. For the first time that night, Eliza thought she might have caught a glimpse of fear in Mr. Carstone's face. Perhaps he now realized what challenging Simon really meant—certain defeat in front of hundreds of witnesses. To his credit, he didn't back away. She could see that Simon was losing his patience. He indicated the man should charge, but Mr. Carstone held his ground. Simon yelled something to him, but it was swallowed by the spectators before it reached her.

Finally, Simon charged him. The man backed up, eliciting a chorus of boos from the crowd. Simon caught him against the ropes and landed the first punch right in his stomach. Mr. Carstone doubled over but recovered himself before Simon could do more damage, although Eliza would have bet anything that Simon was holding back. He'd prefer sport over annihilation.

The attack seemed to make Mr. Carstone's fear turn to ire. He charged Simon and they both staggered across the ring in a sort of bear hug until Simon was pressed against the ropes on the other side. Mr. Carstone pummeled him with a series of punches that had him moving like an automaton, each blow timed perfectly after the one before it to not allow Simon to retaliate. Simon rolled away from him, however, and the man lost his balance and fell forward. Simon tugged his shoulder and turned him around and hit him square across his jaw.

They exchanged blows for a while, continuing to make circles around the ring. Even from as far away as she was,

Eliza could tell that Mr. Carstone was breathing fast, but Simon still seemed fresh. A bell rang and the men retreated to their corners. The pause lasted for a minute or so before the bell brought them both to their feet.

This time his opponent seemed to approach with renewed vigor. He ran over yelling and dealt a hard blow to Simon's jaw. Everyone screamed like mad and Simon stumbled backward. That wasn't supposed to happen. Eliza's hands tightened into hard fists that had her nails digging into her palm. She didn't like to see him like this.

He recovered quickly and returned the blow and added another for good measure, but he retreated again. He was clearly toying with the man and she didn't understand why. When Mr. Carstone hit with his full strength, Eliza was convinced that Simon held back.

"Why is he doing that? He could finish the thing now if he wanted," she said to Lord David.

"Good eye." He nodded in approval. "If he finishes too quickly, everyone will be upset. They came for a good show and he gives them one. It's why they pay so much to see him."

Eliza took in the people around her. They were all mesmerized by the drama playing out before them. It was a drama, she realized. It was sport set to theater. She hoped Simon received a portion of the ticket sales.

Even with the show, it was clear that Mr. Carstone wasn't up to snuff. The fight finished after another couple minutes of back-and-forth, until Simon finally landed a blow that knocked Carstone to the ground. He was moving, but he didn't get back up before the official-looking man called a halt to the game and announced Simon as the winner.

A rumble of applause and cheers went up that seemed to vibrate the entire building. Simon had won. Despite that it had been a foregone conclusion, satisfaction filled her, bringing with it an energy that reminded her of why she had come. The fight was icing on the cake. She had come to see Simon.

"Will you take us back to see him?" she asked Lord David.

He frowned. "That's not wise."

None of this night had been wise. "If you don't take us, then I'll find a way to go back there myself, and my sister, being a devoted and kind sort, will feel obligated to accompany me. I thought I would offer you the opportunity to help."

He glanced at Jenny as if to ask, *Is she always like this?* Jenny laughed and laced her arms with Eliza's. "Come, let us go talk to Mr. Cavell."

They made their way through the sea of people to the doors where the fighters had entered, and Lord David followed them.

TEN

THE BRAWL HAD GONE EXACTLY AS SIMON HAD planned it. Carstone was an overly pompous dandy who had no business challenging anyone in the ring besides other overly pompous dandies. Simon didn't mind it, though. It had earned him a tidy sum that he could put aside, assuming Brody kept his word and released him from his debt after the grittier fight Brody was arranging.

He had been swarmed by congratulations and celebrations since the fight ended. Leigh, Rothschild, and Devonworth had only just left, and he had ensconced himself in the small room off the service corridor that led to the gymnasium. It was a changing room for members who exercised in the gymnasium. The walls were lined with cupboards and shelves, and benches were scattered throughout the room. Simon planned to make use of the shower bath in the back corner before going out to join in the victory celebration. He peeled off his sweat-stained shirt and set about unwrapping the bindings from his hands. Aside from a couple of nicks on his face and a few knuckles, he hadn't been bloodied. His still-tender ribs were already starting to ache; nothing a bit of whisky wouldn't solve.

Finished with the batten, he tugged at the lacing on the front of his breeches, but a knock on the door halted his progress. Muttering a curse at the interruption, he turned off the water and made his way to the door. He never expected to see Eliza Bloody Dove standing there looking at him with her wide and innocent eyes and her absurdly pretty face.

"Wot the hell—?" he started to ask but then slammed the door shut. He had no time to deal with her tonight. He turned to go back to his grooming, but a terrible thought stopped him cold. What if someone saw her out there and started questioning why the American was sniffing around his dressing room? What if they thought he'd compromised her? He'd lose his job. Or worse, to save herself she might very well be forced to share the secret she hadn't yet told. *Fuck.*

He opened the door and she still stood there, though she was frowning this time. Grabbing her arm, he pulled her none too gently into the room and slammed the door behind her, locking it for good measure. He pressed his hands into the door on either side of her, caging her in. She sputtered, momentarily taken aback. He could kiss her now, hard. Make her wish she'd never knocked on his door. Touch her in ways that would offend her and send her running away from him for good.

He took her head into his hand to do that, his fingers digging into the glossy brown hair piled at the nape of her neck. But he couldn't. The dumbstruck haze in her eyes faded into the sweet honeyed look of trust mixed with something like respect that she sometimes got when she looked at him. They were precious things that he couldn't take from her. "Someone should take ye over their knee and give ye a good spanking," he growled.

"Are you volunteering for the task, Mr. Cavell?" She blinked up at him.

God, he'd like to. "Wot are ye doin' here, Miss Dove?"

"Your accent has come out of hiding, I see."

He wanted to wipe the smirk off her face. The problem was, the only way he could think to do that was to kiss her. Since it couldn't be rough, it would be soft and wet and lead to things that were out of the question. He turned to stalk away from her, taking several deep breaths until he had calmed down enough to speak again. "What do you want with me, girl? You shouldn't be here. You could get me into a lot of trouble."

She glanced over her shoulder at the door, uncertainty reflected in her face. "I don't want to get you in trouble. I took precautions. Everyone thinks you're changing and alone." He wasn't reassured by that, a state of events she must have suspected, because she came over to him and put her hand on his arm. "No one saw me come in, except for Jenny and Lord David—"

"Lord David? Of Strathmore? That Lord David?" He paced again to get out the nervous energy her very presence caused in him.

"Yes, but he won't say anything. He's doing his best to impress my sister and wouldn't dare betray our trust in him."

That did very little to reassure him. "What do you want?" He turned quickly and almost ran into her because she'd followed him.

"I told you already. I thought I was very clear." When he merely stared at her, she said, "I want you to take me out for a night."

Impossible.

"I thought I already told you no."

She shook her head. "You said that you would think about it."

He took in a breath for patience. "I cannot take you. It's too dangerous, and don't you threaten to tell everyone the secret you carry. If you were going to you would have already."

"I can pay you." Her eyes were resolute, and she brought her handbag up to rifle through it. His gaze flicked down and was caught by the swell of her bosom. He looked away because he enjoyed looking a little too much.

She pulled out some folded bills. "It's yours if you'll take me. One night. That's all."

He stared at the money, but of its own volition his gaze went back to the swell of her breasts. They weren't too large, but not small, either. He reckoned they would be a nice handful with pink crests and . . . Aware of where his attention was focused, she took in a shuddering breath that broke the spell. His eyes met hers.

"Why is this night in Whitechapel so important to you?"

An internal battle played out over her face. She didn't know how much to tell him, but he wouldn't do this for anything less than the full, unvarnished truth.

"What do you remember about the night we first met?" she asked, her voice low, almost a whisper. It drew his gaze to her mouth and her soft pink lips.

He remembered that he'd called her Angel. "Tell me."

She took in a long and wavering breath. "I'm engaged to be married to a man I barely know. My entire future will be an endless round of social occasions: balls and weddings and teas and political dinners. To top it off, I'm fairly certain I'll have to give up my dream of going to a university. So few accept women, and I can't believe that Mainwaring will countenance such things of his wife anyway. All of that might be bearable

if I loved him. But he is even now cavorting across the Continent and having relations with prostitutes, and he's so proud
of that fact that he and his friends are keeping score on that
blackboard." She pointed in the direction of the very room of
their first meeting.

As he recalled, there had been several check marks added
since that night. There was a twinge in the vicinity of his
heart. It wasn't that he didn't feel for her; it was that he found
it difficult to empathize with her making a decision that she
knew was bad for her. "Then why are you marrying him?"

"Because it would be stupid not to. My fa . . , my *god*father,
Mr. Hathaway, is in charge of my inheritance and he will only
dole it out upon my marriage to a man he finds suitable. He
only finds aristocrats suitable."

"What happens if you do not marry an aristocrat?"

"Then I receive no inheritance and I'll have nothing. I have
no father, Simon." He wasn't prepared for the fist-punch effect
of the sound of his name on her voice. It stole his breath. "My
mother and sisters and I sold everything we owned to come
here for the sole purpose of finding husbands to secure our
futures. There is nowhere to go back to. There is no future
where I don't inherit."

He didn't know Mainwaring well, but he knew men like
him. The thought of her married to one of them was anathema
to him. Men like that wouldn't know how to deal with her.
They'd crush her to control her. "There is. You simply choose
not to want that future."

"Would you choose that future?" she challenged him.
"Would you walk away from two hundred thousand dollars
with an annuity to a future of nothing but insecurity? I'm sure
you're aware that options are limited for women."

Simon could hardly conceive of that sort of money. He

imagined his sister, Mary, her curls and laughter and all the small things about her that he didn't think about unless he had to because it was too painful. If she'd had that choice, she might be alive now. She certainly wouldn't have wasted away in that dirty little attic room in a brothel, her body ravaged by a fever that had set in and refused to leave. Her baby left to die on a diet of watery pap until he'd paid a bloody fortune for a wet nurse to care for her. How could he fault Eliza for choosing the way she had?

"I still don't understand this scheme of yours. What if Mainwaring finds out about this night out in Whitechapel? He won't marry you then, and you won't inherit your fortune."

"Don't you understand? I need this. If I can have just one adventure where I don't have to think about Mainwaring or a future with him, then maybe I can face that future. He has an entire summer to indulge in adventure. I simply want one night. I know it's foolish to ask for more, but surely one night is possible. He won't find out because we'll go where no one knows me. I won't even talk to anyone."

He bit out a curse and she startled. "One night." He held up a finger between them. "That's all you get. One night and then I never want to see you skulking around here again."

She was already nodding vigorously. "Yes, I understand. You'll never have to see me again."

"I don't want to hear one word about the secret we share." She nodded again. "If—" Her smile had widened to the point of near delirium. "No, listen to me." He made his voice as low and serious as he could, but that didn't dim her enthusiasm much. "If after that night anyone comes to me and even so much as mutters the word *Duke*, I will find you and I will make you pay for your betrayal."

She had the audacity to laugh, not at all put off by the seriousness of his manner or the threat he was attempting to convey, and then launched herself into his arms. He had to catch her or they would both go wobbling. "Thank you so very much, Simon. I promise I will never tell anyone who you are. Never." She pulled back enough to look up at him, trust and gratitude shining out of her eyes. He was damned near bathed in its warmth. "Thank you."

He swallowed thickly. The weight of her body felt so pleasant against him that he didn't want to let her go. He could think of several ways that he wanted her to thank him. All of them sexual, none of them advisable.

"What night shall we do it?" she asked.

He was forced to clear the husk from his voice. "Tomorrow. Can you get away?"

"I think so. Should I come here at nine o'clock?"

"No, never come here again." He let her go and forced space between them. She frowned but didn't object. He couldn't decide if she knew what she did to him or not. It was almost as if she was toying with him. He named a street corner near her house. "I'll pick you up there in a cab and we'll travel to Whitechapel together. Eleven o'clock."

"Yes, that makes the most sense. I'll wear something sensible and plain."

"Wear your cloak." He nodded to the black one she wore, the same one she'd worn when they had talked in her bedroom. "You always wear it to cause mischief. Your mother should burn it after."

She laughed. "She'll be free of me soon enough."

He despised thinking of her married to the viscount. She had too much life in her. But it wasn't his business. He had enough troubles without inviting more.

"Put your money away. I don't want it." When she began

to sputter a protest, he added, "Now I have to shower. Get out of here unless you plan to stay and watch." His fingers went back to the ties of his breeches, and her eyes widened as she followed the movement.

"Of course," she said, and hurried around him toward the door. "Until tomorrow night."

He nodded and waited a beat, long enough for her to have left, and turned on the tap. A sluggish stream fell from the spout overhead. He pushed his breeches down, drawers and all, to step into the round porcelain basin. It wasn't until he did that he realized he hadn't heard the door close. He glanced behind him to see her staring at his backside. A blush stained her cheeks when he caught her watching him, and she grinned sheepishly as she ducked out the door.

ELEVEN

ELIZA DONNED HER COAT AND SLIPPED OUT OF THE servants' entrance of Camille's townhome in Mayfair. She hadn't dared tell anyone where she was going. She had claimed to have a sore throat and gone to bed early while Jenny and their mother went out to the theater. Even Jenny, who generally went along with her schemes, would have put her foot down for this one.

Like she'd promised, she wore a light merino gown in dark green. It was on the plainer side but had detailed embroidery along the hemline and bodice. They had traded in all of their truly plain clothes in order to look the part of heiresses. She was not wearing any sort of jewelry, and the cloak could be pulled closed to hide other details if necessary.

Approximately ten minutes after leaving home, she arrived at the street corner where they had arranged to meet. The streets were fairly busy, but no one seemed to notice her. There was no sign of Simon yet. She began analyzing the carriages that passed when a man stepped up behind her. She knew it was him before he'd even said a word. His clean lemon scent wafted to her from behind.

"Where did you come from?" She smiled as she turned to see him. He wore a proper suit and hat, though she noted that it was plainer than what he'd worn escorting her family around.

"Followed you." He smiled back, giving her a glimpse of his gold eyetooth.

"You followed me?" She hadn't seen or heard him at all.

He nodded. "I was in the park waiting for you to come out of the house. I didn't want you to have to walk alone."

She was touched by his thoughtfulness, and a little annoyed that he thought she needed an escort, but his eyes sparkled down at her, centering her thoughts on him. He wasn't entirely put off by this night of adventure. Was it possible that he might even enjoy himself? The idea thrilled her for reasons she'd rather not examine.

"Thank you again for coming with me," she said when he indicated they walk toward a cabstand.

He offered her his arm and they walked like a true couple. The solid strength of him beneath her touch was distracting. It brought back the memory of his long and muscled form as she had last seen him. The pale globes of his buttocks and the powerful muscles of his thighs. She still couldn't believe her audacity in stealing a peek at him.

"We have to be home before dawn," he said as they walked.

She was already perturbed that he'd made her wait until eleven. "But surely no one will see me if we stay a little longer."

He gave a brisk shake of his head as he held out a hand to hail the cab. "The servants will be up at dawn, possibly before. We're already risking much."

"We keep city hours. The duchess's servants won't be up so early."

He gave her a look with furrowed brows. "You've no idea what it means to run a household, do you? There's food to fetch, laundry to do, and hearths to clean and light. Most of that before the household is awake."

She was suitably chastised. She knew how their small household back in New York operated, but they'd only had the one housekeeper and she didn't live with them all the time.

"You still want to be able to marry your viscount, yes?" he asked, mistaking her silence for a partial retreat before she redoubled her attack.

The mention of *him* made her stomach churn unpleasantly. She didn't want him intruding on her night out. "I understand." Simon was right. She was already taking a risk by going out with him. It was foolish to think she could extend the evening further into tomorrow.

He helped her into the cab and climbed in behind her as he gave the driver their direction. Settling back against the well-worn leather seats, she watched London pass by her window. Thoughts of the viscount faded, and the familiar warmth of excitement burned in her belly as she anticipated the night to come. The sights and sounds and people. She could hardly imagine what she would see.

"Before we arrive, there are a couple of things we need to get settled between us." Simon's voice called her back to him. She hadn't realized how much space he'd take up in the cab. He warmed her entire right side, and her leg was pressed to his. His scent surrounded them, mingling with the leather and stale sweat of prior occupants. The light citrusy smell more than made up for the slight unpleasantness. "I need you to promise to stay at my side the entire time. Do not leave me for a minute. Not even to piss in an alley."

She smiled to cover her embarrassment, but a laugh escaped her anyway. "I'll try to hold it."

"This is no jest, Miss Dove. I need you to understand that there will be danger lurking in the shadows and it won't hesitate to reach out and grab you if given half a chance."

He must be exaggerating things, but she nodded anyway and dropped the smile. "I understand, but what do I do if I have to . . ." She couldn't say it. "Go to . . . relieve myself?"

He grinned. "It'll be in an alley, miss, only I'll be there with you."

That did not sound like something she wanted to participate in, so she resolved to indeed hold it even if her bladder burst.

Continuing on with his rules, he said, "We'll pretend you're my sweetheart. If we encounter anyone I know, then I'll say you're mine. Even among strangers, I'll keep my hand on you. It's important that people believe we're together."

"Is this your way of saying that you want to hold my hand?" she asked with a smile.

She saw his teeth when he smiled. He looked away before saying, "I'll be holding your hand and more, possibly. Just be aware."

"Okay, I'll be aware. You can hold my hand and more if need be." A very large part of her was hoping there would be need. The way he'd said *you're mine* was still echoing inside her. "I was thinking it might be a good idea if I don't talk very much. I can do a passable English accent. It wouldn't work for the Queen, but possibly for others."

"Good. We should come up with another name for you, too."

"Something common. How about Mary? If I'm your girl, then we don't need to worry about a last name."

A shadow passed over his face. "Mary was my sister's name. How about Anne?"

Was. His sister had died. She felt immediately terrible for even bringing up the name to remind him of his loss. She had a hundred questions about his life, but she couldn't ask a single one. Not yet. Instead she said, "I'm sorry. I didn't know. Of course, Anne it is."

He looked past her and out the window. Tall brick buildings lined the street on either side of them. The streets were no longer well-kept, and some of the buildings looked to be badly in need of fresh paint. The farther they drove from Mayfair, the worse it became, until there were whole sections of eaves hanging off or rotting wood that needed to be replaced.

The closer they got to Whitechapel, the tenser he became beside her. It was almost a physical change that came over his face. His jaw tightened and his brows drew together, a permanent crease etched between them. For the first time it occurred to her that this jaunt might cost him more than she realized. Should she say something? Should she tell him that he didn't have to do this—whatever this was—to himself? She wavered, uncertain whether or not to mention it. And then it was too late. The carriage came to a stop and he reached into the inside breast pocket of his coat and withdrew their fare.

"Oh no, I can pay." She rifled in the small drawstring bag attached to her wrist.

His eyes widened when he saw it. "Give me that." He took it away from her before she could argue and stuffed it into his coat. "I'll pay." He handed the money up to the driver and the carriage door opened. "Never carry a purse on you here. Keep your money as close to your breast as possible."

She nodded, embarrassed again that she was doing so terribly on their night out. He climbed out first, helped her down, and then they were alone on a strange street corner in a strange part of a city that she barely knew. It was only in that moment that she understood the deep well of trust she had placed in him. There were no other cabs around. Perhaps they didn't come to this dark part of the city. She didn't even know which direction to go to get home. She turned in a small circle. The brick buildings stretched out in either direction, dark and abandoned, or so it seemed.

"This way." He put a hand on her lower back and shepherded her down the sidewalk to a lighted area up ahead. "This is the hay market on Whitechapel High Street," he explained. "It's where most of the nighttime activity is."

Once they turned the bend in the road, the light became something like a city square. Several cobblestone roads seemed to converge with an island in the middle. Shops and stalls lined each side with crowds of people moving along as if everyone knew exactly where they were going. A church spire rose high up in the distance on the far side. Wagons wound through the chaos, bringing loads of hay for the morning market, their wheels grinding the piles of manure that littered the streets. It made for an almost overpowering smell. Her hand rose to her nose.

At her side, he said, "You'll get used to it."

She wasn't entirely certain that she would, but she wasn't going to let it stop her. He guided her along, and a hawker called out to them, offering them hot cups of coffee. The next stall offered colorful scarves and fabrics. That was followed by a cart hung with the most terrifying dolls she had ever seen. Their hair was coarse and made of corn husks and dried grasses, their eyes were simple x's made of black yarn, and their dresses made of burlap. "One for your sweetheart," the woman called out to Simon. He declined and they kept walking.

Across from them, a pub presided over the square. It seemed to be the life of this particular part of the city with a steady stream of people going and coming through its doors. As much as she wanted to see the inside, she wasn't up for it yet.

Simon guided her to the side, in front of a drapery shop that was closed for the night. A huddled form took refuge on the floor in front of the door, but Simon didn't seem to pay the person any mind. "What do you want to do first?"

It was almost too much. She didn't know. The pub later, but she didn't want to jump headfirst into the belly of the beast. She wanted to ease her way in. A sign across the street caught her eye. The stylized white lettering on a black background named it **PENNY AMUSEMENTS**. "Let's go there."

He agreed and they stepped into the street to cross. It was no easy feat since the wagons seemed to have no interest in stopping for them and the manure was so thick that it took some concentration to find a foothold not covered with it.

"Have you ever been inside? What is it?" she asked.

"It changes to keep customers interested. You never know what you'll find."

A tall man at the door garbed in black from head to toe watched them approach, his eyes lighting up at the prospect of a sale. "Come in, come in, and bring your lady friend, sir," he said in a very heavy Cockney accent. "Come in and see the strongest woman in the world. Challenge her and win and secure yourself the prize of the night."

Simon declined but paid him a penny for each of them. The man in black opened the heavy wooden door and they entered

a dimly lit hallway. Music and carousing could be heard further inside, but here they were alone. She took his hand and he
tightened his fingers around hers.

Wax figures lined the hallway, three on each side. The first
was a very dignified and royal-looking woman with auburn
hair. The name placard read Catherine of Aragon. The next
was an attractive woman wearing Tudor dress, but instead of
her head being where it was meant to be on top of her neck,
she held it at her side. Her smile was twisted grotesquely and
her neck had been severed clean across. It was painted red to
look like blood.

Finally, she understood. "Anne Boleyn. These are the wives
of Henry VIII."

Simon gave a brief laugh, an exhale of breath that seemed
louder than it was in their cocoon. "Never let it be said that
we don't enjoy the sport of watching our betters meet their
ends."

"Even centuries later," she added.

His other wives were also on display. Another with her
head at her feet, and one that lay on her side, her womb on the
outside of her body. One with a strong jaw and long nose, and
a final one presented in a more dignified manner in royal
dress.

Up ahead a woman peeled back the black curtain that had
kept them artificially away from the main attraction. "Welcome in, sir, madam." She indicated they should go on inside.
There were rows of chairs facing a small platform meant to be
a stage, and a woman stood on it. Her hair at the side of her
head had been sheared to above her ears while the back had
been braided and coiled on the crown of her head. She wore a
button-down shirt that had the sleeves torn out to reveal the
impressive muscles of her biceps. On her legs, she wore flesh-

ings. It took a moment for Eliza to be certain that she wore anything on her bottom half at all, because the tights almost perfectly matched her light skin color. A canvas stretched across the ceiling above her head declared her name to be *Miss Pearl, Strongest Woman In The World*. There were crude drawings of a woman with her proportions performing all sorts of feats of strength, from raising a man over her head to lifting a cannonball attached to a rope with her teeth.

"Here." Simon led them to seats in the far side of the room that backed up to the wall, she assumed because it gave him a clear view of the door and the stage.

The woman on the stage was in the process of picking up two weights that had been attached with rope to a metal bar. She strained and grunted but finally lifted it over her head in an impressive display of strength before lowering it again. The crowd applauded and an announcer with a speaking trumpet declared that she had successfully picked up ten stone. As he spoke, another man who was part of the show brought out a pair of boxing gloves, which she donned with the ease of practice. The announcer invited any man in the audience who would like to challenge Miss Pearl to a match to approach the stage.

"Which one of you has the nerve to fight me?" she called out. An organist accompanied her words to dramatic effect. "I'll take on any one of you men as long as you weigh under ten stone. You?" She pointed at a man in the second row. His friends had gotten her attention because they'd been pushing him to challenge her. "Do you have the bollocks to fight me?" He demurred. "I didn't think you did. You have the look of a girlie type. More cunt than bollocks." The crowd laughed uproariously.

The man stood up, affronted. Eliza couldn't hear exactly

what he said because his back was to her, but she heard him call the woman a very vulgar name. Miss Pearl insulted him again and he charged the stage. A bruiser as wide as he was tall had been posted at the perimeter of the stage and he stopped the man.

"You have to pay to fight me, idiot." The woman laughed at him.

The man practically sputtered with indignation and rifled in his pockets to pull out some coins. He tossed them onto the stage and was allowed to proceed. As he climbed up, he took off his coat. Miss Pearl made a show of stretching her neck and shoulders as the man punched out, and she was easily able to dodge him. This went on for a couple of minutes with her calling him all manner of names until she finally got tired of toying with him and punched him square in the jaw. He went tumbling from the stage and landed on a few audience members. The crowd loved it.

Eliza leaned over to Simon. "I'm beginning to see where you get your showmanship."

He guffawed.

"Admit it. You could have ended that fight with Mr. Carstone in the first minute."

"Watch the show," he said, and ducked his head as the people in front of him had turned to get a good look. But it was too late.

"It's the Duke," one of them whispered.

"The Duke himself," someone else said but louder.

It didn't take long for the information to spread through the audience. Simon muttered a curse under his breath and indicated they should leave. They rose but it was too late. He commanded the attention of the room. Some looked on in confusion, but it was clear that several people knew him as the Duke.

"The Duke will fight you." The bald man in front of them stood up and called out to Miss Pearl.

Miss Pearl frowned, her brow furrowed. "Is there another challenger?"

"No, apologies, Miss Pearl, but I'm a bit more than ten stone," Simon said. He took Eliza's arm and moved to leave.

"Join the show!" the bald man said. "Who here wants to fight the Duke?"

Calls of enthusiasm followed them as they walked toward the door, Simon's arm snaked around her waist.

TWELVE

꧁

"DOES EVERYONE KNOW YOU HERE?" ELIZA ASKED when they were back outside. She seemed a little afraid of the answer.

Simon tucked her against him with his hand at her lower back. It wasn't something he had realized he'd done until the side of her body pressed to his. She didn't seem to mind the closeness. She stared up at him with her clear brown eyes so full of trust and intrigue. The gold flecks in their depths shined up at him. It was a shame that it couldn't be real. If they were different people, he could bring her out like this often. They could drink and laugh and kiss. Some long-buried part of him wanted to indulge in that frivolity for the evening, but he couldn't afford to let his guard down. Brody was watching whether they saw him or not. Life could never be what Simon wanted it to be as long as he was beholden to that monster.

"Not everyone, no. The ones that know me as the Duke are the blokes that bet on brawls. The ones that would go to a show like Miss Pearl's."

She nodded thoughtfully. "Even still, it seems I misunderstood the aura of your mystique."

He laughed. "The aura of my mystique?" He couldn't help but laugh when she was near even as they dodged the piss and shit that clogged the streets. "Where to next?"

She looked around and her gaze caught on the pub across Whitechapel High Street. The White Hart was well-known far and wide. Loud and crowded, it tended to attract those from outside the rabbit warrens of Whitechapel who came to gawk at the people who lived here. He didn't want to go there. Not with her.

"Do you see the church?" he asked to distract her.

She turned her head to look at the church spire that rose about two hundred feet high into the sky just past the boundary of the high street area. "Yes."

He'd always found the outside of the building rough and forbidding. It was meant to be a respite among the dirty streets that surrounded it, but the forbidding brick and stone had never felt welcoming. It loomed dark and austere in the night. The inside wasn't any better. He hadn't seen it in over ten years, but it had been filled with sculptures, gilding, and stained glass windows. An embarrassment of riches given the lack of basic necessities available to those it cared for.

"St. Mary Matfelon. Legend has it that it was once limewashed, ages ago. Or perhaps one of the earlier buildings that sat there was. It's how the area became known. It was the White Chapel."

She looked at it with renewed interest. "I'd never heard that."

"Why would you have? Most people don't care about this corner of the city." He hadn't meant his voice to sound bitter, but it did.

Her head whipped around and she looked up at him, perhaps seeing too much. "I didn't mean . . ."

"They say we were found there . . . Mary and I." He didn't know why he'd said it. There was no reason to tell her about himself. He damned well didn't remember those early years. If the change in subject was meant to shift course from the awkwardness of his previous statement, it didn't work.

"You were left there?" What else was she supposed to say? She turned to him, and her voice had taken on a soft and curious inflection.

Her tender concern would break him. He could feel a tightening sensation rising in his chest. His hand slid to her hip, and he made sure to keep his eyes straight ahead and not on her as he led her away from the high street. This road was still a main thoroughfare, less busy, but not so quiet as to be dangerous. Or any more dangerous.

He should change the subject, but he inexplicably kept talking. "There's an alcove around the side of the church that is hidden from the street. We were found there with a threadbare blanket. It was near winter. November or December, I reckon. I was an infant; Mary couldn't have been more than a year or two. They said that she held on to me and wouldn't let me go." She'd always been protective of him, even when the foundling house had split them into different rooms once they'd moved out of the nursery. Her with the girls and him with the boys.

"Do they know who your parents were? Your mother?"

He shook his head. "If they did, they never said."

"Perhaps she left you there because she knew she couldn't care for you properly during the cold winter."

"It's kind of you to think so." Sometimes he thought that, too. Sometimes he wondered if she'd died from disease and someone had dropped them there. Sometimes he wondered if she'd ever cared for them at all. If she'd been happy to rid herself of them. He'd never know the truth.

"Where did you grow up? Did you live at the church?"

"The church sent us to a foundling house they funded. We stayed there for a while . . . until we left."

"Why did you leave?" she asked.

"Doesn't matter. That's enough about that."

He was cursing himself for ever mentioning it. He let her go. They could walk side by side. No one would bother her. It was obvious they were together. He didn't need to touch her. But she didn't give him that choice. She took hold of his arm and laced hers through it. He shouldn't like the fact that she did it as much as he was enjoying it. Having her on his arm made him feel about two stone bigger and taller.

She was silent for a moment, her attention caught by a trio of acrobats performing on the pavement ahead. The high street was known for its street performers. They all wore black tights and flat boots as they contorted themselves into unnatural shapes. Then, as a fourth beat cymbals together, one of them was tossed into the air to land on another's shoulders to much applause from the spectators they had attracted. He tossed a halfpenny into the ratty felt hat laid out on the ground as they passed.

"You and I aren't that different, you know."

He should've known she wouldn't give up the conversation so easily.

"You've said something similar before, but from where I'm standing you're wrong." He grinned to soften his words. "You're either lying or prone to delusions, and I can't figure out which."

She smiled up at him, latching on to his arm with both hands. "There is a third option. That I'm telling the truth." He shook his head, but she kept talking. "My mother tells everyone that she was born to some genteel but impoverished family from South Carolina. That they died from a fever. Sometimes it's influenza, or scarlet fever, or yellow fever. She was the only one who survived and was sent to Chicago to be with distant relatives. But the truth is that she was born in Chicago. Much like you, she was left on the steps of an orphanage as a newborn. When she was older, they told her it was likely that her mother had been a prostitute. They frequently left their liabilities at the door. The orphanage had a basket set out for that reason."

He shook his head. He didn't think she was lying to him, but it seemed too unlikely. She wasn't like him.

"How did your mother go from a prostitute's castoff in an orphanage to the ballrooms of London?"

"That, Mr. Cavell, is a long and sordid tale. Suffice it to say that Fanny Dove is a resourceful woman who knows how to use the men in her life to her advantage."

"And that's why you're marrying Mainwaring . . . using him to your advantage?"

The words caused an instant change in her. Her brow trembled and her mouth tightened. "No more than he is using me."

"No," he said quickly. "Of course not. I didn't mean it that way. I can see that he's using you, as well." He spoke to the top of her head, because she was looking down at their feet.

He hadn't meant it in a way that would hurt her. It was simply that the idea of her with that man struck Simon like a fist to the gut and he spoke without thought. Grasping for some way to bring back her good cheer, he said, "Look." She followed the direction he pointed. A cobblestone path turned to the left, a high brick wall on one side and a row of terraces on the other. "Graces Alley. There's a music hall there. Best one in Whitechapel."

THIRTEEN

THE LARGE BUILDING WAS FOUR FLOORS TALL AND seemed to expand infinitely on either side. Even though the tall and heavy double wooden doors were closed, lively music trickled outside to them. On a wooden sign above the door, the word *Wilton's* was written in red paint. The ground floor windows were covered with red shutters to hide whatever was happening inside from those who hadn't paid for their ticket. Carved plaster panels on either side of the door had been installed backward, so that pineapples hung upside down from their stone dishes. Eliza wondered if the quirk had been intentional.

A man in a dark green suit with red piping guarded the door. He called out to them when he saw their interest and promised an evening of music and delightful exhibitions. Simon paid their admittance fee and he opened the door for them. The building's rather plain exterior had not prepared her for what was inside. The entrance hall had a very high ceiling with frescoes of what looked to be cherubs, Shakespearean scenes, and mythological creatures all making a home for themselves on a sky blue backdrop. The music hall was a flurry of activity. To the right, the hall opened up into what appeared to be a pub. Several men stood at the bar, others sat at small tables eating, while others stood along the wall drinking and laughing. The theater was up ahead, and that's where Simon led her.

The corridor opened into a huge room that soared several stories overhead. A giant chandelier hung from the high ceiling and lit the space with hundreds of little gas flames and thousands of dangling crystals. A gallery encircled the area above with hundreds of people seated there. Hundreds more crowded the main floor, which was set with long tables and chairs all around them. Behind them, chairs were set up in rows on the wide steps that led to the upper area.

A man on the stage in formal evening wear was belting out a tune she could barely discern over a boisterous orchestra. She caught the words "Call me Champagne Charlie" as he popped the cork on a bottle of the stuff. People applauded as the liquid spewed out in a fountain and he held it off the side of the stage so the people seated there could catch it with their glasses. A man in a uniform matching the red and green of the man at the door indicated they should go to the left. There were other couples sitting at tables where Simon found two seats for them.

"Do you want a gin?" Simon asked near her ear.

She'd never had gin, but she nodded and he ordered two from the waitress who had hurried over to them. The crowd and the heat from the overhead lamp had her slipping out of her cloak before she sat down. Simon took it from her and pushed her chair in before taking his own seat next to her, the cloak folded over his lap. His eyes were glued to the man onstage. "George Leybourne, *the* Champagne Charlie," he leaned over to say in her ear.

"That's George Leybourne?" She'd heard of him. Some of the music halls back home advertised his songs on playbills out front. She was so accustomed to other people singing his music that it hadn't occurred to her that the performer might be the man himself.

Simon nodded enthusiastically, excited that she knew who he was. "He performs here regularly. A few times a year at least. I see him when I can."

"Did you know he was here tonight?"

"Happy accident," he said.

She meant to go back to watching Mr. Leybourne, but Simon's profile arrested her. His face was lit up in pure happiness. She couldn't remember a time when he wasn't tense. Even when he laughed with her, he gave the feeling that it was pulled out of him reluctantly, despite all the million things that pulled at him. Perhaps he needed this night of adventure as much as she did. Without thinking, she reached over and placed her hand in his where it rested on her cloak. Startled, he looked at her and she squeezed gently. A thank-you for the evening. He squeezed back and held her gaze until she managed to look back at the stage. She thought it was the happiest of accidents that she'd run into him in the service corridor at Montague Club. She was supposed to return to her life after this night was over, but she couldn't imagine not seeing him again.

What would her seeing him again look like? She couldn't turn up at Montague Club again. Someone was bound to find her there. He couldn't come to see her—not that he would.

Mr. Leybourne finished his song with a crescendo that had him drinking directly from the bottle of champagne before tossing it to a man in the audience who eagerly caught it to uproarious applause. Though Simon laughed along with everyone else, he didn't let go of her hand. Even when the barmaid returned with their tin cups of gin, he raised his cup with his right hand and she with her left. He toasted her silently and she clinked her cup to his. Then she took a swallow of the gin and her tongue caught fire. Her eyes watered and she sputtered as the liquid burned all the way down to her stomach where it simmered like a banked lump of coal.

"Have you never had gin before?" he asked, his voice laced with amusement.

"Never," she said when she could finally talk. Several of the people near them looked over, probably in annoyance.

"Goes down something fierce the first time, but gets smoother as you go."

She eyed it dubiously. Onstage, the man announced in his booming voice that it was time for someone named Flying Myrtle to entertain them. The crowd applauded and Eliza looked for her onstage, but the thick velvet curtains never parted. Finally, she realized that most people were looking up, so she did, too, and saw a woman standing dangerously perched on the outside railing of the gallery above. Flying Myrtle was posed in the glow of a limelight with one arm high above her head.

She was a plump woman with shining black hair tied up on her head. She wore a gleaming silver costume with a fitted bodice and tulle skirt similar to what a ballerina might wear, but the skirt was much shorter. White tights fitted to her legs, and on her feet she wore shoes similar to pointe shoes. Offstage, a drummer made repeated low raps on a drum and the woman got into position with one foot out. It was only then that Eliza realized that she meant to traverse a rope that stretched from one side of the gallery to the other.

Eliza watched transfixed as the performer made her way out over the audience. As she walked, knees wobbling, the people under her would duck as if she was about to fall on them. Several people shrieked in anticipation of such an event. The musicians hidden in a pit to the side of the stage played along with her every step and seemed to even anticipate when she'd walk faster or slow down. She moved with grace and dexterity and finally made it to the other side to hoots and clapping. Once there, a man handed her a chair and she started the whole process again, this time with the chair in hand. She balanced it over her head and even sat on it right in the middle of the stretch of rope before walking to the side again. There she bowed and climbed quickly over the railing.

Other musical performances followed. There was a man with a banjo who sang about a sweetheart back home who'd run off with a railroad man. He sounded American. He was followed by a lively performance of dancing girls with ruffled skirts and stockinged feet. Some of the people in the audience even got up and danced along with them. The area in front of the stage seemed to be reserved for men, and several of them got up and danced together, swinging from arm to arm as everyone clapped along. She was struck by how lively and boisterous it all was. The excitement was infectious. It was more thrilling than attending the theater on the other side of town with stilted social mores and no one really paying attention to the entertainment. No one looked at her oddly for clapping along or drinking her gin. Simon was right: it did get smoother the more she drank.

They might not be looking at her for clapping or drinking,

but ever since the banjo man, several women at the next table
kept glancing at her and then murmuring among themselves.

She leaned over and whispered in Simon's ear, "Why are
they staring at me?" She got a nice whiff of lemon and made
a note to ask him what the scent was. It was quite appealing.
Though she suspected some of the appeal was that he wore it.

He looked at her, his eyes first going to her mouth, which
always sent a thrill shooting through her stomach whenever he
did it, then to her hat, and then to her eyes. "It's your hat.
They know you're not one of us and are wondering what
you're doing here."

"My hat?" She touched it instinctively. It was a simple
black hat with a narrow brim that she thought sat rather jaun-
tily on the hair she had pinned up herself. It had a little veil
that was more decorative than functional because it merely
covered the front brim, and a cluster of black feathers.

"It's not up to Whitechapel standards, I'm afraid."

He was right. The women all wore large hats of felt and
velvet with even larger flowers, plumes, feathers, and all manner of decorations. A slow study of the other women in the
crowd found them to be similar. Only a few hats were black.
Most were blue, crimson, green, and even purple, dark colors
that wouldn't easily show dirt and would wear longer.

"Why didn't you tell me?" she asked.

"You're not going to buy a new hat for one night out."

"How do they know *you* are from around here?" she asked,
mildly annoyed.

"I don't look out of place." He waggled his fingers at the
women and they giggled and turned their attention to the
show.

She sat back in her seat, but kept her hand on his shoulder.
It felt too good touching him, but also, she wanted those

women to think he was hers. She wasn't very proud of that part of her, but there it was. He glanced at her hand, but she couldn't tell what he thought before he returned his attention to the stage.

Mr. Leybourne was back, this time without his champagne. He began singing a lovely tune that she hadn't heard before, but that everyone else seemed to know. There was loud applause when he started, and several people tried to sing along, until their friends shushed them. It was the love song Simon had sung the night he was inebriated. The night they had met.

> *If ever I cease to love,*
> *If ever I cease to love,*
> *May the moon be turn'd into green cheese,*
> *If ever I cease to love.*
> *She's as sweet as a rosebud,*
> *And lily flow'r chang'd into one.*
> *And who would not love such a beauty*
> *Like an Angel dropp'd from above.*

She leaned forward again. This time she sat so close to him that her lips touched his ear when she said, "I like it better the way you sing it."

He looked at her, surprised, his mouth so close to hers that they could have kissed. She wanted him to kiss her right there in the theater in the middle of everyone. He wouldn't do it, though. She knew him well enough now. He'd want to, but he'd talk himself out of it and think he was doing the right thing by her.

It was a good thing she was impulsive enough for both of them. Maybe it was the gin, but she didn't want to blame it on that. She kissed him and he jarred from the shock of it, but he didn't pull away. In fact, he kissed her back. His soft lips moved over hers, parting and tasting. The song finished, and the thunderous applause drew them apart.

Everyone rose to their feet, including them, but Simon led her out of the theater like the hounds of hell were chasing them.

FOURTEEN

WHY DID YOU DO THAT?" THE WORDS BURST OUT of him as soon as the doors closed behind them and they were out on the street.

Eliza didn't know what to say. He wasn't walking too fast for her, but he was taking them back toward the main street, and she was having trouble watching her step and his face at the same time. He looked . . . not angry, like she'd first assumed . . . but desperate.

"Should I not have?" she asked.

He glanced at her, his brow furrowed as if questioning the state of her sanity. "We're not courting, Eliza."

He'd called her by her first name. The little skip her heart gave had her pausing to catch her breath. He stopped to give her a moment, but he didn't drop her hand. *He still held her hand.*

"I know that we aren't," she finally said. "Is that the only reason to kiss?"

He looked at her and she felt the heat of it all the way to her core. "We're not doing that, either." There was no doubt about what he meant by that.

Hot flames touched her face, those words stoking the fire that always simmered between them. They called up the memory of his nude backside, and her imagination went ahead and embellished, filling out his front side and remembering how it had felt to be pressed against him that night in her bedroom. Perhaps they should do that. At least once.

"Isn't there a space in between?" she asked instead.

"Not for us." He looked straight ahead and continued walking, his long strides eating up the cobblestones and leading them back to the busier area.

She kept pace beside him, fumbling for what to say that would bring back the closeness they had shared in the music hall. Kissing him had felt natural and right. He'd felt it, too. She *knew* he had. It was why he had ended it. She simply wanted it back.

"But why? Simon . . ." She pulled him to a stop. "I simply want to know you." It was as honest as she could be. What would come of knowing him? Nothing, except she would have the memory of him to ruminate over in the coming years of perpetual boredom.

Part of his allure was the adventure, the fact that he represented something totally different from the life being laid out for her, but that wasn't all of it. There was something about him, the essence of him and who he was, that wouldn't allow her to look away. He was from this place but he had made his way to Montague Club and a new life, driven by some spark inside him that she didn't understand. Yet. She wanted to understand, though. He'd intrigued her since the first night they had met, and she couldn't let it go. She didn't want to let go of this fascination. He was important to her life in a way that she couldn't understand yet.

"You want to know me?" he asked. There was a challenge in his words.

Fine, she'd accept. "Yes, I want to know who you are and what you feel and why it means so much to you to leave here." She raised her free hand up to encompass the area.

He shook his head. "You don't know the first thing about this place."

"It's no Mayfair or Belgravia, but in some ways I prefer it here. The people are real."

"Is that so?" He held out her cloak for her.

She turned and allowed him to drape it over her shoulders. "Yes, it is so. I'm not as naive as you seem to think. I lived near the Bowery back home, and my mother sometimes took us into the Tenderloin district when she had a friend performing at a playhouse there." Though the area hadn't been known as the Tenderloin when she was growing up.

"The Tenderloin?" he asked. His fingers absently tied the edges of her outer garment together.

"A district in Manhattan with brothels, taverns, music halls, and cheap playhouses," she explained. "According to a friend of my mother's, the police get paid extra by the brothels for protection, so they eat beef tenderloin for dinner instead of the cheaper fare a policeman's salary provides."

"What sort of friends does your mother have?"

She smiled, sensing that she might get further with him if she told him a little more of her family secrets. "She was an actress until she met my father." Mr. Hathaway was her true father, not Mr. Dove, but that was a story for a later time. After Mr. Hathaway had taken up with her mother, he'd forbidden Fanny from performing. He didn't want her anywhere near those sorts of theaters to fan the flames of gossip about his illegitimate family.

His gaze fell upon her face as if seeing her anew. "I told you the truth." She took his hands in hers and held them between their bodies. "We are more alike than you think."

He looked away and blew out a breath of air. "It's not the same here."

"No, it's not. I understand that." Before she could stop herself, she touched his face, drawing his eyes back to her. "I know that the poverty you experienced here is different. Growing up without your mother, or any parent. It's not the same. I know that. I only wanted you to understand that I didn't grow up with all of the advantages that you seem to think I did."

For the first time since walking out of the music hall, there was a chink in his armor. A shimmer of longing came into his eyes as his gaze dropped to her mouth and back up to her eyes. Her hand moved to rest on his chest. His heart thumped a steady rhythm under her palm. She wanted to kiss him, but she knew better than to spook a stray kitten.

"Will you show me more of this place?"

"Do you mean to go farther in?"

"Yes."

"It's too danger—" He paused and something caught his eye. There was movement back the way they had come. He grabbed her arm and began walking at a fast pace toward the Whitechapel High Street.

She glanced back over her shoulder but couldn't see very much. It looked like a man was walking behind them, but she didn't see anything that made her think he was following them. "What's happened?"

"We need to leave," was all he said.

After they entered the busy area, Simon made to cross the street, but paused at the curb. Two men were directly across the road from them. She had never seen them before, but they looked hard and menacing. Their eyes locked on Simon, and she knew for certain they didn't like him.

Simon cursed under his breath and changed course again. The man behind them had disappeared into the crowd. Simon took hold of her hand and walked so fast she was practically running beside him. They went toward the White Hart, the pub they had seen earlier that she'd wanted to go in. It occupied a corner with a street on one side and an alley on the other. He took them through the open double doors from the street, threading them through the crowd inside. They darted out the other side and toward the alley.

The mouth of the alley was marked by an arched tunnel that might have been charming in the daylight, but at night it was a little forbidding, like an entrance to another world. The narrow cobblestone lane was barely wide enough for four people to stand shoulder to shoulder. Tall brick walls of tenement buildings hemmed them in on either side and stretched several floors overhead. It felt oppressive, like they were running into the mouth of danger rather than away from it.

A handful of women in tattered dresses lounged against the sides of the buildings. They wore large hats like the ones Eliza had noticed back at the theater. A few of them called out to Simon while giving her curious glances. They were prostitutes peddling their trade as they waited for customers to come stumbling out from the pub.

Simon hurried them through so fast that she barely got a good look at them. It was dark and frightening here with no proper light to show them the way, which meant she had to pay attention to the crumbling roadway so that she didn't trip. The only light here was an open fire far in the distance. It became quieter as they left the merriment of the tavern behind them. The change in atmosphere was immediate. Instead of feeling jolly and festive, the very air felt stifling and dark. Almost as if something cynical watched them from every doorway and window they passed.

"Where are we going, Simon? Why are we here?" she asked, her voice lowered so that whatever was in the shadows didn't hear them.

"Because we can't let them catch us."

It was such a simple statement to cause such terror to grip her heart.

"What happens if they catch us?"

His eyes said it all. Nothing good.

She grabbed up her skirt and sprinted with renewed verve. He took them down one dark alley after another. She knew she'd never be able to find her way out without him. Finally, he slowed and they walked. He kept her close to him, though, his arm at her waist as they moved through the alleys. She wondered if whatever awaited them in the dark might be worse than what trouble followed them.

Several times different men came to attention when they approached. Simon would call out some variation of a greeting that would see them stand down until they passed. Sometimes they'd greet him by name. Twice he tossed a coin over in what seemed like pay for their safe passage. She lost count of how many times they hurried past figures moving in the darkness against a wall. Grunts and soft cries filled the air, leaving no doubt in her mind what was happening. Women found customers at the pubs and brought them to the alleys.

"This is what it's like," he finally whispered when their hearts had slowed. It seemed they had lost their pursuers. His voice was soft but resolute. "The people that live here work hours every day for pay that doesn't cover rent and food for themselves, let alone their families. They're left to make up the difference at night."

She tried to imagine how hopeless it must feel to labor all day and then be forced to turn to prostitution at night in an alleyway. The truth was that whatever she imagined was a pale comparison to the experience of living it. She and her family hadn't had very much, but they'd never been forced to sell their bodies to survive. As much as she sometimes struggled with her decision to sell her hand for a title, it wasn't the same as being taken by a drunk man against a wall that smelled of human waste.

She tightened her fingers around Simon's and he squeezed them gently. The next street was a bit wider, wide enough for a carriage to easily traverse. It was a smaller and grittier version of Whitechapel High Street without the interlopers. An open sewer ran down the middle of the street. Plaster crumbled in the wide gaps between the bricks, and some of the walls were covered in crude drawings and words. The paint around the street-level doors and windows had long ago peeled away.

They had no sooner left the opening of the alleyway than several men solidified from the shadows. Simon tightened his arm at her waist and pushed her behind him. She held on to him and peered over his shoulder.

The only light here was from the moon overhead, but her eyes had adjusted to the darkness. The man before them was of average height with a solid frame. He gave the appearance of being well-fed, which she couldn't say for most of the people they had passed in their run through the maze of streets.

"Good evening, Cavell," he said.

FIFTEEN

SIMON BRISTLED AT THE VERY SIGHT OF JAMES BRODY.
The fact that he was in the same space as Eliza only served
to put Simon further on edge. Brody was unpredictable. Circumstance dictated his wickedness, but it was often comple-
mented by the delight he took in his own moral decay. Most
knew that Brody had a strong hand but thought he could be
reasoned with. They had good reason for thinking that. Brody
wanted them to think that. But Simon had seen with his own
eyes what happened when his tightly moderated control
snapped. He'd seen the man go too far. He'd seen how his eyes
lit up with the ecstasy of unbridled power. Simon had seen him
break a man just because he could get away with it.

"Brody," he said in acknowledgment.

"Wot are ye doin' here?" Brody asked. He gave no clue to
what he wanted.

Simon came back frequently, and it was no surprise that
Brody knew that. Brody had men everywhere, knew what was

happening on every corner of his part of the city. The only surprise here was that the criminal had sought him out.

"Wot do ye want?" Simon asked, though he kept the annoyance from his voice. Eliza's hands were pressed to his back, and he took comfort in the fact that she seemed willing to stay behind him and allow him to lead the talk. He'd turned them slightly so that their backs were facing the wall and not Brody's men who followed them in the alley.

"I've arranged your next task. Thought we'd discuss it." Brody's eyes roved over what he could see of Eliza. "Who's this?"

Simon couldn't appear too defensive; it would only draw more of Brody's attention to her. Instead, he said truthfully, "A new friend. Anne."

"Anne . . ." Brody let the name roll over his tongue. "You're a pretty gal, Anne. Wot are ye doin' with a bloke like this one?"

She shifted and Simon put his palm against her thigh, a subtle indication that she should stay behind him. Her fingers tightened around his coat. "He bought me a gin," she said in a low voice. Her accent wasn't American, nor was it Cockney, but something indistinguishable.

"Bought ye a gin, has he? Ye should make him buy ye more than that before ye go deep into these parts."

"Let's have it, Brody. I need to get her back."

Brody's eyes narrowed on her, but he raised his chin in acknowledgment. "Not in front of her. Come."

The last thing he wanted to do was leave her alone. "She's nothing. Tell me now and let's have this done with."

A stony silence followed. Simon turned and Eliza was staring up at him with her wide eyes. "I have to talk to him or he'll never let us go." He kept his voice low so that it wouldn't travel. "Stay here and don't let anyone touch you."

She gave a firm nod of her head and glanced toward the men that had been steadily creeping toward them from the alley.

"Leave her be, Beck," he said to the one he recognized in the group.

The man shrugged. "Hurry along, then."

Simon touched her hand in encouragement and turned to follow Brody across the street. He wouldn't leave her out of sight and thankfully Brody didn't require this. No one else followed them, leaving them in relative privacy.

"This about that big fight ye mentioned?"

"It's set. You and Rouse."

"Rouse?" It shouldn't come as a surprise. Rouse had a reputation as a strong brawler, and Brody had been angling to set up a fight between them for a long time now. "When?"

"Same as usual. A month hence. Midnight. He'll come here, so we'll have the advantage."

"Why the privacy, then?"

"Because I don't want ye to win. Ye'll lose this one."

"Lose it?"

Brody nodded. "You're too good. Odds are shit if ye win. Ye want a big score? Ye want enough to be out for good? Then ye lose. I'll make yer fee and ye'll leave. And when ye do leave I don't want to see ye here ever again."

Simon shook his head. "I don't lose fights."

"Ye will if ye want to be done with it."

"Ye want me to take a tumble. Why would ye ask it of me?" Most of the people who bet on him were the people here. Men and women who labored in factories and the docks to live in squalor.

"As I recall, it was ye who asked me to arrange something. To get ye out. Well, here is yer chance. Or do not fight and pay the price. Which do ye choose?"

Brody had done this on purpose. He'd arranged the most loathsome scenario he could to make it hurt. Simon ground his molars together. There was nothing for it. This isn't what he wanted, but he'd do it if he had to. The subtle threat Brody had tossed in made it clear that Simon, and possibly Daisy, wouldn't be safe if he refused. "Then ye promise I'll be free. That I'll be out for good."

Brody raised his hands. "On my honor."

"Daisy, too. You'll let her go."

"The brat, too."

"Fine. I'll do it." He'd do whatever it took. He turned to head back to Eliza, but Brody stopped him with a hand on his shoulder.

"Ye could stay," he said. "It's not too late."

Simon paused, knowing what it took for Brody to say that. The plan had been for Simon to run things with him. Brody had never said it, but he'd once trusted him like he'd trusted no one else. He'd meant to share power as much as someone like him was able to share anything. Once, Simon had bought into that plan, but that had changed with Mary's death. He'd promised to get Daisy out and he would.

"It is too late. We both know it." Even if Simon agreed to stay, he'd already lost Brody's trust. He'd be dead once Brody realized he'd never trust Simon like he had before. He'd be killed as a warning to any others who might think to go against Brody's wishes.

Brody dropped his hand and Simon walked back to Eliza. He kept his pace slow and steady even though he wanted to rush over to her. Beck had drifted closer to Eliza. He was standing in front of her, flicking the embroidered edge of her cloak with his filthy fingernail.

"Stand down, Beck. Anne." Simon spoke harshly so that

none of them would get a whiff of what she meant to him and held his arm out to her.

She stepped around Beck who leaned forward to catch her scent. She shrank back from him and hurried toward Simon. She tucked her hand into the crook of his arm. He'd been foolish to think that they could outrun Brody. He was lucky his flight hadn't made the man more suspicious of him.

"I'll see you home," he reassured her.

She nodded silently at his side and he feared the worst, that he'd committed some unforgivable transgression. That she'd never forgive him for exposing her to those men. He should hope that was the case. If she never wanted to see him again, then he'd be well rid of her.

If only that's how he could really feel.

No one appeared to be following them as they made their way back through the alleys of Whitechapel. He didn't bother going back through the hay market. They needed to get out of the area as fast as possible before Brody decided that she meant more to Simon than he'd let on. Brody wouldn't hesitate to use her to toy with him.

Unfortunately, it meant going by the workhouse. He always tried to avoid the looming brick building, but on the rare occasions he was made to pass by, it held him spellbound. Today was no exception. He looked up as they passed. The windows were dark, but that didn't mean someone wasn't looking out. He'd spent many evenings when he was supposed to be asleep looking out the window in the room he'd shared with thirty other boys and imagining a better life. He'd almost found it. He wouldn't let Brody keep him from it by throwing this last hurdle in his path.

"Simon?"

He hadn't realized that he'd stopped until Eliza's voice

broke through his thoughts and her hand rested on his shoulder. She followed his gaze to the building and back again. There was no doubt in his mind that she knew what the building was. The word *workhouse* was carved above the door. Whatever mystique she had attributed to him must have been wiped away. He wasn't the Duke or the boxing champion that Montague Club endorsed. He was Simon, a poor boy with no family who might as well have been born in that workhouse. It was his birthright and the only one he would ever have.

But she didn't shirk from him. Instead, she wrapped her arms around his and when he walked she fell into step beside him. His feet found their purpose again, which was to get her as far away from this place as possible. He took them out of there as fast as he could. She kept pace beside him and he managed not to look at her again too closely. Simon could feel Brody's grip and the grasp of that workhouse lessen about his throat with every step. He always breathed easier when he left.

At the first streetlamp outside of Whitechapel he took her hand and drew her beneath its light. "Are you all right?" he asked in the safety of its warm glow.

She smiled up at him and he was nearly overcome by the trust shining out of her eyes. Who was this woman? He expected fear and censure mixed with repulsion. Not this.

"Yes, obviously. You seem to think I'm made of paper and glass."

He touched her cheek with the pad of his thumb. What had he been thinking? He should have turned her down when she demanded he bring her here. Someone in this girl's life should keep her under lock and key. She felt delicate. Too soft and fragile for the likes of him.

She wasn't, though, and that knowledge filled him with something powerful that he was afraid to examine. "Brody isn't a nice man. I'm sorry you had to see him. I shouldn't have taken you there."

"I've seen bad men before, unfortunately." She cupped the back of his hand with her palm. His gaze was caught by the contrast of her soft hand against the roughness of his own. His were scarred by a lifetime of work and thievery and evil deeds. Hers were pristine. "In fact," she continued, drawing his eyes back to her pretty face, "my father could likely give your Mr. Brody a run for his money."

He did not need to know what she meant by that. He wanted to know, but it was none of his concern. One question would lead to others and where would it end? He gave a nod and took her hand, pulling her behind him as he continued in his headlong dash to get her far away from Whitechapel. The streetlamps came with more regularity, though it was so late the streets here were very nearly deserted. He looked for a hansom cab, but there wasn't one to be found. The area was too residential.

As they walked, his mind churned over what she'd said. She had once told him that she didn't have a father. He'd taken that to mean that her father had died. How could her father give Brody a run for his money? Was the man not dead? It didn't matter. He did not need to know more about this woman who was an enigma to him. He didn't need to understand her.

And yet, the moment they turned a corner and found themselves under a lamp hanging from a storefront, he couldn't resist the inevitable question. She was fascinating to him. He turned to face her, not too close, but close enough that he could read her expression. "What do you mean by that?"

"By what?" It was a reasonable question. Many minutes had passed since they'd last spoken.

"About your father. I thought he was dead."

She glanced at the store behind him and he followed suit. The door was closed. Solid black wood scuffed at the bottom from countless boots. Looping white letters identified it as a coffeehouse, though it wasn't particularly boisterous at this time of night in this slightly more boring neighborhood.

"You want to go in?" he asked.

"Assuming that it's a true coffeehouse and not a brothel?" She raised her eyebrows in question, and a memory of the night they met came back to him. Mainwaring visiting coffeehouses in Italy. Mainwaring was a bellend. He must be the most stupid man imaginable to go off doing that when he had this enchanting creature waiting for him.

"If we go in you'll tell me about your father?" he asked.

She nodded. He opened the door and followed her inside.

SIXTEEN

Eliza had heard that women generally weren't allowed in coffeehouses. That certainly seemed to hold true for this particular house. There was a small group of men in deep discussion at a back table and the man behind the counter. All of them looked up sharply when she and Simon entered. Simon guided her to a corner table near the front window and then went to get them two cups. He put two coins on the bar as he spoke to the man. Whatever he said must have set him at ease, because a few minutes later he poured two cups of coffee from a press machine and pushed them across the counter toward Simon.

"Coffee, milady." Simon set her cup in front of her and took his seat.

She smiled up at him, catching a shimmer of amusement in his eye. Whatever effect the gin had had on her had worn off in the excitement of meeting Mr. Brody. She was glad for that because she didn't want to forget a moment of this night with Simon. In the time since they'd left Whitechapel, he'd regained some of the carefree attitude he'd had at the music hall. She wondered if this is what he was like most of the time, when he wasn't worried about gang leaders and brawls and whatever else seemed to constantly plague him.

Bringing the hot drink to her mouth, she blew gently and took a small sip of the bitter liquid. "Ugh." She tried not to make a face but probably wasn't very successful given the grin he gave her. "Is there no sugar?" she whispered.

"I fear we're on thin ice with the proprietor as it is," he said.

A quick glance at the counter confirmed the man still hadn't recovered from her presence. He kept sending harsh glances their way.

Simon took a drink of his coffee to no ill effect, so she determined to persevere.

"Now, about your father."

"I'll tell you about him if you tell me about Mr. Brody."

He shook his head, his gaze on the window and the deserted street beyond. "Believe me when I tell you that you don't want to know any more about him than you have to."

"But I do," she insisted. When he glanced at her, she added, "To be fair, it's you I want to know about. However, I sense that Mr. Brody factors into your past."

He set his cup down and held it between his hands, his thumb tracing the rim in a way that held her mesmerized. "He does. What do you want to know?"

His blue eyes were deep when they met hers, like the sea on a gray day. His Whitechapel accent had retreated, but he also wasn't using the accent he used at Montague Club. She sensed this was the real him, a mix of the two that elongated some of the vowels and clipped a consonant or two. It was like him, a blend of who he had been and who he was striving to become. "Everything," she said.

The winds between them had shifted in the hours since they'd left Mayfair. In the beginning he'd seemed almost determined to keep distance between them. Little by little that gap had lessened. Now the winds circled around them, pulling them in close together over the table, their voices low and intimate.

"You asked about why we left the foundling home . . . Mary woke me one night. She told me that we had to leave. She looked frightened and I didn't question her. I hated it there. By then we'd been moved to the workhouse. I didn't see her very much and I detested the work."

"You didn't go to school?"

"Some. Enough to read and do basic arithmetic. But by then work took up most of my day." He held up his hands and she leaned forward, caught by the sight of his fingers.

White strips of scar tissue covered the pads of his fingers and the beds of his nails, particularly near his pointer and middle fingers. There were also scars on his thumbs and palms.

"What work did you do?"

There was a sardonic tone to his voice when he said, "I was naughty more often than not, so I got the task of unraveling the old navy ropes that were sent down."

"Why is that a task?" She looked up at his face.

"Oakum. They dip the fibers in tar and use it to line the boats to keep the water out." He glanced at his fingers and turned them over, clenching his hands as if to hide the evidence of his abuse. "The hemp is razor-sharp and cuts like paper."

She hoped the abject horror of imagining such an existence did not show on her face. Instead she took his hand, wishing in some small way to relieve him of the memory.

"How old were you when you left?" she asked.

He shrugged. "Don't know. I'd been at the workhouse for at least a year, maybe more. Eight or ten years old, I expect."

A horrible feeling overcame her. "Simon, do you know how old you are?"

He didn't react for a moment, his gaze taking in her face. Finally, he said, "No, I don't know. It never seemed important."

She couldn't imagine never celebrating a birthday. In their home, birthdays had always been celebrations. They hadn't had much, but there would always be special treats of sweets and gifts. "What's something you can remember? Some event that happened when you were young?"

He paused for a moment, nibbling the inside of his bottom lip as he thought. She'd never envied a lip so much in her life. It sent tingles down her arms to imagine him nibbling her lip in that way. "I can remember when Prince Albert died. I wasn't at the workhouse, so I wasn't yet seven—they sent us all there at seven years old—but Mary was already there."

Prince Albert had died back in '61. She quickly did the math in her head. "If you were only five or six years old, then that makes you twenty-two or twenty-three years old, maybe?"

"That could be." He didn't seem to have a particular interest in the topic for himself, but he asked, "How old are you?"

"Almost twenty." She'd be a wife by her birthday. Pushing that from her mind, she asked, "What happened when you left the workhouse?"

"We lived on the street for a while. I started out doing odd jobs. Then we fell in with a gang of pickpockets. That's how we met Brody. I nipped the billfold of one of his men. Would've got away with it but one of the bastards tripped me and sent it flying. He tried to beat me and I held my own enough that it impressed Brody. After that night we slept on the floor of his office. When we were older, I roomed with the other blokes and he trained me to be a punisher."

"Is a punisher . . . is it just as it sounds?"

"I was his hand of justice. One of them. Much like the blokes that hemmed us in earlier. If someone wronged him, then I made it right."

He didn't say more, but she could see the weight of those words on his face and in his eyes. His shell wasn't as hard as he wanted it to be. She took his hand where it rested on the table. "That's when you decided to leave?"

His gaze jerked away from her and to the window for a moment. She sensed there was more to the story, but he was finished talking about it. "Your turn. Tell me about your father." His gaze settled on their hands. He turned his over beneath hers, and her fingers settled between his. She loved the rough texture of his skin on hers and the way he made her hand feel small.

She wanted to press him for more, but it was only fair that she reveal more of herself to him first. It's not as if he'd show up at a dinner party one night and spill all their secrets to the ton. Even if such a thing were possible—their attending the same dinner party—she trusted him to keep her secrets.

"My mother fell in love with my father, Charles Hathaway, when she was an actress in Chicago. She was young, close to my age, and he was handsome and rich. One can assume he was more idealistic then, to have attracted her attention." It was the only way Eliza could explain it to herself. The man she knew now was nothing like that. She could not imagine her mother ever having her head turned by Mr. Hathaway as he was now. "She became his mistress, though she claims that he promised to marry her. Do you know the Hathaway name?"

He nodded. "It makes the newspapers here some. An old family from New York, if I remember correctly."

"Yes, apparently they were one of the original families. Today they own half of Manhattan. You can imagine his parents were not enraptured with the idea of welcoming Fanny Fairchild into their family. I don't know what happened precisely, but he moved her to New York. He bought her a house and gave her a small allowance, but he eventually left us to rot, house and all. Mr. Dove is not our true father. He's someone my father found to marry her . . . or at least pretend to marry her . . ." It hadn't occurred to her that the marriage might not be real until just this moment. Mr. Dove had died when she was very young. She didn't even have any proper memories of him. She had met his relatives a few times over the years. They trotted down to Manhattan from upstate sometimes to make it appear as if they cared about his children, but there was very little communication. What if the whole marriage had been a ruse?

"Are you all right?" he asked. He squeezed her hand gently.

"I just had the odd thought that I barely know who I am."

He chuckled at that. "No, not you, Miss Dove. You know more about who you are than anyone I've ever met."

That name didn't set right with her suddenly. It was wrong because it wasn't real. Nothing was real but her own name, and she wanted more than anything to be real with him. "Call me Eliza. Please?"

"Eliza." The name rolled over her skin like a caress.

She couldn't hold the intensity of his gaze, so she looked down at their hands. His nails were short and well-kept, but there were small scars on every finger.

"That makes your father a bellend, for certain, but not a killer like Brody," he said.

"I'm sure he'd like to think the same. Which is worse, Simon? A man like Brody who takes advantage of people in horrific situations or a man like my father who helps create those very same situations." At his questioning look, she added, "I mentioned that he owns real estate. Some of those are tenement buildings. Buildings that are cheaply made with exorbitant rents. It's ironic that Devonworth is fighting for water access for such buildings when Hathaway is rumored to have spent thousands fighting *against* a similar policy in the States. He cares only for himself."

Simon's jaw tightened as she spoke. "Did you know him at all as a child? How is he with you?" he whispered.

She had vague memories of him coming to see them when she was very young. Her mother would line them up in their Sunday best and he would nod to each of them. She couldn't remember a conversation she'd ever had with him. Mostly, she had hidden behind Cora. Then the visits had stopped. Cora had gone to see him at his Fifth Avenue townhome last autumn when they had received the note about their inheritances, but he'd never come to see them. Eliza had only met him again here in London, and he might as well have been a stranger to her. She explained all of that and ended with, "He's barely spoken to me."

Simon was quiet for so long that she thought perhaps he didn't know what to say. But then he looked up at her again and his eyes were burning. "Is that how you see your life now? Living with a man who barely sees you?"

"You don't think I should marry Mainwaring, do you?"

He didn't move. His fingers didn't so much as twitch. "That's not up to me," he finally said after an interminably long time.

Gathering her courage, she said, "It's not, but my question

stands. You don't think I should marry him." It wasn't really a question, though, was it?

"You'll be miserable, but that's beside the point. You're not marrying him for happiness."

She shook her head. "No, I'm not expecting to be very happy."

He wanted to say more; she could see it in his face. Instead, he brought his cup to his mouth with his free hand and swallowed very deliberately. She watched his throat work with the action.

"He didn't even ask me to marry him," she said.

An eyebrow rose in response. "Are you not betrothed?"

"He spoke with my mother at the end of the house party Camille gave for us when we first came to England. Then, later, he met with Devonworth and Mr. Hathaway. He never actually asked me." He'd had every reason to assume her consent. The whole reason they were in England was to find husbands. Still . . . it had always irritated her that he hadn't bothered to ask her the question.

Simon licked his lips and then said a bit ruefully, "A man should ask you himself."

"You would have asked me."

His eyes deepened and became heavy as they met hers. He let out a long breath through his nose and whispered, "I would have asked you."

And she would have said yes. For a moment, she allowed herself the absurd luxury of imagining herself with Simon.

Eliza didn't know how long they sat staring at each other. Two of the men got up from the table in the back and left out the front door, the little bell on the door jingling behind them. She glanced away first and Simon let go of her hand. She might have audibly protested, a sound drawn from deep within her at not being able to touch him, but if she did, he didn't appear to notice. He gathered up her half-empty cup along with his and set them on the counter. When he returned, he offered her his hand and she took it.

This was it . . . the end of their night. She might not ever see him again. There would be no reason to see him. She'd promised him that this would be it. She'd leave him alone. He drew her to her feet and she followed him out the door feeling like she'd left half of herself inside. Half of her would forever be in that coffeehouse with him while the rest of her, the ghost of her, would be with Mainwaring . . . married and not at all who she was meant to be.

A light rain had started to fall while they were inside. She didn't mind. She thought—hoped—that maybe they would have trouble finding a hansom because of the hour, but as if he'd summoned it, a cab stopped for them at the corner. The driver rubbed his tired eyes as he asked Simon their direction.

Because of the rain, the driver pulled the leather curtain closed before climbing up on the seat behind the carriage. Eliza tried to look out the window on her side, but her gaze kept going back to Simon, who seemed deep in concentration as he looked out his own window. He hadn't touched her since they had climbed on board, except for where his thigh pressed against hers in the enclosed space. London flew past them faster than it had any right to. They'd be in Mayfair soon, and it would be like the night had never happened.

"Simon."

His breath stilled, but otherwise he didn't acknowledge her.

She closed her eyes before she said the next part. She wouldn't be able to take it if any part of him showed any sort of revulsion. "Would it be all right if we . . . if we pretended that things were different for the next few minutes? If we pretended that we're in love—"

His mouth crushed hers at the same time his arms came around her. She opened to him and his tongue swept inside her. He pulled her onto his lap, and her hands pushed inside his coat, eager to feel him. Her palms explored the planes of his chest, his hard pectoral muscles to his soft but firm stomach. His hands were no less greedy in their exploration. They roamed inside her cloak and she cursed how thick the material of her dress was and how many layers came between them. His palm cradled her breast and her nipple pebbled in response, but she didn't know if he could feel it.

When they paused for air, his hot gaze met hers in the dark, seeking more. She nodded and he made something that sounded like a groan deep in his throat. He kissed her cheek, her jaw, and then her neck. "Simon," she gasped when his teeth touched her skin. He bit right where her neck met her dress, making her break out in gooseflesh.

"Eliza," he whispered, kissing that very spot. Then he sighed and buried his face there.

She held him close, her fingers buried in the hair at the back of his head. She swore she could feel his heart beating against her own breasts. His hat had taken her place on the bench seat at some point.

The carriage slowed and Simon lifted her off his lap a second before the driver opened the hatch overhead.

They had arrived. The night was over.

She waited for him to hand the fare up to the driver and for the hatch to be firmly shut before she said, "You know which bedroom—"

"Eliza." He spoke in a low warning tone that had her smiling. It was the same way he'd said her name when she'd teased him in the hallway at home. Rifling in his coat, he pulled out her purse and handed it to her.

She had been teasing him. He knew where her bedroom was and likely how to come inside without anyone being the wiser. But she hadn't been seriously suggesting he do something like that. Not that she would turn him away . . .

"Good night, Simon."

The dark clouds in his expression parted, and he looked at her like he had a moment earlier. Like she was someone he could love . . . or maybe already did. There was heat simmering beneath the surface, but that wasn't what caught her. That wasn't love. She saw something deeper in his eyes. Something vulnerable and pure. The very presence of it caused a lump to build in her throat. She hurried to disembark the carriage before she did something truly impulsive.

"Good night, Eliza." His voice carried after her, low and deep.

She swore she heard the sound of it reverberating inside her even after she laid her head down to sleep. Her good angel breathed a sigh of relief. The night was done and she was home and now they could get on with it. But her bad angel beat her wings in fury, raging that they weren't finished. This isn't how it was supposed to end.

SEVENTEEN

LIFE WAS MEANT TO GO ON AS IT HAD BEFORE SIMON Cavell had come into Eliza's life. She awoke the day after their night out convinced that it would. She missed him. She had expected to miss him, but that didn't mean she would allow herself to wallow in her feelings. She promised herself that this time her good angel would win. The poor thing deserved an occasional win, even if Eliza wasn't completely happy with the idea of her winning.

She stumbled down to the drawing room the next morning. She had spent what little was left of the night tossing and turning in a restless sleep that had made her irritable but resolved to get on with things. Her mother and sister were already there.

"Good morning, darling." Her mother looked up from her newspaper and offered her cheek for a kiss. She had folded her curvy frame into an armchair with a cup of coffee balanced on the plush upholstery. The creamy liquid in the cup smelled like heaven, much nicer than the strong and bitter brew she had shared with Simon.

Eliza dutifully gave her a peck on the cheek. "Good morning, Mama, Jenny."

Jenny sat on the sofa, also swathed in a dressing gown, a slight but knowing smile on her face as her gaze tracked Eliza to the silver tray service that held an extra cup along with the cream and sugar she'd need to make herself a proper cup of coffee.

"How are you feeling this morning?" Fanny asked.

"Yes, how are you feeling?" Jenny echoed the sentiment but with a certain tone that Eliza didn't appreciate. It made her think her sister had come into her bedroom and found her gone. Jenny wouldn't tell anyone, but she would have many questions, and Eliza didn't know how much she was prepared to share. Her feelings for Simon had changed over the course of the night and become deep and complicated in ways she wasn't ready to examine.

"Better, I think, tired still but no headache." Eliza prepared her coffee and avoided looking directly at her sister as she made her way to the sofa.

"Good, you really don't want to miss many nights out," her mother said. "Once you're married, Mainwaring will undoubtedly tag along and—no offense, darling—he's a bore."

He was a bore. Eliza brought the cup to her lips and savored the first creamy sip. She'd need it to fortify herself, because even thinking about being faced with Mainwaring every day and *not* Simon's mischievous grin was not settling well with her.

"What is it he said at the house party?" Fanny asked.

Jenny sat up straighter and cleared her throat. Affecting an upper-class English accent that Eliza was convinced was taught to these men at their boarding schools, she said, "'Tea in the afternoon is a digestive boon, Miss Eliza, but do not be seduced by the heady flavor. Imbibe any later in the day and 'twill have quite the opposite effect than one intended. One shall find'—"

Eliza held up her hand to stop the recitation. "Thank you for that reminder." He had gone on to lecture them for nearly ten whole minutes on the delicacies of their digestive tracts and how weak bone broths and the avoidance of spices was necessary to preserve their health. She couldn't help but wonder if he'd given any thought to his own health during his coffeehouse visits.

Fanny and Jenny dissolved into bouts of laughter, but Eliza couldn't find the humor in the situation. It wasn't the fact that he was boring that bothered Eliza. Had he gone on about the intricacies of tea production or had he been a purveyor of dietary health to a scientific degree because it was some great passion of his, she could have latched on to his lecture and found some glimmer of information that she hadn't known to explore. But it was the pomposity of his delivery that had stuck with her.

She imagined herself surrounded by a table of their offspring fifteen years into the future while he lectured them on the proper drinking of tea. Or—*heaven forbid!*—what if she'd become a convert at that point and delivered the speech herself? What would she be like after a lifetime with him? Would she be her own person or would he have bent her to his will? What would it be like to raise children with him? To *create* children with him?

"Do you suppose he knows the meaning of the word *seduce*?" she blurted out.

The laughter stopped and everyone was silent. Jenny raised her hand and settled it gently on her shoulder. "Oh, Eliza."

"I wouldn't count on it, darling," Fanny said, setting her newspaper and coffee aside. She rose and joined them on the sofa, sitting on Eliza's other side. "If it helps, Charles didn't know, either."

"Ugh!" Eliza groaned at the same time Jenny said, "*Mother.*"

Fanny rolled her eyes. "You both behave as if you were raised by Puritans. Sexual congress between two people can be pleasurable; it should be pleasurable. We've talked about this."

"Yes, we've talked about this, but I don't want to know anything about Mr. Hathaway," Jenny said.

Fanny sighed. "In this case it is important. Charles is no viscount, but he is from a prominent family. That's applicable because he believes himself to be better, and his family and everyone around him fosters that sort of belief."

"Why is that important?" Eliza asked.

"Because it means that he was accustomed to everyone handing things to him. He never had to work for anything and that includes women. You see it with handsome men often. But in Charles's case he was both handsome and wealthy, and not by his own means. He came to me with a sort of expectation. He expected to be served, if you will."

They both groaned.

Fanny rolled her eyes again but carried on. "So I made him serve me instead. No one had ever done that before. Made him work for anything, I mean. He thrived on the praise and rose to the challenge well. He was very good at—"

"Say no more!" Jenny said.

"Fine," Fanny said. "All this to say, don't discount your viscount yet. It is entirely likely that he may come around."

Eliza did her best not to focus on the content of her mother's words. Instead, she turned her attention to the sentiment. "But isn't the opposite also possible? That he won't rise to the challenge? He'll already have me, so to speak, so there will be no need to challenge himself."

Fanny gave a nod of agreement. "It's possible, but we don't know him well enough to say."

Eliza was afraid that she did know him. She feared very much that she was walking into this marriage with her eyes wide open and she knew exactly what she would be getting.

Fanny must have seen her fear, because she took her hand. "Do you remember when we went to Paris and bought you girls those gowns?"

After Cora had married, they had gone to Paris to visit Mrs. Wilson, Fanny's friend who had taken over Jenny's musical education. While there, they had paid a visit to House of Worth to have ball gowns made. Fanny had never been very clear on where the money for those gowns had come from, but the inkling of suspicion that had tugged at the back of her mind then raised its head.

"Yes?" Eliza asked.

"I paid Charles a visit. I tried to reason with him. Cora had married Devonworth and I assumed . . . well, I hoped that an earl would be enough to placate him. I reminded him that you girls deserved your inheritances from your grandmother and you shouldn't be required to marry as he sees fit to receive them. I'm certain you can imagine his reply. He did fund the gowns, however."

"Our father, our hero." Jenny's voice dripped with sarcasm.

"My point is that you have two choices, darling," Fanny continued. "Marry Mainwaring and receive your inheritance, or don't. If you do choose to marry him, then go into the marriage hopeful for the best. You never know what could be possible, and you'll only give into despair if you expect anything less."

Eliza was as confounded as she was uplifted by her mother's eternally upbeat outlook. Despite growing up with few advantages, the woman had managed to live a full life that had seen her children taken care of and educated and one of them married to an earl. It wasn't a life Eliza would have chosen for herself, but it was a life that had seen more happiness than sorrow, and she didn't know if anyone could ask for more than that.

"What will happen to us if I don't marry him?" she asked.

Her mother shrugged. "Don't look too far into the future. It only leads to sadness."

"But someone must. Mama, this is more money than most people see in a lifetime." This is what happened when she allowed her good angel to win. She asked responsible questions about the future. "Did you ask Mr. Hathaway about Bedford College again?" Eliza had very reasonably offered to take less of her inheritance if her father funded her college attendance.

"The same. I'm afraid he's got his mind set on noblemen and he won't entertain any other sort of future for you girls. He doesn't even want to hear that Jenny is a mesmerizing soprano with perfect pitch."

"Then I don't have a choice, do I? What will become of me if I don't get my inheritance? What will become of you and Jenny?"

"Darling, Jenny will have a fine career. You don't need to worry about her."

"And . . ." Jenny grinned. "Our mother has caught the eye of a certain Lord Ballachulish."

"Lord who?"

"Jenny, no, that is not the least bit true." Though their mother denied it, she was blushing prettily.

"Ballachulish. He's from Scotland and he is smitten with our mother," Jenny explained. "We met Lord Aberdeen last night, and his new wife is the sweetest woman. She's our age, Eliza, and seems to be very progressive in her ways. They even say the Earl and his wife dine with their servants. She invited us for a small gathering at their home after the theater, and their friend Lord Ballachulish was there and seemed quite taken with Mama."

Fanny smiled. "You see, perhaps he'll whisk me away to his castle and you'll not have to worry about me welfare." The last part she said in a Scot's brogue that had them laughing.

"I thought you denied receiving his attention?" Eliza said.

Fanny shrugged and rose to her feet. "I'm off to get dressed. Before I forget, Camille sent a letter." She gestured to the writing desk in the corner. "She's marrying Mr. Thorne in a few weeks, which means we'll lose the house. Start gathering your things because we'll have to move in with Cora when she does."

This was no surprise. Ever since he had proposed marriage to her earlier in the year, everyone had known they would marry as soon as possible. The only issue with this was that it meant that the Doves were effectively being evicted from her dower house, which would revert to the Hereford heir after Camille's marriage. Until Eliza and Jenny were married, they had nowhere else to go but to Cora's. The next couple of weeks would be taken up with packing their trunks and moving to the Devonworth townhome.

"Eliza, darling, your beau sent you a letter as well." Fanny swept out of the room.

"Well, I suppose that's that." Life would go on even though

she feared that she'd left her heart behind in that coffeehouse. Eliza went to find the letter from Mainwaring on the desk. This was the second letter she'd received from him. He'd sent the first one from France and had complained about the richness of the food. She wasn't sure she wanted to read this one, knowing what he had gotten up to in Italy.

"Care to tell me about last night?" Jenny's eyebrows rose almost comically high.

"What do you mean?" Eliza studied the writing on the envelope as if it held the key to avoiding the conversation she knew was coming.

"I know you weren't home. I came to your room to share a rumor I heard. You can either tell me now where you were or I'll badger you until you give in." Jenny crossed her arms over her chest in a display of her willingness to sit there for as long as it took.

Eliza sighed. Flopping down on the sofa next to her sister, she recounted the night out with Simon in the sparsest of terms. She couldn't share how she felt for him.

After Jenny admonished her for how foolish she had been to do such a thing, she dropped the scowl and smiled. "But you had a good time. Right?"

"It was fun."

"Fun?"

Eliza shook her head. "That word doesn't do justice to it. It was . . . I don't even know how to talk about it. He was more than I ever imagined . . ." She didn't know what she meant by that.

Jenny stiffened at her side and watched her. Eliza could feel the intensity, but she refused to meet her sister's gaze. "Are you falling in love with him?" Jenny asked.

Eliza was worried that was exactly what was happening,

but she could hardly admit that to herself, much less Jenny. It would seem foolish. She didn't really know him, even though she felt as if she did.

"I want to see him again," she said instead.

"Eliza, what happened last night? Did you . . . ?"

"No, we kissed, but nothing more. Not physically, at least." There had been so much more. When they had talked, she felt that he'd listened and she had gotten to know him. She wanted to know more of him. She sensed there was so much that she didn't know.

"Then what will you do? You can't go back to Montague Club." Something in her expression must not have mollified her sister. "Eliza, you risk getting caught every time you go back. Unless that's your plan. Do you want to be caught so that the decision to marry Mainwaring is taken from you?"

"No, of course not." She didn't *think* she wanted to get caught. "I just . . ." She had an insatiable need to know him. It was like an invisible string kept pulling her to Simon and she didn't know what to do about it. She refused to break it.

"Eliza, I fear that I should warn you that as much as you like this man, you don't know him."

"I know that."

"Good, then you do realize that risking your future on what might amount to a fling isn't very smart?"

She did. It was why she refused to listen to the fury of that dark angel that urged her to go to him. She would go about her life and lock Simon Cavell into a corner of her heart where he belonged.

"Yes, of course I do."

"Good. Now, let's go get ready. Lady Aberdeen has asked us for tea and I'd like for you to meet her."

"I'll be there directly once I read this." She held up the letter from Lord Mainwaring.

Jenny rose to leave, but Eliza called after her, "Wait! What was the rumor you wanted to tell me last night?"

Jenny grinned devilishly and sank back down beside her. "I overheard Lady Hanford and Mrs. Thistle discussing Lord David."

Eliza vaguely recognized the names of two Society widows. Lord David had been briefly linked to one of them by gossip, but she couldn't remember which one. "What about him?"

Her sister leaned closer. "I can't be certain, but I believe one of them said that he had an adornment." Jenny raised an eyebrow as if Eliza should know what she meant.

"An adornment? Where? Jenny, what does that mean?"

"There." She vaguely gestured in the area of her groin. "His *private* area."

"No." Eliza covered her mouth in shock. "It's not possible."

"I didn't think so, either."

"How would that even work?" Eliza asked.

"It must be quite painful." Jenny started laughing and Eliza followed suit.

"I don't believe it," Eliza finally managed.

Jenny shrugged. "I can't decide if I do or not, but I for one will be looking at him very differently the next time I see him."

They both devolved into laughter again until Jenny managed to stand. "I must go ready myself. Don't be long."

She hurried out, leaving Eliza alone.

Eliza sighed and retrieved the pewter letter opener to cut through the envelope and pull out the single sheet of paper. A sense of dread settled in her stomach while she did. It always did when the subject of her fiancé came up. She scanned the letter quickly. He wrote that the food was too spiced for his taste and that he couldn't wait to come home to her. He made no mention of his coffeehouse visits. He signed the letter with his title. Had he even given her leave to use his name? No, he hadn't.

Their life would be a series of niceties while he trotted off to coffeehouses. She was sure of it. She closed her eyes and forced a calm that she was far from feeling. It would be so very foolish to throw away a quarter of a million dollars on something that wouldn't amount to anything. Jenny was right.

She resolved to move on from Simon, but as she stood, her gaze lingered on the stack of clean parchment waiting to become letters. The urge to write to Simon nearly had her sitting back down. No, she would move on from him faster if she made herself forget him.

EIGHTEEN

TRAINING, VISITING DAISY, AND WORKING. THOSE three things were Simon's entire life for the next several days, and often in that order. They were the only things that mattered. The encounter with Brody had spooked him. Simon did not trust the man. Even though he claimed the final fight would free her, Simon kept waiting for something to happen. He kept expecting that he would visit the little attic room where she lived and she wouldn't be there, so he went more often.

He woke and trained, then hurried to Daisy, then came back to start working until late into the night, except on the days when his shift started early, and then he would peek in on her as she slept and assure himself that she was well. The next day was more of the same. The only part of that routine that came to anyone's notice was the training. He sparred with a relentless energy that caught the attention of nearly every partner he encountered.

Most of it was because he was concerned about what Brody had asked him to do. Aside from a couple of early fights when he'd started out, Simon had never lost on purpose. Throwing a fight intentionally was almost as difficult as winning; especially this fight, because the man he was fighting was good. Dangerous and good. He never wanted to be on the losing end of that man's fists, because sometimes they didn't stop until it was too late. The loser generally received more damage than the winner.

He couldn't deny that some of his passion was pent-up frustration that he couldn't have Eliza. That night in Whitechapel had shown him what he had always feared. That she was a deep and thoughtful person. That what he had suspected had come to fruition. She was so much more than the impulsive behavior that he loved about her. She was sweet and soft and bitter and hard. Every facet of her held him spellbound. She shined like a jewel, and he wanted to hold her in the light, in the dark, and everywhere in between to see how she shimmered.

He wanted to pursue her, but to what end? She was too passionate to settle for a sexual interlude, but even he knew that wasn't the only thing he wanted with her. He wanted more. He wanted everything. For the first time in his entire life, he wanted to spend time with a woman and learn more about her. He wanted to share more of himself with her. At night before he went to sleep he imagined taking her and Daisy to the park. They'd walk hand in hand while Daisy played around them. They'd settle on a blanket to eat their bread and cheese and then feed crumbs to the ducks like he'd seen other families do.

It was foolish to hope for such things. Eliza didn't even know that Daisy existed. He couldn't assume that she would want to join their little family even if he was successful at placating Brody. She had another life all planned with her betrothed. Simon couldn't offer her anything better. He couldn't even offer her safety. If Brody ever thought that he could use her to get to Simon, he wouldn't hesitate.

Those thoughts left him little time to rest because they drew him out of bed and to the gymnasium. Sparring and training was the only time he could focus on anything else. He'd just finished a hard but satisfying sparring session on one such morning. Drenched in sweat and with his lip nicked by an errant knuckle, he sucked on the blood as he made his way to his office. It was a little room off the service corridor outfitted with a wooden desk and chair and cabinetry for files. Much of his tasks involved working the floor and dealing with members and various events, so he kept member files and event diaries. Only one of the shower baths was functional today, so he had let his opponent who had taken more than his fair share of the beating shower first.

He walked into the room intent on sorting the stack of morning post that had been left there for him. The post generally came addressed to the club. The rare letters addressed to him were from members thanking him for his handling of a delicate situation or they were writing ahead to request a special arrangement for when they were in town, which was the case today, except for one letter from someone named Anne Leybourne written in a neat and sloping hand, a feminine hand. The only Leybourne he knew was George Leybourne, the performer he and Eliza had seen in Whitechapel. His heart thundered as he turned over the envelope and broke the seal. It couldn't be from her, but he hoped it was.

Dearest Simon,

I told myself that I wouldn't write to you, yet here I am, putting pen to paper in the hopes that this finds you well. Thank you for everything. I will always be indebted to you.

Should you have need of me in the future, please do not hesitate to write to me. We will be moving to the Devonworth townhome directly, which is where you should look for me.

Yours faithfully,

E

She thought of him. The knowledge should not have made him happy, but it did. He'd half assumed that now that her adventure had been complete, she'd go back to her life with little concern for him. That's what should have happened.

Simon read the note over again at least ten times, trying to read what she hadn't written. Did she long for more time together as he did? Did she relive their kiss? He closed his eyes and remembered the taste of her mouth beneath his and the feel of her in his arms. There was no telling how long he sat there with the note spread open before him, but someone cleared their throat from the open door of his office.

Dunn stood there. "Ready?" he asked.

Simon glanced at the clock on the cabinet. Bugger it. He'd sat there so long he was running late. Dunn accompanied him to Whitechapel to see Daisy most days. It was always best to go there with others if at all possible.

"No, I need a few minutes more," Simon answered.

Dunn grumbled but left him alone. Simon selected a sheet of paper from the basket on his desk and took up his pen.

Dear E,

The words stopped after that. What was he to say? He should wish her well. He should keep his tone even and impenetrable as he warned her away. She was barely more than a girl, and she fancied that she felt more for him than she did. She didn't love him any more than he loved her . . . but, God, what he did feel was sweeter and bitterer than anything he'd ever felt before. He needed some inkling of her true feelings.

The ink in his pen had created an unsightly blotch, so he picked up a new sheet of paper and started again.

My dearest Eliza,
And how shall I find you there?
Yours,
S

He folded the letter into an envelope. He didn't write a return address on the outside. Instead, he simply wrote *S. Leybourne.*

He existed in a dream world until he received her reply. Train, visit Daisy, work. His routine was the same as ever, only Eliza was even more present than before. Her reply came two days later.

My dearest Simon,
You shall find me in half agony, half hope.
Yours faithfully,
E

He smiled when he read it. This time he'd closed the door as soon as he saw the envelope on his desk. He'd snatched it up and opened it before he'd even sat down. He did so now, however, sliding into the oxblood leather chair and devouring the words again.

Half agony, half hope.

He'd been all agony until reading it, knowing that the only way he would ever see her again would be when he happened to pass her in public. Now, inexplicably, hope flickered to life. There was no future for them. That was an unavoidable fact. But that didn't stop hope from igniting. It did, however, stop him from writing her back.

Half agony, half hope.

The words became his mantra.

NINETEEN

IT HAD BEEN OVER A WEEK SINCE ELIZA HAD SENT HER last letter to Simon and over a fortnight since their night in Whitechapel. He still hadn't written her back. She told herself that his nonreply was answer enough. The one letter he had sent hadn't been very forthcoming. What more of a response did she need? He didn't want her.

Though he lingered in her mind, she carefully planned every minute of every day so that she wasn't sitting around moping. She went to teas and dinners and the theater, and she had her family to keep her occupied in the mornings. Once, she and Jenny had gone to a lecture at the British Museum—Egyptology—and she had managed to have the carriage drive them by Montague Club, but that was as close as she had got to him since their night out in Whitechapel.

Her bad angel had been firmly shoved to the deep recesses of her mind. Even the fantasies that she entertained late at night that Simon might come to her in her room again had been laid to rest now that they had settled into Cora's home.

She was forced to share a bedroom with Jenny here, so there would be none of that even if he was inclined to come to her.

Not that he would come here; that would be ridiculous.

She was so certain of that truth that when she heard his voice rumbling down the upstairs corridor of Devonworth's home, she very nearly convinced herself that she was imagining it. A pleasant tingling rippled down her spine, and the small hairs on her body stood on end. She paused at the threshold of her new bedroom and closed her eyes and let the cadence soothe her. *If only it were him*, she thought.

But then she looked up and realized that the door to Devonworth's study was cracked open. The voice came from in there. She crossed the hall on her tiptoes and listened.

". . . assure you that we found everything of note in his suite. If Vining had any other information, he most certainly hid it elsewhere. I doubt he has anything."

She leaned in too close and the door creaked open because it hadn't been shut properly. Damn. There was nothing for it but to reveal herself. She pushed it open farther and stuck her head inside. Devonworth sat in one of the chairs before the hearth, a brandy in hand. Simon and another man sat across from him holding similar glasses. All three men rose when they saw her.

"Good evening, my lord, I wasn't aware that you had company." It was the only thing she could think to say to cover her gaffe.

"Eliza, you remember Mr. Cavell and Mr. Cox," Devonworth said.

She nodded and greeted them both, her eyes latching on to Simon, drinking him in as if he were the oasis to her desert. He didn't reveal anything in his expression, but his eyes held hers, the intensity in them speaking louder than any words.

She wanted to ask why he hadn't written her back, but she didn't dare. Instead she said, "Will they be protecting us again? Has there been another threat?"

"No, nothing like that." Devonworth faced her more fully to reassure her. "I've asked them to follow up on the investigator I hired months ago."

"Oh . . ." She hoped she didn't sound too disappointed. What else could she say to that? She was desperate to stay, to soak up Simon's presence. "Well, I'll be downstairs if you need me."

A flash of uncertainty crossed Devonworth's handsome face. "Thank you. Good evening, Eliza."

She inclined her head to him and both men. But her bad angel stopped her at the door. With her heart pounding, she turned back to face the room. "Would Mr. Cavell and Mr. Cox like to stay for supper?"

The room fell silent. Everyone sat stunned, because what she'd said was highly improper. Cora or Devonworth were the only ones who should issue such an invitation.

Devonworth recovered quickly. "That's a fine idea, Eliza." Turning to the men, he said, "Please join us."

Mr. Cox was the first to agree. Simon murmured a polite refusal, but Devonworth wouldn't hear of it. When he eventually agreed, Eliza smiled to herself and finally met his gaze. His eyes lit her on fire across the distance.

Eliza gave a quick and abbreviated curtsy and hurried downstairs to inform the cook of their supper guests. She carried that warmth with her the entire way.

SIMON LIKED TO THINK THAT HE WOULD HAVE TAKEN the high road, that he would have walked right out of Devonworth's home and gone back to Montague Club without accosting Eliza had they not stayed for dinner. Alas, he was only a man after all. He could only avoid her if she wasn't actively near him. All bets were off otherwise.

As it was, he sat through dinner with Devonworth, Lady Devonworth, Eliza, and her mother and sister feeling very uncomfortable. It wasn't that he was unaccustomed to dining with quality. He'd been at Montague Club long enough to have dined with many lords and second and third sons. He could conduct himself appropriately without embarrassing anyone. It was a learned survival tactic, much like his ability to mute his accent. He had figured out at a very young age to mimic those around him, to do what they were doing, and speak as they spoke. His discomfort came from the fact that Eliza had positioned herself directly across from him where he couldn't easily avoid looking at her. The more he saw her, the more he thought of her letter: *half agony, half hope.*

The wide-eyed longing on her face was enough to make him ask himself silly questions like why did they have to live in agony and why couldn't he have her?

"Tell us how you came to be at Montague Club, Mr. Cavell." Fanny Dove sat to his right, her intelligent and somehow knowing eyes taking him in. He fidgeted with his soup spoon and forced himself not to look at Eliza again. He didn't think Eliza had told her mother about him, but he couldn't tell. From the amount of attention the woman paid him, he had to wonder.

"Rothschild and Leigh were out one evening and they were . . ." He had to think of a delicate way to word the interaction. "They were attacked and I stepped in to set them free."

It had been his own men, Brody's men, who had attacked them. Simon had learned not to draw the attention of the upper class, so he had stepped in and stopped the fools before they had done any real damage. That had been many years ago when the club was in its early days. One of Brody's men had been an upstart who had planned to usurp Simon's place in Brody's esteem and had fought him on leaving the nobles alone. Simon had been forced to subdue the man physically, which had drawn the attention of the two noblemen.

Leigh had sent word to him later to come to him if he was interested in a job. At first, the job had been to train with them, but Simon had quickly gained their trust and respect. When Mary had fallen pregnant, he'd reevaluated their lives and decided that there was no future with Brody. He'd asked Leigh to give him more work. Then Daisy's birth and Mary's death had only confirmed everything for him. When Mary was on her deathbed, he'd tried to leave Whitechapel. Brody had beat him so badly that he had staggered to the club, delirious for days afterward. He'd gone back to Brody after that. But when Mary had died, he tried again and struck the deal with Brody.

He summed that all up with a quick, "They offered me a job as thanks for my help. I've slowly worked my way to a place of responsibility."

"Then you were not a second or third son as so many of your club's members are?" she asked.

"No, madam."

She sniffed. "Well, you wouldn't know it to look at you."

He wasn't certain that was a good thing given the way she'd said it, but then she smiled up at him and he thought he saw approval there.

"Where are you from, Mr. Cavell?" Eliza's sister asked from his left.

"Whitechapel, Miss Dove. Lived there all my life until Montague Club." Devonworth already knew much of his history, so Simon didn't mind telling it in this company.

"You are very young to have the running of the club, though, aren't you?" Mrs. Dove asked. She was poking at his story, looking for holes.

"Depends on what you consider to be young, Mrs. Dove."

"Quite right, I suppose," she agreed.

"Have you ever traveled, Mr. Cavell?" Miss Dove asked.

"I went to Scotland once. Leigh has a family home there, Blythkirk. He's recently renovated it with Lady Leigh's help, and they invited me up for the hunting party when they opened it."

"Did you like Scotland?" Eliza asked, her eyes bright with interest. "I've not yet been there, but I've heard it's a beautiful place."

"It's more beautiful a place than any I've ever been." Which wasn't saying very much considering his only other trip had been an overnight to Kent. "It was peaceful, and I never knew the sky could be so big." He'd wanted to stay there longer.

"Did you hunt?" Miss Dove asked.

He shook his head. "I'm not much of a huntsman." The trip had been his only real encounter with nature. He'd not seen the need to destroy it, when it had given him so much peace.

"No, but as I recall you were quite the marksman," Devonworth put in. "Outshot everyone with targets."

"Is that right?" Mrs. Dove asked, impressed.

Simon glanced up and caught Eliza staring at him. She held his gaze as the conversation continued. The women switched to asking about Montague Club again. His answers were aided by Devonworth, who also had some familiarity with the club. The entire time, Eliza watched him. Her gaze bordered on adoring, and he had to force himself not to look at her.

Half agony, half hope.

He was relieved when the conversation turned to Cox, who

had to answer a similar bevy of questions. Eliza dutifully turned her attention to the man, and Simon allowed himself the pleasure of looking at her profile.

Half agony, half hope. Did she see a way forward for them, or was she simply being impulsive, again?

A footman asked if he was finished with his soup, which forced him to look away from her. Another footman set a plate of roast beef in its place. Something touched his foot beneath the table. It was her foot. He glanced over at her to make certain, and she smiled at him, heat smoldering in her gaze.

This was too much. He was all agony at this point. Still, he did not pull his foot away from her reach even as he redoubled his efforts to concentrate on his food.

By the time the meal was finished, he'd decided that he needed to confront her. He waited. She had to stop looking at him so obviously. The women retired to the drawing room, and Devonworth offered the men cigars at the table. Simon accepted and rose to his feet to watch the women leave. The men stayed in the dining room for about ten minutes until Cox asked about a painting they had seen earlier in the upstairs corridor. When Devonworth offered them a closer look, Simon declined and remained in the dining room to finish his cigar.

Left alone, he stayed on his feet and walked to stand behind the closed door, silently counting the seconds. To get upstairs, the men would have to pass by the open door of the drawing room. Eliza would see that he hadn't accompanied the men. He gave her exactly thirty seconds to make an excuse and find a way to come back to the drawing room.

The door opened on the count of thirty-two. The skirt of Eliza's blue dress preceded her into the room. She paused inside the door and he grabbed her arm and pulled her completely into the room. The door closed and he pressed her against it, holding his hand over her mouth to silence her gasp of surprise.

"I knew you'd come," he said.

She smiled behind his hand and he let it drop between them. He couldn't not touch her, though. His hand found hers of its own accord. "Of course I came."

"Half agony, half hope." He recited her words back to her.

"You didn't write me back," she admonished him gently.

"Why did you write it?" he asked instead of answering her accusation.

A pretty blush stained her cheeks. "It's true."

"What do you mean by hope?"

She took in a breath and her free hand came up to his face. The backs of her fingers pressed his cheek. He had to fight not to lean into her touch. "I meant the hope that I would see you again, but it's become more . . ." She let out a ragged breath. "Sometimes I think of you and a future where we are together."

He clenched his teeth to keep from leaning into the absolute pleasure that her words evoked in him. He reminded himself that they hardly knew each other, so ideas like those had no place between them. When he was certain he could control himself, he said, "That can never happen."

She closed her eyes and pressed her forehead to his shoulder. Her body shuddered in a sigh. After a moment, she looked up at him. "I know, but I wake up thinking about it. I lie in bed at night and think of you."

It was subtle, but a shift happened with those words. Her eyes dilated and there was a husk in her voice.

"And what do you think of?" He wanted to kiss her. That he could do. He could give her stolen kisses. He leaned forward, the rose scent of her teasing his nostrils. He wanted to find the source of it. Was it her hair? A bit of perfume she dabbed on her neck?

"You," she whispered. "And me."

"And what are we doing?" He was so close now he could feel her breath on his lips.

"Touching."

He cursed softly. The allure of her was too much. He kissed her, his mouth pressed to hers, seeking the heat of her. She parted beneath him and he brushed his tongue against hers. She made a soft sound in the back of her throat that nearly undid him. He needed more of her, more of this, more of everything.

His hands went around her and pulled her against him, the hard boning of her corset digging into his fingers. She deserved better than this, better than a door at her back and an overly eager man at her front, but he couldn't concern himself with such things right now. As soon as her fingers plunged into his hair and held him to her, he was lost. He was at her mercy. Whatever she wanted, he would give to her.

"Eliza," he whispered, taking her precious face between his hands and drawing back only far enough to look at her. She was beautiful, her eyes heavy lidded but as mischievous as ever. The light teased out hints of gold in her irises.

"What are we doing?" he asked. Even as he questioned it, he didn't pull back from her. In fact, he settled his hips against her, the rigid swell of his cock pressed firmly against her soft stomach. She writhed subtly but enough to make sparks of pleasure skate up his spine.

"I don't know." Her eyes were wide and earnest. "I just know that I can't *not* think about you."

He groaned and brought her lips to his. He devoured her.

Not kissing her wasn't an option. He wanted to have her on her back on the table and only barely managed to keep his wits about him and stop from doing it. Instead, he reached down and dragged up her skirt. His fingers slipped easily underneath, across her knee, between her thighs. He found the slit in her drawers, the fur guarding her sex, and her soft petals opening to his fingertips. She was slick to the touch and swollen with need. He pushed a little, the tip of his longest finger finding her heat as she yielded to him.

"Simon," she gasped.

It wasn't enough. He needed to feel her, to know the taste and salt of her skin. But this was all they could have. He pushed farther, her body enveloping the length of his finger, gripping him. The fit was so snug he almost groaned. She did cry out softly, and he smothered the sound with his mouth.

He glided out of her almost completely and pushed back in, rubbing the pad of his finger against the texture that made her hips bounce. He'd give anything to be inside her. She flooded his hand with her need, the sound of his finger driving into her making him mad for her. Withdrawing, he rubbed her clitoris, which was rigid and extended by now. She rolled her hips, seeking more, his name falling from her lips.

He hadn't meant to go so far with her. He'd only wanted to touch her, to get a small taste of what existed between them, but now that he'd reached this point, he found that he couldn't stop. He wanted, no, he *needed* to make her come apart. She couldn't be his in any meaningful way, but he could claim her with *this*.

She pressed her face to his chest, her breath coming fast and hard as she rode the pleasure he gave her higher. He could feel it rising within her. He ground himself against her hip, his body throbbing and aching for release, but it was hopeless.

Already, voices were coming through the door. Devonworth laughed at something Cox had said as they came down the stairs. Simon let her go as if she'd turned into live flame in his hands. She fell back against the door, panting, and her knees were wobbly. Her eyes were dilated and glazed. Jesus, he wanted to drive himself into her right there in the dining room, to take her against the door and damn the consequences. He couldn't do that. He wouldn't take her future from her.

He kissed her parted lips before hurrying to the window that looked out over the side garden. He couldn't see anything beyond his own feverish need as he took deep breaths and tried to beat back his own arousal. Blood rushed in his ears, nearly drowning out every other sound.

He'd never done something so foolish. He had no right touching her or doing that in Devonworth's house. He didn't know what had come over him. She moved, adjusting her clothing and getting herself together, and caught his eye in the reflection of the glass. He knew that he would do it again in a second if given the chance. She had that power over him. It wasn't a power he resented. He wanted her to wield it. He'd savor it for as long as he could have her.

The door opened and Devonworth paused mid-sentence, his gaze roaming from Simon to Eliza and back again. Eliza opened her mouth, and he had no idea what she meant to say, because she ran out of the room instead of saying it.

Thankfully, Simon's need for her had been thoroughly doused with her brother-in-law's arrival. He thought he managed to appear well put together when he said, "We should be going, Cox. Lord Devonworth, thank you for having us for dinner." He held his hand, still slick with her need, behind his back.

"Cavell," Devonworth said, a hint of warning in his voice. He suspected something, but he didn't know anything. It was best to leave while he still could.

Cox said his goodbyes and Simon gave an abbreviated bow as he headed toward the front door. He looked neither to the left nor the right; to see her again would tempt fate. He didn't draw an easy breath until they were outside moments later and climbing into the carriage they had borrowed from Montague Club.

"That bit o' raspberry Eliza Dove." Cox grinned. "There's a story to tell there."

"Stuff it, Cox."

His friend laughed so hard the springs of the carriage shook with his humor. Simon held his hand closed, her heat slowly dying on his fingers. Had he been alone he would have tasted her. Hell, had *they* been alone he would have spread her out on the table and feasted on her properly. He nearly groaned at the mental image that evoked. On his deathbed, he'd lie there and regret that he hadn't seen her come apart in his arms.

TWENTY

E LIZA LIKED CORA AND DEVONWORTH'S DRIVER
more than she liked Camille's driver. Camille's driver had
been employed by the Duke of Hereford for decades and was
rather full of himself. He'd been grouchy and had always
looked upon Eliza and her sisters with marginal disdain. She
assumed she didn't like outsiders, particularly American outsiders, and resented having to serve them.

Jones, Devonworth's driver, was more relaxed and given to
smiling. He was in his twenties and had a boyish charm that
she found very amusing. The best part was that he enjoyed
reading novels. She'd found that out earlier in the summer
when he'd seen her holding a book and had discreetly kept
looking at it until he'd figured out the title. Ever since then she
made sure to bring him a book whenever she visited Cora and
they would go out in her sister's carriage. Now that she had
moved in with Cora, she found that she liked him even more.

Because he was less set in the ways of the British upper
class, Jones was very good at minding his own business. He

thought nothing of taking Eliza to the British Museum and dropping her off without a chaperone. To make certain he was occupied, she handed him a dime novel she'd brought from New York, *Buffalo Bill Trails the Devil Head*, before leaving him with the carriage. He accepted it with good cheer, and she watched discreetly from the entrance to see where he parked the carriage down the road so that he could settle in to read. Only when he was occupied did she veer away from the entrance to the museum. He didn't see her cross the road at the corner. And he certainly missed it when she sprinted across the next street and around the corner to Montague Club.

She was here because she couldn't be anywhere else. Simon called to her, whether he knew it or not. Ever since he'd had dinner with them last night and they had shared the private moment in the dining room, she had been consumed by him. Her mother had noticed during the meal that there had been something between them. Fanny had found her before bed and inquired about Eliza's interest in him. It had been on the tip of her tongue to confess everything to her mother. The only thing that had kept her silent was that Simon had given no indication that he wanted to try to figure out a way forward for them. It seemed impossible—probably was impossible—but didn't they owe it to themselves to even consider the possibility?

The idea of them was foolish, but she'd never forgive herself if she married Mainwaring without talking to Simon first. It wouldn't hurt to have one honest conversation about where things stood.

The attractive limestone building loomed across the road before her. Several carriages were stalled out front, busy with the late-afternoon traffic of people arriving at the club. Men in suits were loitering on the sidewalk, talking with one another before they went inside. It might have been less crowded had she been able to come earlier in the day, but there had been a luncheon with the London Suffrage Society that she hadn't felt she could miss. Her only hope of avoiding detection was the kitchen entrance she and Jenny had used the last time.

The moment traffic let up, she hurried across the road. From her vantage point at the street corner, she could see that the kitchen door was closed. Hopefully, it wouldn't be locked. She didn't get a chance to find out, because as soon as she started down the sidewalk it opened. Startled, she stopped walking. Simon's tall frame emerged, and she did a quick about-face so he wouldn't catch sight of her.

Almost as quickly, she turned back around. She was here to see him, after all. There was no need to hide from him. He wore a bespoke suit, the same type that he wore when working at the club. It was different from what he'd worn the night they had gone to Whitechapel, which had been plain and hung looser on his frame. She knew the suit was custom because of the fineness of the broadcloth and how it fit his waist and shoulders, emphasizing the narrowness of the former while drawing just snug enough against the latter. He hadn't yet looked in her direction, and she realized what had made her feel hesitant at his abrupt appearance. There was a look of single-minded determination on his face. He seemed concerned and carried a leather satchel. He crossed the sidewalk in only a couple of long strides and hopped up into the carriage waiting there. It took off at a fast clip before the door was even closed and before she could call out. Wherever he was going, he was in a hurry.

She should go back to the museum, but she couldn't look away from his carriage. It had rolled to a stop at the intersection. Where was he going so fast? She couldn't shake the feeling that something was dreadfully wrong. Her good angel told her it was none of her business where he was going, but her bad angel told her that something was wrong and he might need her. She'd never seen him with such an expression on his face.

Should she follow him?

She paused, vacillating between going back to the museum and hailing a cab. Of course she should go back to the museum. There was always tomorrow. Yes, that is definitely what she *should* do. But it wasn't yet dark, and Jones didn't expect her back for a couple of hours. What harm would there be in following Simon? She'd never have to reveal herself.

No, she should definitely return to the museum. It was the obvious choice. She turned around and started walking back the way she had come. A hansom pulled around the corner, driving idly toward her. She looked back at Simon's carriage just in time to see it turning left. Her decision made, she stepped out into the street to flag down the cab.

"Please follow that carriage," she called up to the man before he could jump down and help her inside. Grabbing onto the handle, she pulled herself up and settled herself back against the seat.

The hansom took off and they were able to keep a fairly good pace. She only lost sight of Simon once, but by then she had already recognized the narrowing streets and buildings in need of upkeep. Simon was going to Whitechapel. But why? She had gotten the impression that he didn't wear his club attire on Whitechapel streets. He had obviously left in a hurry. What would bring him here today?

When the cab came to a stop near Whitechapel High Street, the driver pulled to the side of the road and opened the hatch. His stern face appeared in the square opening above her. "I don't drive here," he announced.

"Fine, I'll get out here." She fumbled in her handbag and pulled out his fare.

His bushy eyebrows came together. "Are you certain, miss? This area—"

"Yes, I'm certain. Here." She shoved the money at him and he shrugged and took it.

She fumbled her way out of the carriage and hurried toward the busy market. Panic began to overtake her because she didn't see any sign of his carriage. It wasn't dark yet, but it was late enough in the day that the streets were crowded. The White Hart pub was busy across the road.

A carriage had pulled up to the alley beside it, and she thought it might be his. Montague Club's carriages were unmarked for anonymity with no crest on the door. It might have been anyone, but all the other vehicles in the market were either wagons or not as sleek and shiny. Pulling her skirts up to her ankles, she hurried across the road, dodging carts, wagons, and manure as she went. By the time she got there, the carriage was pulling off, but she saw Simon's trim form disappearing down the alley. He wasn't running, but he walked very fast. She had to nearly sprint to keep pace with him.

He turned down two more alleys that were too narrow for anything larger than a cart. Finally, his pace slowed as he came to a row of houses. They were narrow and tall and made of brown brick. He walked up to the front door at the third house and knocked. A sign hung out over him, but it was so faded that she couldn't tell what was written on it from where she stood hidden at the end of the block. He glanced around as he waited, and she darted around the corner. Again, she should have revealed herself, but something kept her silent. By the time she peeked back around, the tall door had opened. It had once been green, but the paint had long since faded and peeled away in sections. She couldn't tell who stood inside the door, but, man or woman, they were shorter than Simon. He looked down as he spoke. The person stood back and allowed him to enter. He swept off his hat as he stepped inside.

Once the door closed behind him, she hurried to the building. She didn't allow her good angel a say as she raised her hand and knocked on the door. An older woman opened it. Her silver-streaked hair was pulled back into a tidy bun and her black gown quite conservative with a high neck and long sleeves.

"Yes?" she asked when Eliza didn't speak right away.

Eliza opened her mouth, but realized she probably shouldn't ask for Simon. What had she hoped to find out anyway? Her impulsive flight to find him had overtaken her good sense.

"Are you a new girl, child?" the woman asked. She spoke in the East End accent Eliza had come to expect, but it was tempered somehow, as if she wasn't native to the area but had lived there a long time.

"Yes, I am new." Eliza nodded and used the same contrived accent she had used that night with Mr. Brody.

The woman sighed. Her voice was kind, but stern as she said, "Only customers come through this entrance, dovey. Go round to the back." Then the woman gave her a thorough once-over and shut the door in her face.

Customers? What sort of house would have customers? A sickening hollow opened up in her stomach. There was really only one thing it could be, but she didn't want to believe that Simon would frequent such a place. Still, she hurried around the block to the back of the row of houses. She counted to the third house down and knocked on the door. A feminine voice yelled inside, though Eliza couldn't make out the words. That was followed by heavy steps. A series of locks were being unlatched; she could hear the springs and metal tapping against wood. When the door finally opened, heat from the kitchen to the right wafted over her. Ahead, the corridor loomed, dark and narrow, creating a straight path to the vacant front door.

The woman who had opened the door appeared to be the cook. She wore an apron and an affronted expression that Eliza would dare to appear there and disturb her. A trickle of sweat rolled down her brow, and she wiped it away with a hand reddened from the heat of the kitchen.

"I—I was told to come in the back," Eliza said.

The cook huffed and waved her in before slamming the door behind her. Then she appeared to forget all about her as she returned to the kitchen and continued scolding the scullery girl who was on her hands and knees cleaning up a spill.

Eliza glanced toward the front of the house again and saw no sign of the woman in black. The woman's voice drifted down the corridor to her from a front room, coupled with a man's voice, but the man was not Simon. This was her chance. She needed to find him before someone stopped her.

A narrow and steep set of servants' stairs was tacked to the side of the corridor, so she took them and cautiously made her way to the second level of the home. The upstairs was narrow with several rooms turning off of the corridor. One of the doors opened to reveal a young woman in a dingy white shift with nothing else underneath. The lamplight spilling from the room lit her sparse frame from behind.

"Who'r you?" she asked, her brows drawn together.

"Anna—Anne," Eliza answered, stumbling over the name she and Simon had decided she should have in Whitechapel.

"We already have one of those." The woman's gaze narrowed.

"I can change my name."

The woman huffed and disappeared back into her room without another word. Eliza stared for a moment at the other doors, wondering if Simon had gone into one of them. Maybe he was even now undressing to take one of the occupants to bed. She hadn't thought he was someone who would visit a prostitute. Not these poor women, anyway, who were likely forced into the job by circumstance rather than choice. She hadn't thought he was someone to take advantage of that, having seen the genuine desperation from the other side, but perhaps she had been wrong. Though, honestly, it wasn't only that that disappointed her. It was that he could touch her the way he had last night and then come here today.

What was she supposed to make of that?

That it is none of your concern and that you should return home. Eliza pushed that voice of reason aside. She'd come too far to turn back now.

A footfall echoed on the stairs, and she looked up to see a man's shoe go past on the landing above. Perhaps it was him. She hurried around and up the next flight of stairs to the top floor. She got there just in time to see the man, presumably Simon, disappear up a narrow set of stairs set into the wall that led to the attic.

She followed, her heartbeat pounding in her chest, and quietly walked down the short corridor to the bottom of those stairs. A quick peek confirmed that the man was Simon. She pressed her back to the wall and waited as he knocked on the single door at the top of the stairs. It opened and she glanced again to see a dark-haired girl who couldn't have been more than fifteen inside the attic room, her face pale and thin. Her eyes lit up when she realized Simon stood there, and she stepped back to let him in, then the door closed behind him.

Cold prickled over Eliza's scalp and down her spine. The

girl was so young. Why would Simon be visiting her? He couldn't really mean to bed her, could he? Before she could properly consider all of the reasons, one of the doors on the corridor opened. An older man stepped out, adjusting his clothing as he did. She closed her eyes as she turned her head away.

"Are you new?" he asked in a tone that indicated he was entirely too interested.

"No, I'm not new. Get out of here," she snapped, keeping her voice low so that it wouldn't travel up to the attic.

He frowned but finished tucking in his shirttails as he walked toward the stairs to go down.

She waited for him to disappear from sight before she glanced back up the steps to the closed attic door. She wavered for a moment before ascending the steps. She had already come this far; she wasn't about to turn back now.

Once at the top of the attic stairs, Eliza raised her hand to knock, but decided not to. She didn't want to give them time to pretend they were doing something else. If he was sleeping with this girl, then Eliza needed to know. She needed to see the seduction with her own eyes. Then she would berate him for being a cad and leave. At least it would settle the question of her future.

Sick to her stomach, she pushed gently and the door opened inward, as nothing had been latched from the inside. The room was not as small as she had thought it would be.

A narrow window was directly across from her; late-afternoon sunlight spilled across the bare wood floor. A small bed was pushed to the wall on one side of the window with a table on the other side. The bed was empty. The girl sat at the table and Simon sat adjacent to her. A third set of eyes looked over her as well. An even younger child in Simon's arms. Both he and the girl came to their feet at the sight of her.

"Eliza?" he said.

The girl's eyes went wide with fright. The blanket she had been mending plopped to the ground, a needle poking out of it with a tail of red thread falling limply to lie on top of the blanket.

"Simon?" Eliza's gaze was wrenched back to him and, more specifically, the child in his arms.

The little girl wore a simple yellow knee-length dress. Her light-colored hair had been neatly combed and left to fall in airy ringlets down her back. She couldn't be more than three years old.

"Who is that, Papa?" the child asked in the soft tone of a toddler. Her blue eyes, so like Simon's, were wide with curiosity.

Papa. The little girl had called Simon Papa. Eliza wrenched her gaze away from the child to Simon. He looked as stunned as she felt. His face was a frozen mask of shock, and he hadn't moved since he'd catapulted to his feet.

"Simon." This time it wasn't a question. Eliza was too stunned to ask questions.

Simon had a child. A daughter. Had she been prone to fainting, she would have fallen dead away and rolled down the stairs.

TWENTY-ONE

✣

"Papa?" Daisy reached up her plump baby hand to cup Simon's cheek.

He looked down at her sweet face, her round eyes large with concern, and tried to recover himself. Though he didn't think he'd get over seeing Eliza *here* anytime soon. "This is my friend Eliza."

Daisy nodded and smiled, seemingly pleased by this answer. The spell that held them all still had been broken. Eliza realized that perhaps standing with the door open wasn't appropriate. With a sheepish look on her face, she stepped fully into the room and closed the door. The other option was to turn around and leave, but having come this far, he didn't expect her to leave until she got answers. He knew her well enough to guess correctly which option she would choose.

Eliza stared at him. Her eyes were soft now . . . almost vulnerable, exactly the way he felt. No one had ever seen Daisy from his other life, the life he lived outside of Whitechapel. It wasn't that he wanted to hide her, but that he was forced to hide her away here. Eliza was the first person he cared about to meet her. Because Daisy lived here, the room had always had a reverent aura to him. Eliza had stumbled upon this sacred space, and he couldn't decide how he felt about it. It felt as if she was seeing a very tender part of him.

"This is Daisy," he said. "Mary's daughter." He paused to allow the meaning of that to set in. Understanding flickered across Eliza's face as did a good bit of relief. Had she thought that he'd fathered the child on the young girl? "And this is Henrietta. Daisy has christened her Heni. She helps take care of her."

Henrietta looked back and forth between them, uncertain, but she bobbed a quick curtsy. "Good evening, ma'am."

Eliza had yet to find her voice, but she managed to mumble a greeting to Henrietta. He'd found the girl working here as a scullery maid when it had become clear that Daisy was outgrowing the need for her wet nurse. Downstairs girls often became upstairs girls when they became of age, so he'd offered her the choice of tending to Daisy instead, which she had readily accepted.

Heni picked up her fallen mending and gave Eliza a wide berth. "Please take my chair," she said, and walked to sit on the chest at the end of the bed.

"Thank you," Eliza said, but she still looked to Simon for permission. She was the trespasser, and he suspected that she was only just coming to realize how much she had transgressed here. He nodded and held out a hand toward the chair. She murmured another thank-you and sat down.

"You followed me?" he asked after he'd retaken his seat with Daisy settled on his lap. He didn't know how to feel about that. A part of him had lit up when she'd appeared in the door. It didn't make sense. This was an egregious invasion of his privacy, but all he could feel was glad. At last, he could share this with someone . . . with her . . . the woman who had begun to haunt his every moment, waking and sleeping.

Daisy looked over at her curiously as she munched a piece of bread.

"I'm sorry. I had no right." Eliza's cheeks burned. "I had just gotten to Montague Club when I saw you leave. I meant to turn around . . . to come back again tomorrow, but something about you . . . you seemed concerned, almost upset, and so I followed you."

She shouldn't have. She knew that, if the contrite look on her face was any indication. He tried to get a handle on the pounding of his heart and his sheer joy at seeing her, because it was not good that she was here. It was dangerous. He also couldn't forget the look of outrage and jealousy that had marked her features when she'd opened that door.

"Then it was your concern for me that brought you here?" he asked.

"At first, yes." She didn't want to say the rest. She nibbled her bottom lip with uncertainty. He had to force himself not to look at it and not to imagine biting it himself. "Then I realized this was a b . . ." She glanced to Heni. She couldn't say the word *brothel* in front of others. "I realized what this place is. Well, then I was angry that you might be a customer here."

He let out a huff of laughter and shook his head. "Daisy wasn't feeling well when I saw her this morning, so I've come back to check on her. She's much better now, as you can see."

Daisy munched the last of her bread and reached for a piece of crumbled cheddar that sat in front of her on the table. Loaves of bread and bricks of cheese rested there with a basket of strawberries and one of gooseberries, along with a clump of watercress and some roasted hazelnuts in a cone made of newspaper. He'd brought them for her and Heni, part of the groceries that he kept them supplied with every few days. He didn't want them eating the shite found in Whitechapel. The bread here was made of mostly alum and chalk with only a smidgen of flour. The cheese was molded, and there was very little fruit to be found.

"Yes, I can see that. She's very lovely," Eliza said.

Daisy, who was always impressed by compliments, smiled at her, revealing her tiny white milk teeth. Eliza smiled back at her and something happened inside him. He couldn't say what it was, only that his chest felt heavy and warm and he couldn't breathe for a moment.

He didn't know what showed on his face, but when Eliza looked up at him her smile faltered. "I should go."

"No." The word was between them before he was aware of uttering it. His tone had been hard and final. "You shouldn't be on the streets alone. I'll see you home."

He girded himself for her refusal but, much to his surprise, she remained silent on the matter and nodded. Relieved that they wouldn't have a row about it, he bounced Daisy lightly on his knee. She giggled and looked up at him, and he was nearly overcome with his affection for her. Every time she got sick, he braced himself for the fact that she might not survive. It was a terrible way to live, but he couldn't seem to help himself. Early death was a part of life here. It's why he made such an effort to get her nutritious food. It's why he'd nearly bankrupted himself to supply her with real breast milk and not the watery gruel given to babies here when their mothers were forced to work in factories for most of the day. Running his fingers through her silky hair, he pressed his palm to her forehead. The child had slept most of the morning but seemed much improved now. There was no fever that he could tell. He pressed his lips to her forehead to check again, just in case.

Eliza made a soft sound. He couldn't tell what it was, but her eyes were dark and velvety, shining out at him when he met her gaze. For the next several minutes, he spoke with Daisy and Heni about their needs and reassured himself that his niece had overcome the slight cold she'd had. About midway through his conversation with Heni, Daisy offered Eliza a strawberry and Eliza accepted, eating it slowly. For one brief moment he allowed himself to imagine a future with them both, sitting at a breakfast table and enjoying a quiet moment together. He shook his head to clear the thought away. There was no future until after the last prizefight in a fortnight. That's all that mattered now.

"Eliza and I need to be going. I've work to get back to."

Daisy's brow quivered with concern. She loved him very much and never liked to see him go. He felt much the same. After the fight, he'd bring her to Montague Club and keep her there. Perhaps they'd find a flat in one of the new buildings nearby. "Don't fret, love. I'll see ye again in the morning." He kissed her cheek and then tossed her into the air, one of her favorite things. She giggled as he hoped she would.

"Promise?" she asked.

"Promise." He kissed her cheek again and handed her over to Heni. "Come," he said to Eliza.

Eliza stood and held out her hand to Daisy. "It was lovely to meet you, Miss Daisy. I hope I can see you again soon."

Daisy smiled at her and looked up to Heni who nodded in encouragement. Daisy took Eliza's gloved hand. "Lovely to meet you, Miss Liza," she parroted back to her in her baby voice.

Everything in him stilled, and then a warm flush crept over

ELIZA AND THE DUKE   183

him. His mind went back to those domestic images he had created in his head. A home together. Eliza in his arms every morning. Daisy with a room full of toys and dresses that was all her own. It was too painful to imagine things that would never come to pass. It's why he never allowed himself to dream of things he couldn't have. Until Eliza had come along.

TWENTY-TWO

WITHOUT ANOTHER WORD, HE LED HER THROUGH the brothel, hopeful that they wouldn't run into Mrs. Jeffries, who ran the place. By unspoken agreement, they walked down the back stairs and exited out the back door. He took hold of her hand when they were outside and started walking to Commercial Street where he'd arranged for the carriage from Montague Club to meet him.

"I can't believe you followed me." He tried to make his voice sound harsher than he felt.

"I understand. I can't quite believe it myself. I've been told I can be impulsive."

He glanced over at her and laughed. She smiled. "I can't quite believe you're real," he muttered under his breath. She heard him, if the color in her cheeks was any indication. God, she was lovely.

"I never would have suspected that Daisy existed," she said. "Why does she live here and not with you at the club?"

"Because of Brody." The name had him looking around as if that alone could summon the man. It wasn't dark like the last time they had come to Whitechapel, but the streets were so close together that the air seemed darker and still. He tightened his hold on her hand.

"Is he her father?"

"No, her father's a jack. A sailor. Mary loved him, but when he came back from sea and saw her with a swollen belly, he denied the babe could be his." Simon had gone at him for that, but after the beating, the bloke had set sail on another ship and never returned.

"Oh, well, then, why does Brody have a say?" she asked.

"He didn't want me to leave and doesn't want me to stay at Montague. He resents the fact that he can't use me as he did before. I've cost him much in unearned wealth."

With her free hand, she touched his hand that held hers. He looked down at her fingers, taking comfort in the touch, before looking up at her. "You cared about him, didn't you?" she asked.

A lump rose in his throat causing it to feel tight and achy, but he quickly pushed the pain away. "He was the only father I ever knew. For a time I thought he felt like I was his son." He shrugged. "I was wrong." He'd been wrong about so many things in his life, but that had hurt the most.

"Or perhaps he did feel that way and he's hurt that you left?"

Simon shook his head. "That wouldn't change a thing. He's gone too far. He claims that I owe him money for leaving, and he won't let Daisy leave until I pay for her freedom. It's why I've agreed to that final fight. He's promised that we'll both be free of him."

"Wait a moment." She came to a stop, forcing Simon to stop with her. "You have to participate in a prizefight to be allowed to take Daisy out of here?"

He nodded.

Her brow furrowed and she brought his hand to her chest, hugging it to her breast. He forced himself to take a deep breath and not focus on how soft and warm she was. Still, he found himself drawing closer to her as thoughts of last night burned their way through his mind. The way she had felt beneath his hands . . . riding his fingers.

"But isn't it dangerous?" she asked. "Isn't it a leap of faith? If he's truly so bitter about you leaving him for another life, then how do you know he isn't planning something terrible? How do you know he doesn't mean to hurt you in some way? How can you trust that he'll follow through with his promise?"

Everything she said was correct. His smile was tinged with sadness. "It's good you understand that Brody can't be trusted."

"*Simon.*"

Simon stared at her like he might stare at a simple child. "Wot choice do I have, then, Eliza?"

Understanding dawned on her face. "You don't have choices, do you? Choice is a privilege granted to those lucky enough to have a little bit of power," she said.

The tight ache returned to his throat. This was why he'd never be allowed to have her for his own. The sadness was chased by anger. He wanted to punch something. Brody came to mind.

"You've not been born to privilege, but you've made powerful friends. You could talk to Mr. Thorne or Lord Leigh. Surely, you know the Duke of Rothschild would help you."

"What would they do? Send police to the streets of Whitechapel to root him out? Put everyone—Daisy, themselves, and their families—in danger? No, I'll deal with him on my own." His jaw set rigidly and he started walking, but she refused to budge, drawing him back to her.

"Simon, wait. There must be something—"

"No, Eliza, there's nothing that can be done. Ye don't understand how it is here. If I don't do what he wants, I may very well return to find Daisy gone, and I can't risk it."

The terror reflected on her face was enough to reassure him that she understood now. He wouldn't have to pick her up and tote her out of there, which is what he'd been on the verge of doing. They couldn't stay here, and she needed to know how dangerous it was for her here. She squeezed his hand and followed along beside him.

They emerged onto the pavement lining Commercial, and he looked for the carriage along the crowded street but didn't see it.

"What is stopping you from taking her out of there?" Eliza asked, a quiet hesitation in her voice.

He was silent for a moment, contemplating how much to tell her. "The house has a watchman. He follows Heni and Daisy whenever they leave. Brody will know about your visit soon enough now." His grip on her hand tightened again, as if he could feel her being pulled away from him. She glanced around them as if looking for the man or the men who had followed them the last time they'd come to Whitechapel.

Her body tightened; he could feel her tense next to him. "Promise me that you'll never come here again. He's much too dangerous." When she didn't answer immediately, he turned to her and took hold of her shoulders. "Please, Eliza."

She nodded. "I promise. I mean it this time."

He let out a breath and turned back to the street. He spotted the carriage. It came slowly down the lane, separating itself from the other traffic to approach them.

"Did you ever try to leave?" she asked. "Before . . . when you were a child?"

"Once, a long time ago," he answered. "I beat up a man for Brody. He was a rival, led a gang." He paused, debating whether or not to say more, but she deserved to know. She *should* know. Perhaps it would make her keep her distance. "The man died. As soon as I found out, I resolved to leave. The next day, I ran away and used the money I'd saved to buy a train ticket to Dover."

"But you came back."

"I came back for Mary. I couldn't leave her here alone. She ran away from the workhouse and took me with her. I could do no less for her." He hadn't been thinking clearly when he'd left for Dover. He'd panicked. When he'd come back, she hadn't been ready to leave because she still believed in Brody, so he'd stayed. Every day he wondered what their lives might be like now had he forced her to leave with him. Would she still be alive?

Eliza nodded as if she could possibly understand what his life had been like then. "Where did you go?"

"The sea. I'd always wanted to see it. I took the train from St. Pancras to Dover, got off, and walked to the shore. There was a little stone house there near a cliff. It seemed abandoned, so I rested there. Fell asleep and woke up the next morning. That's when I knew I had to come back."

They were silent as they waited for the carriage to navigate its way through traffic. After a moment, she asked, "Have there been others . . . that you killed?"

He'd been waiting for that question. "A few." He looked at her to gauge her reaction. She didn't meet his eyes, and he felt

the need to add, "They were all during fights with bad men."
All of them had been Brody's rivals, men who would've killed
him if he hadn't killed them first. Still. Death was death. "I'm
not proud of what I've done."

She looked up at him, and there were tears shining in her
eyes. Something about that made pain slice through him so
acutely that he caught his breath.

The carriage pulled to a stop at the curb. Simon cleared his
throat and called up a greeting to the driver and opened the
door.

"I'll take you home," he said.

"Jones, Devonworth's driver, is waiting for me at the British Museum. He thinks I've been there all this time."

"To the British Museum," he called up. "Keep driving until
I tell you to stop."

The driver, McCullough, agreed. Simon helped her inside
and climbed in behind her. The inside of every carriage that
the club owned was as plush and comfortable as the club itself.
This one had a tufted velvet interior in dark crimson. The buttons and knobs for the windows and the little carriage lantern
were gilded and shining. It was truly like stepping from one
world to another.

The moment the door closed and the carriage took off, she
turned to him. "I want you to know that I don't fault you for
anything you've done. I can't possibly understand the life that
you've lived. I just want you to know that I admire—"

He covered her mouth with his hand to stop her. He
wouldn't possibly survive adoration from her. It would undo
him. "Don't, Eliza. This has to end now, tonight. There is no
future where I'm not me and you aren't destined for more."
Her eyes became liquid and he had to look away.

Taking his hand from her mouth, she put it in her lap and

held tight. "Then I want to make the most of the next few minutes," she said.

Startled, he looked back at her. From the look on her face, she meant more of what had happened last night. He couldn't deny her that, because he wanted it more than he wanted his next breath. He drew her into his lap and kissed her.

TWENTY-THREE

IF ALL THEY HAD WAS THE TIME IT TOOK THEM TO drive back to Bloomsbury, then Eliza intended to make it count. She kissed Simon with her whole heart. When he pulled back to catch a breath, she chased his lips. He laughed softly into her mouth and nibbled her bottom lip, scraping it pleasantly with his teeth before he gave it a tug. The answering dart of need that shot through her was unexpected but welcomed.

She'd never experienced this sort of kissing before. Her kisses with Olek had been fumbling at best and left her feeling nearly drowned. Simon made kissing an art form with just enough teeth and tongue to keep it interesting. His tongue was velvety and smooth, and she loved when it brushed up against hers. It felt indulgent. She could have gone on kissing him all day, but they didn't have that long.

She pulled back when she really couldn't breathe anymore. His eyes shined out at her like jewels, mischievous and deep. "Will you touch me like you did last night?" she asked. It came out in a whisper, because somewhere in the back of her mind she knew that it was naughty to ask for such a thing.

He grinned at her. Without saying a word, he leaned over and released the tie holding the heavy curtains open on the far side of the carriage. Then he did the same on the other side, effectively hiding them from the world. Early-evening light seeped in through the cracks. A small lantern was set in the front wall of the carriage, too small to give much light, but enough that the yellow glow caressed the angles of his face.

Somewhere along the way she had forgotten that she'd originally deemed him not classically handsome. He was breathtaking. His nose was better than straight because the slight bump in the bridge was evidence of a life well fought. She loved how it gave him history and character. His brow might be prominent, but she loved to watch it crinkle when she perplexed him, and how it made his eyes deep set and mysterious. His lips were perfectly soft and firm at the same time. She kissed him again, marveling at the flicker of heat inside her when his tongue plunged into her mouth.

One arm was at her back, while his other hand worked its way under her skirts. His rough palm slid over her calf and knee before his fingers delved between her thighs. There was entirely too much fabric. It bunched around his arm and her waist and made her start to sweat in the summery heat of the vehicle. A bead of it trickled down her spine, but then his fingers found her and she forgot to notice. He pressed against her, the cotton fabric of her drawers between them. She braced her left foot on the ground to widen her legs and make room for him.

His fingertips teased her, moving up and down her sex in a maddening rhythm that had her arching her back toward him.

The damned fabric was still between them. "Simon, please," she complained.

"Shhh . . ." he said against her lips and took her mouth in a deep kiss. "You'll get what I'm ready to give ye," he teased her.

She throbbed for him and she could feel that the underwear was soaked. "We don't have time," she whined against his lips.

He shushed her again, but at the same time he finally found the part in her drawers and dipped his finger inside like he had done last night. He teased her, only giving her enough to intensify her ache. She squeezed her eyes shut, too enthralled with his touch to continue kissing. His lips found her cheek and then her ear. She shivered when his hot breath touched her there and then his teeth tugged at her earlobe. God, she loved his teeth.

Her body ached and pulsed, ready for more, but he continued to tease her. He pushed in only to the first joint of his finger and then pulled back out, over and over again. "Simon."

"More?" His breath fanned her ear.

"God, yes."

He withdrew and pushed back in, this time all the way until the heel of his hand was cupping her. Her hips bucked of their own accord to encourage him, and he obliged her wordless prompt. His finger slid in and out of her in a rhythm that was as pleasant as it was maddening. Pleasant because it felt good, maddening because it only made her want more. She basked in the feeling of being full of him, while at the same time beginning to realize that she wasn't nearly as full as she wanted to be.

And he knew. "Can ye take another?" he asked, his lips brushing hers as he spoke.

She nodded and made a sound she didn't recognize. "More. All of them. I don't care."

He chuckled, and a second, broad finger joined the first. For a glorious moment she was filled, her body stretched tight around him. Her arm had found its way around his shoulders and she held tight. When he moved them in a sharp and jolting rhythm that had the pad of his fingers pressing against that place inside her, she wanted to move her hips with him, but the bulkiness of her skirts hampered her. She leaned back to get better leverage but was thwarted by her bustle.

"Damn," she muttered without meaning to.

He pulled back enough to look at her.

"This position . . . this bustle," she explained. This might very well be the only time she had with him, and her clothes were hindering her and ruining everything.

He gave a tight nod and pulled his hand out from under her skirts. She groaned in dismay. "Take it off," he whispered.

Yes, of course! She could take it off. She moved onto her knees on the floor and reached behind her to find the tapes of the bustle. She had long ago taken to wearing a low-profile horsehair bustle when not in a formal gown, one that most women wore when traveling. It was much more comfortable and less restrictive. But even it was too much for *this* in a carriage.

His fingers joined her trembling ones, and together they were able to remove it. He kept working, and she realized he was untying her underskirt as well. Good riddance. She scooted out of the underskirt and tossed both garments on the other seat. Grabbing handfuls of her skirt and pulling it up to her waist, she climbed into his lap, this time astraddle him. One of his hands found its way to the back of her head, tugging pleasantly at her hair, while the other ventured between them and under her skirts, finding her wet and aching center. He entered her with two fingers almost savagely, but it was what she wanted. She had waited for him for so long that she was primed for every drive of his fingers up into her. She cried out and didn't care if anyone heard her on the street as they passed.

He bit her neck and whispered, "Quiet, Angel. Ye have to be quiet."

She didn't want to be quiet, but she understood the need for it.

"Can ye take another?" he whispered, tempting her most viciously.

She looked down at him, not certain what to say. "Yes, probably. I don't know."

His fingers stilled for a moment and then his thumb caressed her, teasing her clitoris. She had touched that place before, at night alone in her bed when no one was around, but it had never felt like it did now when he stroked her there. She gasped.

"Do ye want to try?"

She nodded, unable to say a word because her body throbbed and clenched at him, greedy and aching to be filled. Slowly and gently, he pressed a third finger against her opening. Her body stretched to accommodate him, inch by sweet inch, and he pushed it inside her until she was completely stretched and full. This time he moved much more gently, his fingers stroking her and pushing her higher with every thrust.

"Ride my fingers, Angel." His voice was husky against her ear. His other hand cupped her breast, squeezing and kneading through the layers of corset and bodice. She hated her clothes.

She rocked against him, feeling heat and excitement spiking higher within her. Hot, openmouthed kisses trailed down her neck, emphasized by the scraping of his teeth more often than not. She held tight to his shoulders, burying her face in his hair, the fresh lemon scent of him washing over her. She would remember that scent for years to come. His hand had moved to her hip and helped her keep rhythm as his fingers continued their magic, driving her higher and higher. A coil of pleasure had begun tightening in her belly. Each shove of his fingers constricted it and wound it more. She felt crazed with need, reaching for something just out of her grasp until a wave of pleasure crashed over her. It rocked her from the inside out. Her body clamped down on his fingers, fluttering around him and grasping. He muffled her cries with his mouth.

He continued stroking her, gently moving in and out of her sensitive passage, until she had come down. The trembles of her body slowly eased. He withdrew and she fell against his chest, the rocking of the carriage slow and even. He brought his hand to his mouth and sucked the taste of her from his fingers. She gasped at the hedonism of it and how much she liked it.

"Simon."

He looked down at her, his eyes dark and wide, dilated with his desire. His jaw was tight and his body rigid against her. She moved her hips and felt him there, pulsing and hot inside his trousers. Suddenly, she wanted nothing more than to give him what he had given her. She reached between them, but the second her fingers found him, he took her wrist in his hand and pulled her away.

"I want to taste ye." His voice was rough with need.

Hadn't he done just that when he'd brought his fingers to his mouth? He couldn't mean what she thought he might mean . . . could he? She nodded and he grabbed her hips and set her off of him. Then he moved to his knees on the floor of the carriage, much like she had been moments earlier. Turning to face her, he took hold of her hips. "Like this."

He guided her to sit on the edge of the padded seat. His eyes met hers as he raised her knees, spreading her legs apart. She still wore her stockings, boots, and drawers, but she felt terribly exposed and she liked it. She liked being this way for *him*.

He took one of her hands and showed her how to hold herself open for him. She did as he wanted as he worked to move her skirts out of the way. She couldn't see between them with the fabric of her dress piled over her knees, but she could feel. She could see the hot lick of his gaze as he took her in. His hands went to the back of her thighs and pushed them farther apart. His face seemed hungry and focused when he looked down at her sex. The skin was pulled tight across his jaw, and his eyes were hot, liquid fire. He took hold of her drawers right where they parted and gave a hard yank. The fabric ripped apart; she imagined it split right up to her belly.

He glanced at her as if to say *sorry*, but he didn't speak. She didn't care. She would walk naked to her carriage if it meant that she got to experience this. Then his eyes fastened on her sex, naked and exposed to him, as he shrugged out of his coat and tossed it to lie with her own discarded clothes. His shirt was stretched tight across his shoulders, his black waistcoat emphasizing the narrowness of his waist. What she would give to see him nude, to do this with him in a proper bed with all the time in the world. Taking hold of her hips, he angled her a little more, pulling them just off the edge of the seat, before he bent down and kissed her there.

She wasn't prepared for how strange and decadent his mouth would feel on her there. She barely got her mind around it before he stroked her with his tongue, tasting her. She bit her lip to keep from crying out again, but it felt so good a keening sound escaped from deep in her chest. He lapped at her like that for several minutes until her hips were moving again of their own accord, only for him to tighten his grip and keep her still. He made a rough humming sound in his throat and moved to her clitoris, settling there with his tongue swirling around the swollen bud as he alternated between licking and sucking her.

It was all she could do to hold on to the edge of the seat. "Simon, please." She could feel that same wave of need rising inside her again, but there was nowhere for it to go. There was nothing driving it tight. She rocked against him, but there was nothing to fill her up, nothing that her body could clench around, and apparently that was very important. At the moment, it was more important than her next breath.

She didn't realize that she was saying his name over and over, a litany of a prayer, until he rose over her. "Eliza," he groaned, breaking the spell.

"Please, Simon." She looked at him through a haze of need. "I want you inside me."

He stared at her, silently debating, she was certain of it. A thousand emotions played over his face. To push him over the edge, she let go of the seat and reached for him blindly. Her fingers stroked the front of his trousers and he jerked, but he didn't pull away. Instead, another groan tore from deep in his chest as he pressed into her touch. She cupped him, the length of him burning her through the fabric. He was harder than she imagined he could be and probably throbbing as much as she was.

She used strength she didn't know she had to press herself up and kiss him. "Now. I need you."

He made another sound, half pleasure and half pain, his

hips pushing against her touch, grinding himself against her palm. "Have ye ever had a man inside ye?"

"I'm not certain."

He laughed, a strangled sound that tumbled pleasantly down her spine. "Ye don't know?"

She shook her head. "There was a man—a boy, once. We were sixteen. He did things, but it didn't feel like what you do to me. He might have, but I was never certain."

"Was there pain?" he asked.

"A little, for a second, and then nothing because he'd finished." He'd rolled to the side, a dead weight, and she had wondered how anyone could risk so much for something that had amounted to nothing.

Simon was serious again and shook his head. "I don't have a condom. I won't put a baby in ye."

Somewhere in the deep recesses of her logical mind, she knew he was right. But just then, with his need so obvious and her body alive and trembling with need for him, the price of carrying his baby didn't seem so very high. His fingers caressed her as he spoke, which did nothing to lessen her desire and everything to heighten it.

"You can withdraw," she offered.

The crevice between his eyes deepened. "What do y—"

"My mother and sisters told me about such things. Simon, please." As if on cue, the carriage turned a corner and she had no idea where they were, but it was a stark reminder that their time was precious because they were running out of it.

He looked down at her sex again and touched her gently, reverently. She took on the fastening of the front of his pants, afraid that he might deny her. She couldn't see what she was doing, so she fumbled until his fingers joined her. Together they got them open and his erection filled her hand. She squeezed, drawing a gasp from him as he leaned over her.

"Or I'll go off in yer hand," he whispered.

She let him go at the threat. Her hands moved back to grasp the edge of the seat and brace herself. She didn't quite know what to expect.

"Eliza, Angel." She could barely hear her name over the blood that rushed through her ears. Simon was about to be inside her. She was about to become one with Simon. Her heart pounded.

She felt his fingers fumbling between them and then the blunt end of his erection brushed against her. Her hips jumped at the sensation. He held her still with one hand and guided himself with the other, his eyes on the place where he would join her. In one slow glide, he pushed the tip of himself inside her.

He was solid, his erection more rigid than his fingers. He pulled back and then pushed forward, stretching her as he worked his way into her inch by inch. She could feel herself clamping on to him, greedy for all of him. She couldn't keep still.

He looked up at her, meeting her gaze over the pile of her skirts between them as he took hold of both her hips to hold her steady. "You're so bloody beautiful." His voice was hoarse with longing. As he spoke, he pushed forward until he was seated all the way inside her. There was no pain like before, only minor discomfort as her passage was forced to expand and accommodate his girth. His knees were splayed wide on the floor, and she sat in the cradle of hips.

"Good?" he whispered, leaning forward to kiss her lips. She could taste herself on him.

"Yes." Her voice trembled. She didn't even recognize it.

He rested for a moment, giving her time they didn't have to adjust to him. His eyes were deep pools of affection that held hers. Finally, he moved. At first it was a slow pump of his hips as he tested her. She bit her lip at the pleasure that rolled through her. He pumped upward again, hard and deep, impaling her on his length. This time she couldn't keep her cries in.

He watched her face as he did it again and again in a rhythm that started slow and built to something stronger and deeper. With each lunge upward, his pelvis created friction against her clitoris, driving her higher. Eventually, she relinquished her hold on her knees and trusted him to hold her while she clawed at his shoulders as he panted over her. He kissed her, his tongue doing to her mouth what his cock did to her sex. His hands gripped her hips so tight to hold her for him that it might have been painful had she not enjoyed it so much.

Her body gripped him tight, reaching for more. "Come, Angel." His voice was harsh and commanding and she loved it. She wanted to come apart.

The threads of her very being were unraveling. She no longer knew that they were in a carriage, that they were in the middle of London, that she'd have to leave him in minutes. He was her world. His body in hers, his breath in her lungs, and his taste on her tongue. He was everything.

Then his hand worked its way between them and the rough pad of his thumb stroked her swollen clitoris and she went flying. He let her go and his arm tightened behind her hips, holding her still so he could ram into her hard and deep. He pulled out at the last possible second, she looked down in time to see him fall back, and then felt the warmth of his release against her inner thigh.

After he was finished, he held her, his face pressed to her breasts and his breath coming hard and heavy. Her muscles felt like jelly and she was too weak to do anything but lie against the seat and attempt to find her own breath.

TWENTY-FOUR

❦

S IMON WAS THE FIRST TO MOVE. THE CARRIAGE HAD
turned a corner, making them sway so that he had to catch
himself on the seat to keep from crushing her. He brushed his
lips against Eliza's cheek and leaned over to peek out through
the slit in the curtains. The air inside was humid and warm,
thick with the scent of their frantic coupling.

"The museum is outside," he said.

She didn't know how long the carriage had been circling
the area, nor did she know how long it had been since they had
left Whitechapel. She should care. Jones would be waiting for
her, and he might very well sound the alarm if she was gone
for too long.

Simon rifled in his coat pocket and pulled out a handkerchief. Turning back to her, he wiped the inside of her thigh
where he had spent himself. A pang of guilt gnawed at her.

"Did I make you—"

His gaze shot up to her. "Make me?" Then he leaned forward, a slow moseying stroll that ended with him on top of

her again and his mouth an inch above hers. A smile touched his lips. "Did it seem as if I didn't want to?"

She almost smiled, but he kissed her first, so hard and deep that excitement zinged through her belly. Then he was gone and tucking his shirt in while he fastened his trousers.

This was it. They were finished.

She couldn't quite get that through her head and make her limbs work properly at the same time. The second he had released her, her legs had fallen to the floor and she'd slid down to sit on her bottom with her skirts a mess around her. He shrugged back into his coat, his broad and thick shoulders disappearing before her eyes. His hands scraped through his hair, trying to bring some semblance of order to the mess she had made of it. Then he looked around for his hat. She had no idea where it might have ended up, but happened to glance over and see it undisturbed where she had been seated before he'd pulled her into his lap. She handed it to him wordlessly, even though seeing him fully clothed again made her want to cry. She'd never see him again like this.

"Simon."

"Eliza . . ." There was a warning tone in his voice that gave her pause.

He turned to look at her and took note of her lack of movement. Reaching over, he took hold of her under her arms and drew her up to her knees. He retrieved her underskirt and held it open for her at the waist. Silently, she moved to sit on the bench seat and he worked the petticoat over her feet and ankles and pulled it up her legs. Standing was out of the question, so she hiked up the skirt and moved to her knees on the floor again so that he could tie it in the back. That done, he helped her don the bustle and handed her the tapes so that she could tie it around her waist. When they were finished arranging her underthings, he pulled the fabric of her skirt smooth over everything. Then he faced her and everything stopped again.

"Simon."

He kissed her again. This time gently. It was so gentle that her heart ached. "We have to go," he said when he pulled back.

She nodded, and he stroked her cheek and then her bottom lip. He didn't say anything, but the same affection that had been shining from his eyes earlier was there for her to plainly see.

Her hat was the final item, and he picked it up from the other seat where it had been hiding under her clothes. She took it and worked the hat pin into her tousled hair. Jones was going to wonder what had happened to her in the museum, but it couldn't be helped. She wouldn't change anything that had transpired in the carriage.

When she was finished and settled on the seat, Simon used the flat of his fist to bang on the roof. The carriage came to a stop after a moment, and Simon tied back the curtain. "Do you see your carriage?" he asked.

It was near the other end of the block, thankfully. After pointing it out, he opened the door and helped her out.

"I meant what I said . . . half agony, half hope," she whispered.

The corner of his mouth twitched upward. "All agony here."

What could she say to that? She hurried away and kept her head down as she approached the carriage. Jones came to attention and, instead of their usual greeting, she said, "Please take me home," without looking up.

He opened the door, and only when she was safely settled inside did she let her mind wander over the last half hour. She was sore between her thighs, but in the most pleasant way imaginable. She had experienced something with Simon that she didn't think she'd ever find again.

They arrived home quicker than she could have imagined. She hurried inside and up to the room she shared with Jenny before anyone could meet her. Once there, she took off her hat and then her torn drawers. There was no way she'd be able to mend them so that the maid wouldn't know something had happened. It was too warm for a fire, so she couldn't burn them, either. With a soft curse, she stuffed them under the mattress and swore that she would burn them later.

She moved to the vanity to fix her hair and sat down, her attention caught by her reflection in the mirror. She hadn't thought that what had transpired between them would actually change her physical appearance, but it had. There were the obvious changes. The marks on her neck that he'd left with his mouth. She touched one, remembering how it had felt when he'd kissed her there. She liked that he had marked her. Her only regret was that they would fade. Well, perhaps she had two regrets. The other one being that he also hadn't been able to mark her in other, less obvious places because she'd had to stay mostly dressed.

But it was her eyes that had changed the most. There was a knowledge there that had been missing before. Not a sexual knowledge, though that had certainly changed. But a deeper knowledge. One that she might have never known had Simon not come into her life. She loved him. That fluttery feeling that had been infatuation and lust had morphed into something deeper. She could hear her mother say now that it was only the sex making her feel that way, but she had felt it before the sex. She had felt it when she'd seen him with his niece. She had felt the first stirrings of it when she'd caught him watching Mr.

Leybourne at the music hall, and later that night in the coffee-house when he'd been so interested in her.

The door to the bedroom opened and Jenny came inside. She startled at the sight of Eliza sitting there. "There you are. I thought I heard the carriage, but I didn't see you. I had planned to leave this for you."

Jenny walked over and placed an envelope on the vanity top when Eliza didn't reach out to get it. The return address was somewhere in Italy. Mainwaring's name jumped out at her in his stark and perfect handwriting.

A lump formed in her throat, and she had to cover her mouth to stifle the unexpected sob that followed.

"Eliza? What's wrong?" Jenny sat on the narrow bench beside Eliza and put her arms around her. "Is it Lord Main-waring? Did he do something?"

Eliza shook her head. How was she supposed to marry him now? The hopelessness of the situation took her over. Before she could think better of it, she told Jenny everything.

TWENTY-FIVE

SIMON WAS ACCUSTOMED TO HOBNOBBING WITH THE upper crust. It was his job and he did it well. He was able to seamlessly switch his accent to mimic theirs when he wanted. He made use of their tailors on Savile Row and he dined in St. James's when invited, but he rarely attended balls or other social functions. He never felt comfortable in those sorts of settings where everyone stood around talking about their days at Eton or Cambridge or their latest trip to the Continent. Mimicry wasn't history. He hadn't gone so far as to claim to *be* one of them. He refused to make up a history that wasn't his. Which is why he generally avoided the events.

The wedding breakfast of Jacob Thorne to Camille, Dowager Duchess of Hereford, was the rare exception. Thorne had asked him to come, and Simon hadn't been able to refuse. The man had taken him in and given him refuge from Brody. Aside from that, they were friends. It wouldn't have been right to miss it.

The Earl and Lady of Leigh had offered their home for the

occasion. Their home was situated in a neat row of white stone–fronted townhomes near Belgrave Square. As Simon had heard it, Leigh had inherited this smaller but no less grand residence along with the title from their father, while Thorne had inherited the money and the mansion that had become Montague Club.

On this bright morning in July, an unexpected line of carriages had backed up around the square as people came and went from paying their regards to the happy couple. The Season was nearly over because Parliament would be breaking for the summer in August, so many had already left Town for their country homes. It was surprising to Simon that the marriage of an American duchess—former duchess now—to an aristocrat's illegitimate son would garner so much attention, though it probably shouldn't have been. People had been talking about Camille ever since she had married her first husband, and Thorne was popular because of Montague Club.

With the town house in sight, Simon abandoned his carriage and tucked his gift under his arm. It had been damned near impossible to sit still in the same carriage where he had taken Eliza only a week earlier. He had a difficult time not reimagining her as it was. In his quiet moments alone in his bedchamber, he swore that he could still smell her and taste her. No amount of lemon oil could chase those intoxicating memories away. The carriage only worsened things. He could hear her cries, feel her soft thighs beneath his hands, remember the way she so sweetly begged to be fucked.

He took in a deep breath and forced those images out of his mind, determined not to disgrace himself by arriving with an erection. Picking up his walking pace to pass several couples making their way down the pavement, he hurried up the front steps to have his obligation done with as soon as possible. It wasn't that he didn't want to wish the couple well; it was that he was terrified of seeing Eliza.

A footman greeted him at the door, and he handed over the wrapped present, a pair of silver candlesticks that had cost him dearly since all of his pay was earmarked for Brody. The next step would be to greet the bride and groom, then he'd make his way back out with, hopefully, none of the Doves the wiser. The entry hall was massive with high ceilings and marble floors. The walls were lined with white lacquer panels, broken by insets of blue wallpaper and priceless artwork. He tried not to think how one of those paintings could purchase his and Daisy's freedom. Several groups of people hovered here, holding glasses of champagne and chatting. He inclined his head in silent greeting to the few gentlemen he recognized. No Doves were present.

The front room off to the left was the designated spot for meeting the couple. It was decorated in cheerful tones of yellow, gold, and the same blue from the hall. Thorne and his wife stood at the far end, surrounded by well-wishers so that neither of them had noticed him yet. Simon quickly scanned the room. The only Dove he saw was Devonworth's wife. She hadn't seen him yet because she was deep in conversation with an older woman he didn't recognize. He made certain to stay behind her and out of her line of sight as he joined the short queue and prayed that it moved fast.

Every new person who entered the room made him flinch. It was as if he expected Eliza to pop out from behind a curtain. Finally, he made it to the front of the line.

Camille, now Mrs. Thorne, was dressed in white with a crown of orange blossoms. Her blond hair was pulled up attractively and she glowed with happiness. "Best wishes to you," Simon said to them both.

Thorne shook his hand and they spoke for a few minutes about the entertainment establishment he had recently opened in Paris and their honeymoon plans. Then it was time to move along because other people were waiting. As he turned to leave, Thorne added, "Leigh and Rothschild are here, possibly in the drawing room."

Simon promised to find them, but what he really intended was to find the door. Lady Devonworth looked up from her conversation and her eyes sharpened with interest. He muttered a greeting as he walked past and resolved to leave. He didn't know how much of their relationship Eliza had shared with her sister, but if she had shared any of it, he imagined Cora would waste no time in telling her of his presence. It was best to leave immediately. No good could come of seeing her again.

He paused at the threshold, intending to turn for the front door.

"Ah, there you are, Cavell." A gentleman who was a club patron turned from the group of men he'd been conversing with to bring Simon into their huddle. "You've greeted the married couple, have you? Does this inspire you to wed? You're getting on in years."

The group laughed and he was forced to humor their quips as he claimed no desire to marry. He might have been able to leave after a couple of badly done jests had Eliza not chosen that moment to appear from a room off the hall and dart into another one farther down. She hadn't looked in his direction, which meant she hadn't seen him. He could leave. But he was transfixed by her and what he had seen. She wore a gown of pink silk with an overlay of what he thought was called tulle. It was filmy and emphasized how the silk underneath clung to her form.

A moment later he was able to excuse himself from the group by claiming he'd seen another acquaintance he needed to speak with. In truth he was mesmerized by her and she wasn't even present in the hall anymore. He'd take a quick peek into the room she'd disappeared into and quench his thirst for the sight of her. She'd never have to see him. A passing footman all but shoved a glass of champagne into his hand and directed him to the breakfast buffet. Simon took a glass, more to placate him than anything else, and continued down the hall.

He glanced inside to see that the room itself was small. It was lined with bookshelves from floor to ceiling and held a small desk that faced the window. Lady Leigh was a writer; perhaps this is where she worked. It was clearly an antechamber to a larger room that could be reached through an adjoining door, which he assumed was the drawing room Thorne had mentioned. Eliza leaned casually against the desk as she spoke to Lady Leigh, who was very obviously with child.

Eliza looked up the moment he appeared in the doorway and came to attention. Lady Leigh looked over.

"Simon, I'm so very happy that you came." Lady Leigh had long since taken to calling him by his first name. She demanded he address her as Violet, but he only did when they were in private company. They were of similar age, and she had been very kind by advising him in current fashion and mannerisms. She came over and kissed him on the cheek.

"I wouldn't miss it. It's good to see them both happy." Though he spoke to Violet when he asked, "How are you feeling?" his gaze went back to Eliza, pulled there against his will.

"I'm well, thank you." She must have realized his true focus, because she said, "Simon, this is Miss Eliza Dove."

"We've met." He'd shagged her in a carriage, to be more

precise, but no one could know that but them. "How do you do, Miss Dove?"

"That's right. I forgot that you worked for Devonworth for a brief time. I'm glad that whole situation has been put to bed," Violet said.

"Hello, Mr. Cavell," Eliza said. Her voice was calm but she fidgeted with her skirt. "It's good to see you again." Her cheeks were flushed.

How were they supposed to stand here and make small talk with others when he knew her taste and how distinctly she gripped his cock? Or that as she stood there her anatomy was such that the pink inner flesh of her cunt would be distended from between her lips like an erotic taunting and he knew exactly how she liked to be sucked and licked? It was torture.

He hadn't said anything. He'd been too busy imagining what was hidden beneath her gown. "I'm happy to see you again, as well."

Violet stared at him.

He struggled to remember where they were and why they had come to be here. "Did you . . . did you enjoy the c-ceremony, Lady Leigh?" He downed half the champagne in his glass.

"I did indeed," she said, an eyebrow raised in suspicion as she glanced between him and Eliza. "My apologies, but if you'll excuse me, I've forgotten that I must speak to Lady Fairhope before she leaves." She hurried out the door that led to the hall and discreetly drew it closed behind her.

He didn't know what to make of that. Obviously, the countess had seen something between them. They were hardly alone, however, with the door to the drawing room open.

"How are you?" he asked Eliza again. "Really?"

She attempted a smile and looked down as if she'd suddenly gone bashful. "Good, and you?"

Horrible. In agony even more than before. But he couldn't tell her any of that. Instead he put his hands in his pockets so that he wouldn't take hold of her unintentionally.

Keeping his voice low so that it wouldn't travel to the drawing room, he said, "Thank you for the gifts that you sent Daisy and Heni. You needn't have done so, but they were pleased to receive them." She had sent a small crate of food—a cured ham, fresh items from the greengrocer, bottled ginger beer and lemonade—along with a few books and ready-made dresses for them both.

"You're welcome. I hoped that it wouldn't upset you."

He loved that she had done it, that she had thought of Daisy when she could have easily pushed both of them out of her mind. His only concern was that she might have harmed herself in some way to do it. She had said that she wasn't wealthy. "How did you come to do it?"

She smiled, her deep brown eyes roaming his chest in a way that made him want to hold himself still for her inspection. "I spoke to Cora and she gave me her pin money, but don't worry. I didn't explain who they were, only that a friend had a relative who needed some items."

"A friend."

Her gaze shot up to his. "Isn't that what we are?"

Yes, he supposed that was an accurate term, but he didn't like it. Not when he knew how she felt wrapped around him. Not when he knew her viscount would soon know her as intimately, if not more so.

"Eliza . . ." *Bloody names.* "Miss Dove—"

"*Miss* Eliza. My sister Jenny is here."

He huffed out a breath. "Would a friend know the taste of your—?"

Her eyes widened and she rushed over to cover his mouth with her fingertips. "Don't!"

He sucked the tip of her finger into his mouth. Her gaze honed in on the sight of it disappearing there. When he flicked the tip, licking the salt from her skin, her eyes dilated. It had been a dangerous and heady thing to do, because now he was half-rigid with wanting her. Even the voices wafting in from the other room did nothing to cool his ardor for her. In fact, the very idea that they might be discovered made his longing for her more acute.

When he finally released her, she didn't move away from him. Her hand dropped to rest lightly on his chest. The fingers of his free hand found her arm, and he lightly stroked the silk of her skin. "I've thought of nothing but you," he whispered. He shouldn't be saying any of this. He was a glutton for punishment where she was concerned.

Her eyes were half-closed and she swayed into him, her hip bumping the rod in his trousers and bringing it to roaring life. He was nearly drunk on her and they had hardly touched. Images of taking her over the back of the chair came to mind, and his hand clenched so tightly around the stem of his glass that it shook.

"Simon," she whispered, and it had that tone, the same one from the carriage. "Why do you say such things?"

It was a very good question. "I do not know." Only he did know. It was the truth and he was a jealous fool and he despised that Mainwaring would have her.

"I think of you, too, every day. I am all agony," she said, tossing his words back at him.

"Eliza," he groaned. His hand dropped to her waist, her

stomach, and down to her thigh. "I would give anything to have you be mine."

"Then why didn't you give me the choice?"

There was a knock on the doorframe. Simon managed to put a foot between him and Eliza before the Duke of Rothschild appeared. He looked from one to the other. "Cavell, Miss Eliza, I hope I'm not interrupting."

She recovered before he did. "Of course not, Your Grace. If you'll excuse me, I'd like to get some champagne."

Simon greeted Rothschild as he watched Eliza hurry from the room.

The duke walked over and took Eliza's original spot against the desk. "August and I have had the pleasure of spending a little time with the Dove sisters since they've been in England. They're charming."

"Yes, very charming." Simon felt like a boy who'd been caught with his hand in the biscuit tin. What was happening between them must have been obvious.

"I'm grateful you appreciate our Miss Eliza. Have you decided to court her?"

"I'm aware of the stipulations of her inheritance. I don't fulfill those particular requirements."

The man looked at him, seeing far more than Simon was comfortable with, but he'd just been with Eliza. She was so very good at breaking down his shields, and he hadn't yet had time to build them back.

Rothschild considered him a moment and then asked, "You don't think she'd choose you over her inheritance?"

It was almost cruel the way he said it, though he likely didn't mean it to be. "Choice is a luxury some of us don't have."

"Touché, Cavell." The duke inclined his head, conceding

the point. "It was wrong of me to presume that you hadn't asked her."

That is very much what Eliza herself had said. But it would be foolhardy and selfish to put her in that position. Why would she choose him and an uncertain future when she could have her every need met? Except Mainwaring wouldn't fulfill her needs.

He shook his head to physically stop those thoughts. Until this last brawl was finished, he had nothing to offer her, not even himself. He wasn't free.

"Well, you could always carry on with her after the wedding."

Simon couldn't imagine sharing her with Mainwaring. The idea made him so angry that he wished they were in the brawling ring instead of Leigh's home.

Rothschild smiled, and Simon didn't know if he'd been intentionally provoking him. "Come, let us get you a drink stronger than champagne." He put his arm around Simon and led him to the drawing room.

TWENTY-SIX

THE PRIZEFIGHT WAS TAKING PLACE IN A LARGE brick warehouse near the docks. The air smelled of old fish and decay, the sort of stench that constantly clung to the Thames. Despite the fact that she and Simon had no future—she had discussed this ad nauseam with Jenny and they had both concluded it was true—and Eliza had promised him that she wouldn't go back to Whitechapel, she could not *not* go to his brawl.

Eliza had left Cora's home a couple hours earlier. She had known the fight was tonight, but not the time nor the precise location beyond the fact that it would be in Whitechapel. Her plan had been to get as close to the area as a hansom would take her and then find her way on foot. She reasoned that a lot of people would be attending, so it wouldn't be difficult to find.

Happily, she needn't have worried. Mr. Dunn had fallen into step behind her not long after she had left to go to the nearest hansom stand. Not content to let the foolishness play out, Eliza had turned to confront him.

"Mr. Dunn, I am both surprised and unsurprised to see you here."

He had grinned with a hint of sheepishness about himself. "Simon asked me to come because he knew you would likely try to attend the brawl."

"Then you've come to stop me?"

"That was Simon's intention, but I've a mind of my own."

Her interest piqued, she had asked, "Then what do you intend?"

His smile had widened. "I reckon a man should have the woman he loves at his side on an evening such as this."

She had been too stunned to do anything but fall in stride beside him as he led her to a hansom. Now they were at the fight together and she was very thankful for his presence.

A lump had lodged itself in her stomach ever since she had seen Simon at the wedding breakfast about a week ago. It had only increased in intensity as the days wore on. She feared that Brody would do something underhanded and Simon would have no one there to help him. Not that she could be much help, but she could at least witness the crime if one were to happen.

This irrational fear had only worsened when Cora and Devonworth had left for Italy a couple of days after the wedding. They had received a note that Devonworth's younger brother—Mainwaring's travel companion—had found himself in trouble with the authorities in Rome and they'd gone to retrieve him. That only meant that Mainwaring would be returning early. That meant her wedding to him would happen sooner rather than later.

Both combined was enough to put her off food for days. She simply had to see Simon again and assure herself that he made it through this.

"Stay near to me now, bird." Mr. Dunn's rough voice was low enough that it only reached her ears, she hoped. Some of the men near them looked as if they might take it up as a personal challenge.

She tightened her grip on his arm and followed his weaving through the crowd of men, women, and children who were here to watch the fight. Most of them were honest, hardworking people. The men were most likely dockworkers and laborers. The women she imagined worked at the nearby match factory, the shops, and the alleys of Whitechapel. Children darted through the crowd in packs.

Brody must have men here, too, and the brawler from Devil's Acre would have brought some. They would be here to cause mayhem if the possibility presented itself. Eliza had minded Simon's warning about her purse and kept a little drawstring pouch in her bodice this time so that it couldn't be easily nicked.

The brawl hadn't started yet, but the area around the warehouse was already busy and crawling with people hoping to get inside. Hawkers worked their way through the crowd selling everything from meat pies to little dolls made from flour sacks that were meant to be the prizefighters. Their yells, intended to be heard above the din of the crowd, only added to the feeling of chaos. This wasn't at all like the fight at Montague Club.

"Do you see him?" she asked the very second they made their way inside.

Mr. Dunn was taller than her, but even he couldn't see over the people in front of them. He shook his head and said, "Hasn't come out yet."

The air held a formidable energy. She assumed it was due to the amount of money wagered on the match. She had found that when fortunes were at stake, people could be unpredictable and given to outrageous things.

The smell in the warehouse was as pungent as that outside. The fish and earthy decay was replaced by sweating bodies, smoke of various kinds from cigarettes to cigars, and the pungent scent of mold. The warehouse appeared to be old and dilapidated with crumbling mortar between the bricks. Brick pillars lined the inside, but one of them had crumbled at some point in the last decade and left a mountain of bricks that several boys stood upon to get a better view. Wooden crates lined the edges of the large space, piled three and four high. Some young men and boys had worked their way to the top of those stacks and sat there looking down on them. One group found sport in spitting down wads of tobacco-browned saliva on unsuspecting victims and would laugh uproariously when the person inevitably yelled in outrage.

Eliza drew closer to Mr. Dunn and directed him away from that side. He laughed when he saw what was happening and obliged her, making a line past the group ahead of them that had turned to watch the boys on the crates. This helped them get closer to the front and brought the fighting ring into sight. Eight metal stakes were planted in between the cobblestones with a double line of rope stretched tight between them to form a square of roughly fifteen feet on each side.

Tall barrels had been set outside each corner and one at the midpoint of each rope section, presumably to keep the crowd back. A young man stood on one of the corner barrels calling out bets while a man at his side wrote them down. There was a set of wooden risers on the opposite side from Eliza and Mr. Dunn. A group of around fifteen men stood there to get a better view. She recognized Brody immediately. A burning cigar was clamped between his teeth and a conniving grin curved his lips. She disliked this man immensely. The men surrounding him were likely all on his payroll. Men who wouldn't hesitate to do evil deeds. Men who wouldn't hesitate to harm Simon, Daisy, or even her if Brody instructed them to. She didn't know the odds of any of them recognizing her from their one encounter, but she kept her head down so that they wouldn't notice her, just in case. Mr. Dunn also seemed to pull back into the crowd, making sure they were in the third row and not as in the open.

Nerves swirled in her stomach, and not the good kind like when she saw Simon. This place seemed very dangerous, the tension on the verge of explosion, and she didn't like that so much of the success or failure of the night was carried on Simon's shoulders. What would this crowd do if he lost? What would they do if he won? There would be no pleasing everyone. What would Brody do if Simon didn't perform as he wanted? It didn't bear thinking about.

The warehouse was filled to the breaking point, and she could see shadowy figures outside the windows and spilling through the large open door that indicated there were at least a hundred people outside trying to see what was happening. The press was very nearly cloying. Sweat trickled down her back and she tugged at the collar of her high-necked dress trying to get some air.

Thankfully, an older man in a suit came out and climbed through the ropes to the middle of the ring. He held his hands up as if to call for quiet, an impossibility with this crowd. He looked to be a former fighter himself. His arms seemed muscled under his coat and his stomach padded with a thick layer of muscle and fat. His very presence demanded respect, and some did quiet down, though a din still continued from the back. He inclined his head to Brody, who held up his hand, tipping the cigar in a gesture of goodwill.

From her vantage point, Eliza had a clear view down a dark corridor that led to a back door. The warehouse wall made up one side of the corridor while a room made up the other. A man had come in through the back door flanked by two men. He was shirtless and wore knee breeches and thick hide boots. He had a swarthy appearance, his skin weather-beaten and tanned, as if he'd been a sailor at some point in his life. His multicolored hair was cropped short but frizzed at the neck with streaks of gray and blond intermingled with dark. His full beard was black, and that coupled with his complexion put her in mind of the pirate Blackbeard.

His appearance at the ring was met with a combination of huzzahs and hisses. Unlike Simon's last opponent, this man appeared well muscled and as if he knew his way around a fight. His expression was closed and drawn tight with anger and an innate hostility. He was focused on winning this brawl and not on fawning for the crowd. In fact, it appeared that he might want to take on a few of the men who were taunting him.

"That's Rouse," Mr. Dunn leaned over and said near her ear.

"Is he the favored?" she asked.

Mr. Dunn shook his head. "No, the Duke is favored, always."

She smiled in pleasure at that. Of course Simon would be favored. He was good, but he also had an appeal that most other people didn't, certainly not Rouse.

After a few minutes more, there was movement down the corridor. Her heart recognized his shadowy form before her eyes had the opportunity to focus in on him. It fluttered and sped in her chest, slamming itself against her ribs. Simon emerged and the crowd cheered, a deafening roar that rolled through the warehouse. He was shirtless like his opponent, but he wore similar breeches and boots, though his were considerably less worn. The hair on top of his head had been pulled back in a queue again, but a couple of days' growth of beard covered the lower half of his face. He was alone. Was that because Brody had decreed that it would be so, or was it because Mr. Dunn was acting as her nursemaid?

She yanked Mr. Dunn's shoulder and pulled him down. "Go to him," she yelled to be heard over the excitement.

He only gave a harsh shake of his head, but she could see the concern etched into his features.

The spectators began chanting his name. "Duke, Duke, Duke."

Simon raised his arms in acknowledgment, and the entire place erupted in anticipation. It was a palpable thing that filled the air, like the cloud of smoke that hovered over them. Simon himself looked different than she had ever seen him. He was fierce and vicious, his face a mask of brutal masculine beauty.

The fight at Montague Club had been a match between gentlemen. This one was different. This was a brawl between seasoned fighters. He bounced on the balls of his feet as he approached the ring, a look of grim determination on his face. She hadn't realized how very little Simon had been engaged with the other brawl until she saw him now. He almost appeared a completely different person. Primal and unrefined.

The air had stilled in her lungs. She couldn't look away from him. This was who he had been. This was the man he had been when he'd run the streets of Whitechapel. When he'd fought for Brody. When he'd killed those men. When he'd watched Mary die. When he'd taken on the responsibility of raising Daisy. He still was this man. He was also the Simon she knew from Bloomsbury. Somehow they both lived within him.

She loved both sides of him. She *loved* him.

Air fled her lungs in a whoosh. The blood in her head must have done the same because she stumbled. Mr. Dunn frowned down at her as she caught herself against him.

All this time she had been courting Simon.

All this time she had been falling in love with him.

All this time she had wanted to get caught.

She knew that now. She knew it in a way that made her feel whole and pure. He was the future that she wanted. Every time she had sneaked out to see him, risking discovery, her reputation, and her betrothal, had been because pursuing Simon had been more important to her. He'd been more important. He was worth more to her than the dowry from her useless father.

She would tell him so after the fight. She only hoped that he wanted her in the same way.

TWENTY-SEVEN

SIMON CLIMBED BETWEEN THE ROPES FOR WHAT HAD better be the last bloody time. The sounds of the crowd were near deafening, but it had long since stopped filling him with any sort of electric charge. He fought now only because he had to, because Brody couldn't let him go. Although sometimes fortune smiled on him and he faced an opponent that he was more than happy to punch in the face. Rouse was one of them.

Rouse lived in Devil's Acre now, but he'd once worked for Brody in Whitechapel not long after Brody had taken Simon and Mary in. Rouse was filled with piss and vinegar and had a mean streak that made the workhouse supervisors seem tame. Older than Simon, he had made a sport of terrorizing him and the other boys who'd been part of Brody's underlings then. Simon still had the cigarette burn scars on the back of his head, neck, and arms to prove it. It had been the best day of his young life when Brody had finally cast Rouse out and he'd run to Devil's Acre.

Rouse gave him an evil and bitter grin and said something that Simon couldn't hear over the roar of the spectators. It figured that this was the fight Brody wanted him to lose. One final insult before Simon was gone for good. Anger surged from his head to his fists to vibrate in his fingers. He'd bloody well get a few good licks in before he let the bell-end win.

Brody stepped to the edge of the risers, a god among the people who had come to see the fight, and some of them settled down as they watched him raise his arms for silence. Not to be outdone, Purcell, Brody's equivalent in Devil's Acre, also stepped out from the crowd. He hadn't been allowed on the risers. Brody liked to keep his rivals in their place. Brody tipped his hat to Purcell in a mockery of fair play.

"We've come here tonight to celebrate two great men, our very own Duke and his opponent." Several jeers and hisses followed that, and Brody held up his hand for quiet, though it only barely helped quell the din. "Rouse. Rouse and I go back many years. No offense to you." He pointed toward the man and Rouse spit toward the ropes. Several men called out in dismay but Brody only laughed.

Simon paced his end of the ring, frustrated that this was taking so long. Brody's display of showmanship was almost as bad as that bloody dandy Carstone. Brody droned on about this fight being years in the making and his cooperation with Purcell, but Simon didn't hear much of it. None of it mattered. This was his last night in the hellhole. After—if he could walk immediately after the beating he was required to allow Rouse to inflict—he'd go to Daisy and take her out of here. Fleetingly, he wondered if Dunn had managed to stop Eliza or if she'd even attempted to come.

"Watch out!" someone screamed. The yelled warning came

a second before Rouse's meaty fist impacted the side of Simon's head.

The crowd didn't like that. Simon fell back against the ropes, woozy and dizzy. The man from the crowd who had shouted was on the outside, propping him up. "The mug attacked while Brody was still talking. Cheat!" he yelled.

Simon recovered just in time to avoid another well-aimed punch that would have broken his nose. He whirled, rolling himself down the ropes, and Rouse almost went flying through them. The men nearest the ring yelled in protest at the underhanded move by Rouse, but it was no use. The fight had started whether he was ready or not. There would be no putting this bull back in his stall.

Good. The sooner they got this over with the better. Simon spun again to avoid a thick fist and ducked, landing a blow to Rouse's midsection. He was rewarded with the man's harsh exhale of air. The man's torso fell forward and Simon punched him in the jaw. A spray of blood and saliva flew across the ring, much to the appreciation of the enthralled audience.

The energy that he thought he'd long stopped feeling surged through him. It was cold and dark and hungry. It demanded to be fed. It hungered for Rouse's pain and blood. Simon was happy to oblige. In those short moments when his fist met flesh, he was able to give Rouse the pain that ate him up inside. The pain of not having Eliza. The pain of losing Mary. The pain of knowing Daisy suffered because he wasn't enough to get her out of here. But most of all, as the welts and crimson drops of blood peppered Rouse's body, it was payback for the hell his life had been when Rouse had worked for Brody.

"Back off!" the official screamed in his ear.

Simon realized he'd had Rouse against the corner, his back against the barrel outside the rope. He released him immediately and stepped back to give the man a little time to catch his breath. Simon needed to calm down. He was meant to lose this fight, no matter how much pleasure he derived from beating Rouse's arse across the ring.

He smoothed his hand over his forehead, pushing back a lock of hair that had fallen loose of its binding. A quick glance at the crowd confirmed that most of them were on his side. They shouted encouragement, and he had to look away because he hated that he'd be letting them down. Fucking Brody.

Rouse was coming to his senses, and the official backed up, giving him space. Simon meant to turn back and goad him into punching him, but his gaze caught on the one face he hadn't expected to see. Amazingly, impossibly, Eliza stared out at him. He couldn't see her completely, only her precious face peeking out between the shoulders of the men in front of her, but it was her. Dunn was standing beside her.

"Why are ye here?" he shouted to her. His voice didn't carry, but Dunn knew what he asked. The man shrugged and looked away.

Eliza smiled at him, her angel face full of love and encouragement. *Dear God, keep her safe*, he prayed. He didn't have time to consider her longer because Rouse pushed off the ropes and barreled toward him. Simon lunged away from the man's left hook.

They exchanged blows for the next several minutes, Simon retreating when appropriate to make it seem as if Rouse could get the better of him. The truth was that Rouse wasn't the man he'd once been. Gin and opium had left their marks on him. He was more sluggish and less measured than Simon remembered. While still formidable, as evidenced by the bruised ribs Simon knew he would sport in the morning, Rouse's fight was more brute strength than cunning. He counted on his every punch doing significant damage rather than his own defenses.

It was a pity Simon would be forced to lose to him. Simon took a punch to his gut and doubled over. He used the opportunity to glance toward Brody, who gave him a subtle nod. It was time to end the fight.

Simon charged Rouse, putting his shoulder low and knocking his opponent back toward the ropes. It would be his last move. Rouse would charge him and redouble his efforts, and this time Simon would fall to the ground. Knowing Rouse, the man would hop onto him dealing blow after blow until the official pulled him off.

But that isn't what happened.

Rouse caught himself on the ropes and lumbered his way across the ring, appearing groggy and sluggish, which made no sense. With the exception of the first punch he'd landed that night, Simon's fists had been restricted to the man's torso, not his head. He hadn't been trying to maim him, only taking out his frustration on his meaty midsection.

Rouse let out an inhuman-sounding yell and rushed forward, his shoulder catching Simon in his chest. Rouse probably outweighed him by a stone, but he was shorter, which meant he was broader. The blow hurt but it didn't knock Simon off his feet. He absorbed the man's speed and held them both upright. Rouse's feet seemed unable to hold him up.

"What the devil's wrong with ye?" Simon half shouted.

"Fuck off," Rouse smirked, blood tinting his teeth pink. Then he fell forward, half-bent as if Simon had hit him, but it was a fiction. Simon had merely been holding him up.

Frustrated, Simon punched his arm. "What are ye doing?"

Rouse fell to the ground and spat out blood that Simon was certain he'd manufactured somehow. His teeth might have cut the inside of his jaw when Simon had punched him, but that puddle was too much blood for the simple injury. The man had worsened it. He must have worried it with his teeth. The official ran over to check Rouse, who was now making a performance out of seizing and groaning as if in the worst pain of his life. Simon knew it was a performance because when the official looked over to Purcell for guidance, Rouse flashed him a knowing look.

Jesus Christ. Rouse was throwing the fight!

The crowd all but knew it was over. No one thought Rouse would be getting up to try again. Massive cheers went up through the warehouse, even though Simon's win wasn't official yet.

"Get up!" Simon demanded. Reaching around the official, he grasped Rouse's arm. "You're not hurt."

"Get off me!" Rouse shouted. He grinned for a split second.

The bastard had lost on purpose. Just as quickly, his expression changed and he managed to look half out of his mind when the official's attention came back to them. Simon wondered how much Rouse had won for his trouble.

"Can you fight?" the man asked Rouse. He kept asking and Rouse wouldn't answer. He groaned and pretended to be injured.

Simon backed away from the scene, hoping that it might miraculously change. That Rouse might not actually be intending to throw the fight. He looked up and his eyes caught Brody, who had gone pale with shock. He'd lose a fortune if Rouse didn't get on his feet.

How much money had Simon cost him?

Simon looked for Eliza in the crowd. She stood there cheering with the rest, not yet understanding what had happened. Simon had won when he was supposed to lose. Brody rigged the fight so that he could win big with Simon's loss. Since he'd lost the big payout, he wouldn't let Simon be free now. In fact, he'd kill him.

Dunn knew. Simon had shared the plan with him, the only one he'd shared it with.

Time slowed. Even the sound of his heart beating in his ears had a curious echo, slow and steady. As he watched, Dunn leaned down and spoke to Eliza, his lips next to her ear. The excitement on her face distorted, transforming to stillness. The sort of quiet expectation that accompanied the dawning of loss. That terrible knowledge that preceded the sensation of pain after a horrific accident.

She met his gaze and they both knew. He was a dead man.

TWENTY-EIGHT

THE LOOK ON SIMON'S FACE CONFIRMED WHAT DUNN had said in her ear.

Simon was meant to lose.

She didn't know why or how, but she knew that Brody had arranged for Simon to lose. That night when he had cornered them in Whitechapel and taken Simon aside. He must have told him then. Simon would lose and that's why Brody would win so much. The odds were on Simon winning. His loss would be a much bigger payout. It would likely be a fortune. But now . . .

"What happens now?" She couldn't look away from Simon. She couldn't get over the feeling that this might very well be the last time she saw him. That Brody would want him dead and he had the power to make such a terrible thing come to pass. Everything in her revolted at that. She had not come this far to lose him now.

"Brody kills him." Mr. Dunn spoke so matter-of-factly that

she recoiled at the sound. Each word was a rock whipped right into the center of her heart.

"No." There was so much she wanted to tell him, but they had run out of time. Stubbornly and stupidly.

The official got to his feet. This was it. He would call the fight now. He looked to Brody and his words were lost to the chaos of the night. No one around them needed to hear the words, not when Rouse's crumbled form stayed on the ground and Simon stood there, hale and whole.

"We have to go to him." She didn't know if Mr. Dunn could hear her and she didn't care. She darted through the men in front of her before Mr. Dunn could stop her. If Brody meant to harm the man she loved, he'd damned well have to go through her to get to him.

Simon saw her and he sprang into action, vaulting over the ropes to meet her. Dimly, she was aware of the men on the risers on the opposite side jumping to the ground, but Simon had taken her arm and he was ushering her down the corridor with Mr. Dunn right behind them. They ran outside and slammed the door behind them. It was old and wooden and probably wouldn't hold for long. Mr. Dunn wrestled with a full barrel of something that sloshed as he moved it, the veins of his neck straining with the effort, and set it before the door, a temporary blockade. Whoever followed them would have to take the time to either break down the door or wade through the mass of humanity that obstructed the front entrance. It would buy them a little time; she hoped it was enough.

"You have to run away, Simon," she said as they headed hand in hand down an alley.

Footsteps pounded on the cobblestones behind them. She didn't know if it was ten or a hundred, friend or foe. It was like the warehouse had exploded and all the rats were escaping.

"No, I have to go to Daisy," he said, not even looking at her. His head was on a swivel, looking for Brody's men to hop out of the darkness.

"I'll go to Daisy," she said.

He kept running, not even running, really; he was measuring his steps to hers and she was slowing him down.

They turned down another alley. The whole place was a maze of them. Grabbing his arm, she forced him to stop. When he finally met her gaze, she said, "Listen to me. I'm slowing you down. You have to get far away from Whitechapel. I'll get Daisy and take her home with me. You go hide. Go to Leigh or Rothschild, but not back to Montague Club." Brody might be desperate enough to attack there, but he'd never be bold enough or foolish enough to infiltrate the residence of a duke or earl.

"It'll be better if you and Daisy are not together." This was from Mr. Dunn. He looked around as he spoke, scanning the shadows for threats. "Brody will want both of ye. Daisy can go there. You have to leave."

Simon nodded. "If we separate, he'll be forced to halve his men."

"Yes, precisely," she said with enthusiasm. "I swear to you that I'll see to Daisy. I'll keep her safe for you."

A shadow came over Simon's face. He caressed her cheek. "I can't let you put yourself in danger, Angel."

"For Chrissake, she already has, ye arse," Mr. Dunn pointed out, and Eliza wanted to kiss him for being on her side, but she couldn't look away from Simon.

Without another word, Simon leaned down and kissed her full on the mouth with the desperation they both felt. It was tender and rough and over far too soon.

"I love you," she said, and something wonderful happened to his face. Even though they were on the run with certain death in their future if they were caught, a relief that was full of peace and deep affection came over him.

"Ye have to go. Now!" Mr. Dunn urged, breaking the spell.

"Here." Eliza dug into her bodice and ripped out the coin purse she had pinned there. It might be all the money he would have. She pressed it into his palm, and he brought her hand to his mouth and kissed it.

"Now go," she said, fighting back the tears that burned her eyes.

He took a couple of backward steps, reluctant to leave her, but there was no other choice and they both knew it. They couldn't delay any longer. She hiked up her skirts and turned north to go to Daisy. Mr. Dunn fell into step beside her as she had known he would. Simon would want him to make certain his niece was safe.

A quick glance over her shoulder assured her that Simon had disappeared into the night. It was only then that she realized she had no idea where he might go. She sent up a silent prayer for his safety. In her heart she felt that they would be together again. She prayed that it would be true.

She sprinted as fast as she could, but it still seemed like it took hours to make the nearly two-mile trek. She was gasping for air when they approached the brothel's narrow street. Remembering what Simon had said about a watchman, she searched the sidewalk and the rooftops as they approached. It didn't appear that anyone had spotted them. There was no one running to approach them or running for help. Hopefully, Brody had called all of his men to the warehouse for the brawl.

Several men loitered at the front door, but they seemed to be entertained by the two women flirting with them. Mr.

Dunn led her around the back. She thought they might knock, but he indicated she should stand back and he kicked the door open. She flinched at the crack of splintering wood, but recovered quickly. Mr. Dunn stepped inside to confront the irate cook, and Eliza understood why he'd kicked down the door. The woman would never have let them in. No doubt the gray-haired woman Eliza had met would come to see what all the bother was about. Eliza didn't wait around to find out. She ran up the stairs and all the way to the attic.

The door was locked from the inside, so she was forced to knock. A sleepy Henrietta met her after the third time.

"I'm so very sorry for barging in like this." Eliza pushed her way inside and tried to keep her voice low. "Mr. Cavell is in a bit of trouble and he asked me to come take Daisy home with me. You, too, if you'd like to come." Eliza found Daisy's slight form on the small bed, still sleeping where Henrietta had left her when she awoke to open the door.

"But we aren't allowed to leave. Mr. Brody—"

"I know. Mr. Cavell told me everything. I'm sorry, I don't have time to explain it all properly, but Brody is angry and believes that Mr. Cavell betrayed him. He's had to run for his life and I have to take Daisy home to keep her safe from Brody. Please come, too." She shuddered to think what would happen to the girl when Brody found out that she'd let Eliza take Daisy, because Eliza wasn't leaving here without the child.

Daisy woke up as the girl debated her options, roused by their voices. "Auntie Liza?" she asked, her voice soft and warm with sleep.

Eliza's heart clenched. Simon must have been talking about her with Daisy. "Daisy, I apologize for waking you, but I have good news. We are going on a very short trip to visit a lord and lady." She decided in that split second that it would be best to take the girls to Lord Leigh's residence. Violet was close to Simon, and Lord Leigh was privy to some of Simon's history; it would be easier to explain things. She didn't know if Brody had managed to figure out her real identity. If he had, he very well might attempt to get Daisy back since Devonworth was out of the country and not there to stop him. It wasn't a chance Eliza was willing to take.

Daisy's brow furrowed in uncertainty. "Will Papa be there?"

Eliza swallowed. "He's not there yet, but I think he will be soon." *Please, God, don't make that a lie.*

Daisy smiled, but looked to Henrietta for confirmation.

"Please come," Eliza said to her. "It will make things easier for Daisy and I promise that you will be well taken care of."

Henrietta nodded, and the next several moments were a flurry of activity. They had one small cloth bag and they filled it with all the things they wanted that they might never see again. When they were packed, after Eliza had assured them both that there were clothes and books and food where they were going so they needn't take it all, Eliza picked Daisy up and covered her with the small blanket that Henrietta said she didn't like to be without. Daisy put her head on her shoulder, her tiny hand patting Eliza's back as if to assure her that everything would be fine.

Eliza tightened her hold on the small body in her arms, overcome with the same love she felt for Simon because this was his child. They made their way down the steps to the back door. Mr. Dunn had finished his argument with the cook, but had taken up arguing with the gray-haired lady. They both fell quiet when the three of them appeared on the stairs.

"Get on with the lot of ye, then," the lady spat out and stomped back to the front of the house.

The whole thing had taken probably five minutes, but Eliza kept expecting Brody to appear. The alley was empty when they emerged. Mr. Dunn led them deftly through the twists and turns to the street where she and Simon had boarded the carriage from Montague Club. They found a hansom, and somehow the four of them managed to squeeze inside.

They would be safe now. She only hoped that Simon was safe and had outrun Brody's men.

TWENTY-NINE

THE FOLLOWING DAYS WERE INTERMINABLE. NO one had heard from Simon at all. Mr. Dunn had dropped them off at the Leigh town house and gone back to White-chapel to investigate what had happened. He'd returned with very little information except that no one had found Simon, including Brody. Then he'd refused to stay and had gone back to Montague Club to work and wait for Simon to send word.

Eliza had been forced to explain Simon's duplicity to Lord Leigh when she showed up on his doorstep with a child and a nursemaid. There had been no getting around it, not when she needed his help to keep Daisy safe. He hadn't been angry, not that she could tell. He'd appeared more thoughtful and con-sidering. He'd then sprung into action and ordered up extra protection for the house and the club. August and her husband the duke came over the morning after their arrival, and they all did everything they could to help with Daisy and Henrietta and finding Simon.

Violet had accepted the disruption in stride. She had

immediately made room for them by giving each of them a bedchamber. Daisy had made it very clear that she wasn't quite willing to give up sleeping next to Heni, but she delighted in the adjoining room she had been given, even if she did slip into Heni's room at night to sleep. The lace curtains and canopy over the bed thrilled her. Even more, Daisy had a new playmate that she enjoyed immensely. Violet and Lord Leigh had a daughter, Rosie, who was about a year younger. Rosie was equally enamored of Daisy. They played together despite the age difference and were nearly inseparable except to sleep.

Eliza's hours were well filled. Henrietta needed a new wardrobe, as did Daisy, so they had seamstresses in and out of the house. There was no talk about the future, because so much was uncertain, but she had talked to Violet privately about helping the girl attend school when she was able. Then there was the matter of finding toys for Daisy and figuring out both of their favorite foods—Henrietta enjoyed scones with strawberry jam while Daisy preferred nothing at all as an accompaniment to her jam.

It would have been a peaceful time, but a pall hung over them. Simon wasn't there and she didn't know if he was safe. She had taken to tucking Daisy in every night so that Henrietta could stay downstairs and play cards with Violet, Jenny, and Fanny. Her mother and sister came over every day to visit and had brushed off any concerns for their safety. They didn't believe that anyone would be foolish enough to invade a Mayfair home, and they were probably right. She hadn't seen the need to worry Devonworth and Cora while they were on their trip, so no one had sent word to them. There wasn't anything they could do from afar, and news of trouble would send them running home.

Every night without fail, Daisy asked if she would see her papa in the morning. It broke Eliza's heart.

"Daisy is a very bright child to have spent her whole life locked away in an attic." Violet held her coffee cup while she watched the children play outside the breakfast room window. A sunny room with windows on two sides that was at the back of the house, it had a view of the beautiful walled garden where Daisy and Rosie were playing with Rosie's nanny.

"She is very bright." Eliza couldn't help but smile as she watched them. Daisy jumped off the edge of the low brick wall of a planter and giggled after she landed on her feet. Rosie and Nanny applauded her efforts. In her new clothes, Daisy looked very much like the cosseted daughter of a caring family. It was no less than she deserved. "Henrietta says they were allowed to go out a few times a week while Brody's knave lurked nearby."

Her words took on a bitter twist that got Violet's attention. "We haven't had much time to speak of it with so much going on, but given this turn of events and the way you two were at the wedding breakfast . . . well . . . what are your thoughts for the future?"

"I'd need to speak with Simon, but I hope he's in my future."

Violet's smile broadened. "I don't mean to push you toward a decision—"

"No, you didn't," Eliza hurried to reassure her. "I love him. I don't doubt that at all."

Violet nodded and thankfully did not ask how she had spent enough time with him to know this. Eliza didn't want to explain everything that had happened over the summer. "I only ask because there has been some chatter already. Our servants are faithful, but information can only be contained for so long. It seems that some people know that we have a child and her nanny staying with us. No one knows her identity and I would never tell anyone. However . . . it is also speculated that you are staying here."

Eliza sighed and sat back in her chair. "Is that all there is for people to do in this town? Gossip about everyone else?"

Violet laughed and set down her cup. "I'm afraid there's a fair lot of that. It's worked in our favor that Parliament is on break and most families have returned to the country. It should keep the speculation from spreading like wildfire, more of a controlled burn, but we do need to come up with something if you plan to . . . well . . . Mainwaring will return soon."

"Oh no, I'm not marrying him anymore. I've already decided." That thought had solidified in the days since the brawl. She had nothing but time to think at night as she tossed and turned in bed, worried out of her mind for Simon. She'd send word to Mr. Hathaway once things with Simon were settled.

"Why don't we take things one step at a time? Mainwaring hasn't returned yet, so we don't need to do anything on that front, but you should speak with your mother about him."

"I suppose you're right. I should begin arranging everything so that when Simon—"

A maid appeared at the threshold of the room. "My lady, a wire has come for his lordship." She held a small, folded piece of paper in her hand.

Lord Leigh was already out for the day, likely seeing to things at Montague Club. Apparently, the club was abuzz with chatter about Simon and his whereabouts. No one had told them about his identity as the Duke, but according to Rothschild and Leigh, speculation ran rampant from the rumor that he worked in some sort of secret service to the Queen to the one that he might be a criminal on the run. She had no idea how those rumors got started, but they made her laugh.

"Thank you, Beatrice, give it to me," Violet said, and held out her hand.

Beatrice handed it over and gave a short curtsy before leaving them alone. Violet seemed almost bored. This must be a very common occurrence. Lord Leigh had contacts and business dealings far and wide. Still, Eliza couldn't shake the idea that this one was meant for *her*.

Violet scanned the words on the page. Her lips tipped upward at the corners and there was a devilish sparkle in her eyes when they met Eliza's across the table. "It seems that our estate in Scotland had a visitor arrive last night."

Everything inside her stilled. "Is it him?"

"I knew he would turn up." Violet handed over the telegram. It was from the estate manager, a short two lines advising of an unexpected visitor, a man who had visited last summer, and asking for advice on how to proceed.

"It must be Simon," she said, crushing the paper to her breast as if it were Simon himself. "I have to go." She came to her feet, her mind racing with all the things she'd need to do, but then she realized she wouldn't need to do anything except pack a change of clothes and buy a train ticket. If her calculations were correct, she could be there by very late that evening. "What about Daisy? Should I take her?"

"No, it's best to leave her here since we don't know that he won't be found by Mr. Brody. I'll see that she and Henrietta are taken care of." Violet rose at a much slower pace due to her pregnancy. "I'll talk to Christian and Mr. Dunn. Someone will need to go with you. Perhaps you should see your mother before you leave."

Eliza didn't want to do any of that. She wanted to leave as

soon as possible, but there was one other thing she needed to add to her to-do list. Now that she had found Simon, she needed to officially end things with Mainwaring, which meant she'd have to wire Devonworth for advice. He'd helped arrange the contract and had signed it along with Mr. Hathaway. He'd advise her on how to proceed. She changed course for the writing desk in Violet's office where she picked up a piece of parchment from the basket and a pen.

I have decided I cannot marry Mainwaring. I love another. Please advise. She wrote it with a flourish and made a little swirl beneath it, not that it would translate well in a telegram. She might not look as much like their mother as Jenny did, but she had inherited her flair for drama.

"Can you see that this gets sent today?" Eliza asked Violet, who had come to stand in the doorway.

"Of course," Violet answered.

"Thank you, Violet." Eliza hugged her. "I don't know what I would do without your help."

Violet shook her head. "Thankfully, you won't have to do without it. August is looking into a tutor for Henrietta, and they're supposed to be stopping by this afternoon. Daisy has a fun day planned with Rosie. You go to Blythkirk. We'll both be here to take care of everything until you return."

Eliza hurried up the stairs. She would see Simon before the night was over.

T HE NEXT HOUR WAS A MAD DASH TO GET TO THE train station. Eliza wanted to leave immediately, but it made more sense to plan. She knew that, but she had trouble waiting that long. She had already told Daisy and Henrietta about the quick trip, though she hadn't told them Simon was definitely there, since she didn't know. Now she paced the entryway until Violet came to bid her goodbye.

Violet said, "I sent a footman to tell your mother. She wants you to stop by before you leave."

Perfect. More delay.

"Also, Mr. Dunn will be traveling with you. He'll be bringing some of Simon's clothing and personal effects."

Eliza nearly groaned at how much longer this would take, even as she understood the need. Simon would appreciate having his own clothes.

"Also, there's this." Violet put a small leather satchel in Eliza's hand. It felt as if there was a glass jar inside. "Don't take it out here," Violet whispered, and glanced to a footman who hovered nearby.

Curious, Eliza opened the satchel and peered inside. The faint tinge of vinegar met her nose. The jar was full of contraceptive sponges.

"Do you know what those are?" Violet asked.

Eliza found herself blushing, but she nodded. "Yes, my mother explained them to me."

"Good." Violet's brow unfurled in relief. "We needn't speak of it, but I wanted you to have them."

"Thank you, Violet. I appreciate everything you've done."

"You're very welcome. Now go, and I expect my husband will be close behind you."

They hugged and Eliza hurried out the door to the waiting carriage. The servants had already loaded her small trunk onto the back.

It took them only a few minutes to reach Cora's house. Eliza took off like a charged wire as soon as the carriage door opened, and hurried up the steps. Jenny greeted her the moment she stepped inside.

"Do you think it's him? Is he the visitor?" her sister asked.

"I think so." They danced in a happy circle in the entryway.

"Good, you're here. I thought I heard you." Her mother appeared at the top of the stairs dressed in a deep green traveling costume that made Eliza very suspicious.

"Why are you dressed that way?" Eliza asked as Fanny descended the stairs.

"Because we're coming with you," she answered.

Eliza glanced at Jenny, only just now noticing that her sister was dressed for travel. "But why?"

"Because you need us," Jenny said. "Surely, you have room for one more trunk? We economized." She indicated the trunk that had been set by the front door.

This really wasn't what Eliza had imagined when she'd decided to go north to Simon. "What about your social commitments?"

"What commitments?" Fanny asked. "It's the dead of summer. Scotland will be fun."

Eliza decided they would waste more time arguing and stormed out the front door. Jenny fell into step right beside her and said, "I believe her Scotsman, Lord Ballachulish, has returned home. Perhaps she hopes to make a detour afterward."

Eliza found herself laughing as they all climbed into the carriage. Their trunk was loaded quickly, and from there they traveled on to acquire Mr. Dunn. Thankfully, he was waiting near the door and came running out the moment the carriage stopped at Montague Club.

"Oh, good morning, ladies." His eyes widened in surprise to find all of them in the carriage. After a few exchanged pleasantries and another trunk loaded, they headed off to King's Cross.

THIRTY

Blythkirk, Scotland

SIMON CAME AWAKE THE MOMENT HIS BEDCHAMBER door opened. A shaft of yellow light from the corridor fell across the thick Aubusson rug, and he leaped to his feet while grabbing hold of the hunting knife he'd found downstairs and left on the bedside table. Despite three days of running and one day of sanctuary at Blythkirk, he wasn't convinced that Brody's men wouldn't track him down. The estate was operating on a skeleton staff, and there would be very little to stop them should they decide to come in and get him.

A woman's form stood in the doorway, backlit by the gas sconce in the corridor. "Simon, it's me."

It couldn't be, but it was her voice. She came into the room and closed the door behind her. "Eliza?"

She walked slowly across the rug. Soft moonlight filtered into the room from the windows on the other side of his bed. It painted her in shades of silver, giving her an almost ethereal glow. He softened his grip on the knife and then placed it back on the table. "How are you here?" he asked, still not completely certain she wasn't a dream. "What time is it?"

"Around two o'clock in the morning. I was at Lord Leigh's home when we received your telegram. I took Daisy and Henrietta there."

"They're safe?" He finally came to his senses and lit the small bedside lamp. Her smiling face came into view. God, he'd missed her face.

"Yes, they're safe and being cared for. I took the train directly here as soon as we could after receiving the wire from the estate manager. Jenny, my mother, and Mr. Dunn all insisted on coming, too."

"He mentioned he was sending the wire, but I never imagined that you'd come." He had expected Leigh to come alone, but this was the nicest surprise he could imagine. "I can't believe you're here." He reached out to touch her, but was afraid she might dissipate beneath his hand.

She closed the distance between them and pressed her cheek to his palm. "I don't know why you're surprised."

He laughed. "I don't know, either, Angel. You always seem to find me."

She laughed, too, but there was a hesitancy about her, an uncertainty that had never been present in her before. She might very well be the most confident person he knew. "I'll always find you . . . always be with you . . . if you'll have me."

That familiar ache came back to his chest, as it did so often when he was with her. It was both painful and joyful. "Angel . . ." But he couldn't finish that sentence. He couldn't tell her no because he was selfish. He wanted her. She turned and placed a kiss in his palm. "I was so afraid that I'd never see you again," he admitted. Before he could get ahold of himself, he stepped toward her and gathered her into his arms.

Burying his face in her hair, he breathed deeply of her. He loved how she always smelled of roses. For the first time since he'd last held her, he felt whole.

She whispered his name over and over. She dropped the small satchel she'd been carrying to the floor and her arms went around his waist. They stood like that for several moments, holding each other and relishing that the past few days apart were over. He rubbed his face in her hair, unable to stop himself from feeling her. He wanted to feel her all over.

"Are you hurt? Your eye looks painful." She pulled back to look up at him.

Rouse had hit him high on his cheekbone right below his eye. It hadn't swelled closed, but it was still swollen and hot. "It's not as painful as it appears."

"What happened to you when you left?"

He told her how he ran until he found clothes hanging on a line. He'd taken a shirt and coat and kept going until the sun came up. Then he managed to catch a ride with a vegetable farmer returning to Tottenham after delivering his load. From there he'd taken a mail coach farther north. Finally, after meandering for two days, he figured no one was on his trail and he deemed it safe to take the train for Scotland. "I used the money you gave me for the ticket." He'd nearly starved until he'd got here, but he needn't tell her that. He knew the precious few coins would only be enough for a ticket, so he'd stolen bits of food when he could. A heel of bread here, a tin of beef there. The estate manager had recognized him from his visit last summer and welcomed him. Simon had requested that he word the wire to Leigh so that he didn't use his name, just in case.

"I'm glad you're safe. I was so worried about you," she said with all the love in the world shining from her eyes.

"I worried about you," he said, taking hold of her pointed

chin. "I had no way of knowing that you were safe and that you'd got Daisy and Henrietta." He dipped his head and took her lips. He'd meant for it to be a tender, searching kiss, but he was too hungry for her. He'd been afraid for so long that he'd never see her again.

She kissed him back with the same desperate energy. Her hands tugged at his borrowed nightshirt and he obliged her. He broke the kiss to pull it off over his head. He was nude beneath, and she stepped back to look at him.

"I've wanted to see you like this for so long."

"You almost did," he reminded her. That day in the changing room at the club she had stayed to watch as long as she could before she'd closed the door. "After you left, I imagined you were still there with me."

She grinned and a blush stained her cheeks. He took her hand and lowered it down over his chest and the bruises that still lingered on his torso, across his flat stomach, and down to his cock. He was hard and ready for her. As much as he wanted to take her now, he was determined to go slowly this time.

"What did you do when you imagined me there?" she whispered.

"This."

He wrapped his hand around hers, closing her fingers tight around his erection. He showed her how to stroke him with a slow squeezing motion that made him hiss in a breath. He let her go and found the buttons up the front of her traveling dress. He dipped his head to kiss her neck, savoring the heat of her skin under his lips. Over the past days, he'd wondered if he'd ever taste her again. He closed his eyes when she stroked him again, her touch becoming more confident.

Her jacket fell open and he slid it off her shoulders. She stopped touching him long enough to shrug out of it so he could toss it aside. He kissed her then, a melding of lips and tongues. As he explored her mouth, his fingers tugged at her skirt, loosening it until he could push it down as well. She moved back to step out of it and quickly rid herself of her underskirt and bustle. Suddenly, he wanted nothing more than to see her. The real her without clothes between them. He wanted to touch every precious inch of her skin.

She turned away and worked the fastenings of her corset, and he stripped it away from her the second she was done. His mouth found her neck. He pushed the thin strap of her chemise down her shoulder and nipped at her tender flesh. She gasped in pleasure and he did it again. That prompted her to back into him, the soft curves of her backside pressed firm against his cock.

"Eliza," he whispered. He couldn't get enough of her.

She turned in his arms and he raised the chemise over her head and tossed it aside. His palms found her breasts. They were perfect, slightly more than a handful. Her nipples pebbled against him. His tongue swept into her mouth, brushing against hers. He wanted to keep kissing her, but he wanted to see her more.

He pulled back and admired the plump bit of flesh filling his hands. "You're beautiful, Angel. Even more beautiful than I imagined." He dropped one hand to trail his fingertips down over her rib cage and the soft, slight protrusion of her stomach. He loved how soft and supple she was. How everywhere he touched was a new texture. She watched him with her dark eyes, the lamplight picking out flecks of gold in their depths.

Leaning down, he took a firm, pink nipple into his mouth. He'd wanted to do this in the carriage, but it'd been impossible then. He vowed to make a feast of her tonight. He laved her other one with the same tender attention. Then he dropped to his knees to take off her boots. She sat back against the side of the bed as he unlaced the first one and took it off. He massaged the arch of her foot with his thumbs and looked up to see her smile of appreciation. Removing her second boot, he did the same. She made a soft moan and the sound went straight to his bollocks.

"Will ye make that sound when I'm inside ye?" He grinned up at her.

She gasped and looked toward the bed and then back at him. "I—I think so." Her bashful smile might have put him over the edge all by itself, but then she tugged at the tie of her drawers.

He groaned, physically in pain now, and pulled the white cotton fabric until it fell down her hips. He couldn't tear his eyes from the triangle of dark hair hiding her cunt, so he fumbled and the drawers got stuck on her feet. She giggled and rested a hand on his shoulder as she leaned forward to free the offending garment. The second she had sat back upright, he lifted her thighs over his shoulders and spread her wide. Her sex was pink and swollen, her clitoris engorged already, and he'd barely touched her. He looked up to gauge her reaction. She watched him with eyes wide and so dark with need they were almost black. As their eyes held, he took her swollen nub into his mouth and sucked. She cried out and her fingernails dug into his shoulders. He couldn't get enough of her. After a moment, his tongue dipped inside her, tasting her need for him. She arched, her hips coming off the bed a little as she pressed herself against his face. He'd do this all night for her if only he didn't want her so badly. He alternated between sucking her and teasing her clitoris with his tongue until he could feel his release rising in his bollocks as they got painfully tight. He let her go and came to his feet.

"There," she said, pointing to the discarded satchel on the ground. He'd forgotten all about it.

He was aware of how she watched him walk to pick it up, her eyes eating him up across the short distance. Back at the bed, he pulled out a jar.

"Sponges," she said.

How had she got these? It was a question for later. "I've only ever used condoms," he said. He'd heard of women using sponges, but none of the women he'd ever been with had offered. Nor would he have accepted. He preferred condoms because they helped with disease, but with her that wasn't an issue. "Do you know how to use them?"

"I think so."

He opened the jar and set it on the table. The sharp tang of vinegar met his nose. He pulled out one of the small sponges and unraveled the string attached to it. As he did, she moved back farther onto the bed to make room for him. He joined her there, pressing his knee into the mattress as he watched her.

"We insert it and then we can . . . you can release inside me without fear of a child." She rushed ahead to say that last part, unused to these sorts of discussions.

He wasn't accustomed to them, either. He'd never experienced this sort of intimacy before. This talking and learning each other during sex. His couplings had always been transactional. Usually, women only wanted him because he was the Duke, and when it was over they went their separate ways.

"Shall I do it?" he asked, and she nodded.

He climbed over her and she lay back against the pillows. Once again his mouth found her nipple, sucking one and then the other until she was arching into him. His hand found its way between her thighs and she parted for him. She was slick and hot, anxious for him. He stroked her anyway to make certain, then he pushed a finger into her, followed soon by another when her hips started moving with him. Finally, he pushed the sponge into her, seating it deep before pulling out of her.

Lifting himself, he looked down at her. She was beautiful. Her hair was a mess around her, having fallen free from its pins at some point since she'd arrived in his bedchamber. Her face was flushed with lust and her body eager for his. She grasped at his hips and he fell forward onto an elbow. With his other hand he notched himself at her cunt and flexed his hips, pushing into her. Her mouth parted and she angled her hips up to take more of him, but she was tight. He worked into her slowly, inch by inch until he was certain she could take him without discomfort, and then he thrust forward as far as he could go.

He squeezed his eyes shut at the intense pleasure of being completely sheathed within her. They had all night. She could stay in his bed until morning, unless her mother came at some point and pulled her away, but that was the only way he'd give her up. It was a dream come to life. She was so soft and warm beneath him. He couldn't stop touching her. His palm grazed her hip, her waist, her breast. He gave her nipple a gentle tug and she gasped his name.

He couldn't stay still then if he wanted to. He rolled his hips, rocking into her, and she answered the move, her hands skimming down his back to squeeze his arse. He couldn't stop the shot of electricity that darted down his spine and coiled in his bollocks.

"Eliza," he groaned. "You feel too good."

He thrust again, this time harder, and she made that moan in the back of her throat. The sound vibrated through him. He bucked against her, harder, deeper.

"Simon," she cried. "Please, more. I waited so long for you."

He was lost. He'd crossed the precipice and there was no

going back. There was no stopping this mad runaway train they were on. He adjusted his grip to her shoulder and the other gripped the headboard. He worked his hips against her and fucked her hard and deep in a rhythm that seemed endless.

She clawed at his back and wrapped her legs around his waist, opening herself to him, trying to take as much of him as she could. She felt too damned perfect. He could feel himself barreling toward release, and they had only just started. He withdrew to try to stop it, the hard ridge of his cock sliding over her clitoris. She cried out again. "Simon, I need you. Come inside me."

That was all it took. He slammed into her and she gripped him so very tight, her body clenching him mercilessly. He took her hard, so hard that the headboard slammed against the wall brutally, but he didn't care. He needed her and she was coming apart in his arms, her cries echoing in his ears until he smothered them with his mouth. Her fingernails left marks down his back. He drove into her over and over again until her own orgasm had stilled and his began, draining him of everything he had to give her. His life, his happiness, his future. His heart. She held everything he was in the precious sanctuary of her body.

He fell over her and she buried her fingers in his hair, nuzzling her face against his. He'd never felt this closeness with another person before, as if their very souls had joined. They stayed that way for several minutes until their breaths slowed. He wrapped his arms around her and moved off her so that he wouldn't crush her and pulled her with him. He couldn't let her go. He never wanted to let her go. His body curled around hers.

"I love you, Angel," he whispered.

THIRTY-ONE

THEY STAYED IN BED MUCH LONGER THAN NECESsary the next morning. Part of it was that it was the first night of good, deep sleep Eliza had gotten in days. It was so easy to sleep with Simon at her back keeping her warm. But as the sun rose higher in the sky, she became more aware of him in bed with her and sleeping became less important.

She'd never before considered that a man could take a woman from behind, but that morning Simon showed her it was possible. They had been sleepy and warm and half-aroused from touching each other in their sleep. He'd reached over and taken a sponge from the jar and pressed her forward into the blankets. She'd barely had to open her eyes at all before that glorious wave of pleasure was cresting over her and his grunts of need and fulfillment were filling her ears.

They had tried to rise afterward, but washing themselves had turned into washing each other and they had fallen back into bed. This time she had sat astride him, like in the carriage, but there had been no clothing between them and no uncomfortably narrow bench seat to deal with. He'd lavished extensive attention on her nipples while his hands were filled with her bottom, guiding her hips. She quite liked that position.

By the time they made it downstairs, breakfast was already finished, but plates of sausages and eggs had been left for them. They ate quickly before going to the drawing room where everyone was waiting. Her mother was reading a newspaper while Jenny and Mr. Dunn sat at a table playing some sort of gambling game that he was teaching her.

Fanny looked up first. "Good morning, darling, Simon. You're looking well considering the recent brawl."

Eliza tried not to blush. She could feel the heat sweeping over her and she tried with all her might to fight it. Every person in this room had to know what they had been up to. She had been given her own room, but it must have been obvious that she hadn't slept there. She'd only hurried over to get dressed right before they had come down. Some kind soul had left the trunk with Simon's clothes outside his door instead of knocking and bringing it inside. Even now they stood too close together. Simon was at her back, one hand at her waist while the other was entwined with hers.

They both muttered their good mornings and went to sit on the sofa together. Mr. Dunn and Jenny both looked over at them, pleased as punch, judging from their expressions.

Fanny laid the paper aside and said, "Now that you are both here, I feel that we need to discuss how we move forward."

It was a perfectly reasonable suggestion, but Eliza wasn't yet prepared for that conversation. She and Simon hadn't talked about the future at all last night. She had intimated that she wanted him with her, but he hadn't directly replied to that.

I'll always find you . . . always be with you . . . if you'll have me.

"But I thought we could take a couple of days—" Eliza began, only to fall silent when Fanny gave a slow shake of her head.

"I'm afraid we are short on time, darling." She paused and looked to Jenny, whose face had gone serious.

Oh dear, this would not be good.

Fanny continued, "Lord Mainwaring returned last night. Violet sent a wire this morning. It seems that when his friends had their trouble in Rome, he boarded the next train home and has been traveling all this time. He's looking for you."

Beside her, Simon squeezed her hand, but she could feel his entire body go stiff.

"Then that is good." Eliza tried to keep her voice even. "I had planned to have Devonworth tell him that the marriage is off, but this way I can do it myself." It was the right thing to do.

"Eliza." Simon's voice was so soft that only she heard it.

Fanny charged on. "I'm afraid that we'll need to speak with Charles about this first. He signed the agreement, he'll need to break it, and we'll have to convince him to do so."

The last thing she wanted to do was speak to Mr. Hathaway, but if that was what needed to happen, then so be it.

"Eliza?" This time Simon's voice was low but firm enough to be heard. "We should talk about this. Privately."

His heart was in his eyes. They were soulful and deep and the prettiest blue she had ever seen. Fanny nodded and Eliza and Simon rose. She had no familiarity with the house, but he did. He led them across the hall to a small parlor with windows that faced the side of the property. Aside from a few hedgerows, the landscape here had been left largely uncultivated. A sea of tall green grass spread out before meeting rolling hills in the near distance.

She wanted to be out there. Anywhere but here in this room where she very much feared Simon was planning to tell her things she did not want to hear. He walked up behind her and put his hands on her shoulders. She closed her eyes against the ache that swelled in her throat.

"You don't have to toss away your future for me." The words were low and hollow.

"Toss away my future?" She whirled to face him. The pain that shone on his face made her hurt, too.

"I can't give you what Mainwaring can. I can't make you a lady, or open the many doors for you that he can. I can't give you a fancy wardrobe or a fine home or even the means to educate your children."

"None of that matters to me, though, not without you. If I were to marry Mainwaring, I would be miserable. That's why I needed this summer. I don't want any of those things."

His brow rose. "You don't want to educate your children?"

She shook her head. "You're thinking too much about this. Of course I want that. I want a home. With you. I don't care how fine it is. I don't like wearing ball gowns anyway. They make me feel like a peacock and they're very uncomfortable."

He grinned at that, but she hadn't changed his mind. She could tell by the resigned tone of his voice when he spoke. "I've had some time to think about it since I've been here, and the way I see it, I only have one option. I can't go back to London, not as long as Brody is there. I need to leave the country. America, perhaps. San Francisco might be far enough away. I've heard that it's growing and there are clubs. I could find work there."

She didn't like how often he'd said *I* in that speech. "That sounds like a fine idea. I'll go with you. There should be some work for women, too. I could be a shopgirl, or sometimes we gave piano lessons back home. I could do that."

"We couldn't afford a piano."

"Then I'll be a shopgirl until we can."

He shook his head.

"You'll need someone to help with Daisy." She thought it was a very reasonable thing to point out.

"I only have the money I earned from the exhibition fight. Brody drained everything else away. It's enough to get me and Daisy there and settled for a bit, but it's not enough to promise you a future."

She placed her hand on his back. "Simon, I love *you*. I love your pain and your history and every scar you've earned. You will make something of yourself. I know that you will, and I want to be there with you while it happens. I don't expect luxury."

"But I cannot promise you anything. You mentioned college, and I can't afford to send you."

"It's not as if Mainwaring is a viable option for that. I'll go later."

A sound that was suspiciously like a sob caught in his throat. He drew her against him, his arms around her so tight that she melted into him.

"I can't ask it of ye," he whispered against her ear. "It's not fair to ye."

"You haven't asked. It's a point that I'm starting to find quite irksome."

He drew back to look at her, amusement lighting his face. "God, I love you."

She smiled and took his face between her palms. He hadn't shaved yet this morning, and the overnight growth of beard felt nice abrading her skin. "Good, because let me explain this to you. I want to make this as clear to your mind as possible. Let's imagine for a moment that you leave for San Francisco and I don't. Which of these do you think will be the more likely scenario? Do you suppose I'll stay here depressed and moping, or do you think I will borrow the money from Cora and book passage and find you in San Francisco?"

Laughter tore out of him in a reluctant burst, and he crushed her against him, his chuckles shaking both of them. When he got hold of himself, he held her tight as he brushed a strand of hair back from her cheek. "Perhaps I should save us both the trouble. Eliza Dove, will you run away with me to San Francisco?"

"Simon Cavell, I thought you'd never ask."

A shadow of a smile lingered on his lips, but it melted away as he dropped to his knees before her. "And will you go there by my side as my wife?"

"Yes!" She spoke a little too loudly. Laughing, she tried again in a more reasonable tone. "Yes, Simon, yes." She leaned down and kissed him.

"What this, then?" The voice belonged to Mr. Dunn.

They looked up to see that he along with her mother and Jenny had come into the room, no doubt drawn by Eliza's outburst.

"I've asked Eliza to marry me and she said yes." Simon came to his feet and kept her firmly in his arms.

Her mother's hands went up to cover her mouth in happy surprise, and Mr. Dunn came over to congratulate them and shake Simon's hand. Fanny recovered herself and hugged them both and even gave Simon a kiss on his cheek. Jenny was more subdued; she smiled, but it didn't meet her eyes, and she congratulated them, but the joy was missing from her voice, which confused Eliza.

It wasn't until they had all settled down and Mr. Dunn had left them to find a servant to bring champagne that Jenny voiced her concern. "I understand that you love each other very much, but . . . and forgive me . . . but I don't see how this marriage will solve any problems."

Ah, that made sense. Jenny always had to think ahead. Her life had been led by her ambitions to become a singer. It wasn't an easy path, and she'd had to plan strategically in advance to make things work out for her. Jenny had taken it upon herself to write to Mrs. Wilson in Paris to arrange her studies there. Jenny would need to know the details had all been arranged before she could be happy.

"Perhaps I can explain," Simon said. Then he launched into how he could never return to London. Instead, they would go to San Francisco. He mentioned what he'd heard about the opportunities there and his confidence in being able to find a suitable position at a club.

This was followed up by the questions Eliza expected from her family, questions that Simon himself had asked. Mr. Dunn had come back by this time. He listened patiently without asking a single question.

Finally, Jenny asked, "But how will you pay for the passage and your rent until you're settled?"

"I have some savings," Simon said. "Don't worry, Jenny, I promise I'll take very good care of your sister."

The conversation went on for a bit, but eventually Jenny excused herself and Eliza followed her. Something was wrong and she needed to know what it was. It didn't feel right that Jenny would be upset by something that made Eliza so happy.

They had barely made it into the hallway before Jenny turned and said, "Can't you wait until Cora returns before you leave?"

"I'd like to, but it seems that time is of the essence. Brody will be looking for Simon, and we can't wait around until he finds him."

"But you won't see her again for God knows how long." A look of desperation came over Jenny's face. "You're leaving and that was never part of the plan and you can't even return to visit. You must know that once you align yourself with him publicly, you will be marked, too?"

Eliza hadn't quite considered that, but it made sense. "Yes, I suppose you're right, but what choice do I have, Jenny? He's leaving and I don't want to lose him or this. He's special to me."

"I thought your family was special to you."

"That isn't fair. Of course I love you and Mama and Cora. I want to see you more, but Simon will be my husband, and Daisy will be my niece, though more like my own daughter. One day, we'll have our own family."

"A family we will never know. Is that what you want?"

"No, it isn't, but we don't always get things exactly as we want them."

"But you don't even know him that well. Eliza, you'll be moving halfway across the world."

Eliza held up her hands. "Look, Jenny, I understand that things didn't work out with you and the man you loved in Paris, but Simon isn't like that. This isn't like that. Simon actually wants to marry me and spend his life with me."

Jenny gasped and Eliza felt bad that she had said those mean words. She didn't know very much about Jenny's past love. Their affair had taken place in Paris in the years Jenny had lived there with Mrs. Wilson. She only knew that Jenny had fallen into despair over it for weeks or maybe even months.

"I'm sorry. That wasn't fair to you," Eliza said. "I didn't mean to bring that into this."

Her sister still looked stricken, her face taut, but she said, "I think that you need to think very hard about this. This path will be more difficult than you imagine."

Emotion caused her voice to waver. "I know my own mind on this, and I want to be with Simon. I wish our future could be in London, but I'll take what I'm given."

Jenny pondered this for a moment and asked, "Then you would stay, if given another option? If somehow, miraculously, everything could be worked out and Simon could return to Montague Club?"

Eliza smiled. "That would be a dream come true. I'd live there with him and finally get to see the inside of that place properly. Then I'd go and enroll myself in Bedford College."

"I think we should ask Mr. Hathaway about this," Jenny said. "See if he'll relent and give you your inheritance."

Eliza couldn't help but scoff. "He'll be angry that I've ended things with Mainwaring. He won't agree to Simon."

Jenny was quiet again, something about her face calculating. "It couldn't hurt to ask, and we do need to speak with him about your decision regarding Mainwaring."

Eliza reluctantly agreed. "Fine, but I think it will cause much frustration and do nothing to help."

"You're right, I'm sure, but let's have a telegram sent to him anyway. You'll make your case about Mainwaring and I'll appeal to his decency. He should be back in London now since he was anticipating your wedding later this summer." Her expression clearing, she added, "Let's go back tomorrow and arrange to meet with him. If he says no, and I'm sure you're right about that, then I'll support what you want to do, whatever that may be."

Eliza nearly squealed in happiness as she drew her sister

into a hug. "Thank you, Jenny. Thank you so much for being a very good sister."

Jenny hugged her back and tried to smile but failed miserably. "Don't thank me. I don't know that I would have helped you this summer had I known it would take you away from me."

Eliza laughed even though tears burned the backs of her eyes. "I love you so much, Jenny."

"Don't cry. I refuse to cry," Jenny said through a sheen of tears. "Go back. I'll be there soon."

Eliza hugged her and returned to the impromptu gathering as a footman arrived with champagne. Jenny came back a little while later. She drank champagne and toasted them, but something still didn't seem right with her. Eliza figured that it would take some time for her to come around to the idea of Eliza moving. She couldn't blame her for worrying about it. Eliza knew that it wouldn't be easy, but she was ready for whatever the future brought them, because she and Simon would face it together.

THIRTY-TWO

JENNY DIDN'T LIKE WITHHOLDING INFORMATION from her family, but sometimes it was necessary. In the flurry of activity that morning, she'd been able to walk into the post office next to the train station and send a telegram without anyone being the wiser. No one but the recipient needed to know about it. At least not yet.

Mr. Dunn had accompanied Jenny and Eliza as far as Leeds, where he split off for Liverpool. With Simon's savings in hand, he was going to book passage to America for Simon, Eliza, and Daisy. The plan was for him to wire once the arrangements were made and then everyone would travel there to see the family off. In the meantime, Simon had sent a telegram each to Lord Leigh and the Duke of Rothschild in the hopes that one of them could help him secure a quick license to marry. Fanny had gone off to visit *a friend*, which everyone suspected was her Scotsman, before meeting them in Liverpool.

Jenny and her sister carried onward to London. Once there, they would split up. Eliza would go to the Leigh residence in

Belgravia. Jenny would go to the Devonworth home in Mayfair. They hoped to arrange a meeting with their absentee father tomorrow.

That was the plan as Eliza knew it. She didn't know that Jenny had made alternate arrangements. Those arrangements consumed Jenny's thoughts on the entire journey to London. It was that telegram that had a servant in familiar royal blue livery with gold piping waiting for her on the platform at King's Cross Station.

She stood for a moment outside the train, her only luggage the leather Gladstone bag she carried with her. Despite the fact that she had anticipated this moment all day, she wasn't quite prepared to follow it through now that she was here. She gave the servant a wide berth as she escorted Eliza outside to the carriage that Violet had sent for her.

"Are you certain you won't let me take you home?" Eliza asked as she climbed inside.

"No, it'll be too far out of your way and it's late. We're both tired. Go on and I'll take a hansom."

Eliza argued, but the cabstand was right there and her eyes were drooping. Jenny had the unfortunate luck to have accidentally taken the bedroom next to Simon's. She had heard firsthand how little sleep the couple had gotten the past two nights.

Jenny waited for the carriage to disappear into the night before she hurried back to the servant. The middle-aged man appeared befuddled as he scanned the platform with its passengers dwindling by the minute as they all hurried off to their obligations.

Gathering herself, she marched over to him and he took notice of her when she stilled several yards away. "Madam," he said.

"Yes, I believe I'm the one you're looking for."

He nodded as if he'd suspected all along. "Very good, madam."

"Is he here?" she asked.

"In the carriage, madam. May I carry your bag?"

She thanked him and handed it over and he indicated the direction they should go. He followed at her flank, indicating when a turn was necessary, until they emerged on the sidewalk. An unmarked carriage stood waiting at the curb, it's black lacquer finish gleaming under the streetlamps. She breathed in relief. She'd asked that he not arrive in his usual carriage, the one with his family crest. She couldn't be seen getting into that.

The servant opened the door and a gloved hand emerged from inside. "At your service, Miss Dove."

She shivered. She couldn't help it. There was something about the smooth yet deep tenor of his voice that did it to her. It didn't happen every time he spoke, only the first time when she hadn't seen him for a bit. The soft texture of it slipped over her skin like silk, but it seeped inside her, too, vibrating and quivering.

She accepted his help and climbed inside to sit across from him. The door closed behind her, and it took a moment for her eyes to adjust to the low light. Slowly he came into focus, transforming from dark shadow to shades of black and white. The strong line of his jaw and the high press of his cheekbones against his skin seemed primed to attract the opposite sex. His appeal was only enhanced by the deep, intelligent set of his eyes and the perfect proportions of his mouth, lips full but not excessively so and the shape always given to only just smiling.

"I'm glad you're here, Lord David." She only barely managed to not look down at his . . . his private area. That rumor was too outrageous to be believed.

The carriage pulled out into the light evening traffic, swaying beneath them.

"How could I not be intrigued? You've never sent me so much as a calling card, then a mysterious telegram appears demanding my appearance in an unmarked carriage."

"Yes, well, I couldn't be more specific. Where are we going, by the way?" she asked, and glanced out the window to see which direction they were heading.

"I've given my driver orders to take us to Mayfair and then through the park if we need additional time to talk."

"Yes, good, that will do nicely."

"Don't say you're going to keep me in suspense, Miss Dove. I've thought of nothing else all day."

She refrained from rolling her eyes at him. He'd probably roused himself from a drunken sleep approximately three hours ago. After stumbling out of the bed of the woman who'd been unfortunate enough to fall victim to his charms the night before, he'd gone home to dress and do it all again only to be greeted by the telegram waiting for him. At most, he'd been intrigued for two hours, but that was a generous assessment.

She couldn't say any of that, however. She was here for his assistance, after all, and insulting him with the truth would inevitably start them off on the wrong foot. He always seemed to get offended when she called attention to his poor behavior.

"I've asked you to meet me because I have a proposition to make you and we'll need privacy to discuss it."

"Privacy?" She loved the way he said that. She'd heard enough English accents over the course of the past months that she should have been immune to it, but this was him, and everything he did resonated with her in a different way. "I'm intrigued," he added.

"Good, because I'm afraid you won't have very much time to consider your answer."

She had decided on the train that she might as well tell him everything. It was only fair that he knew what he would be getting into if he agreed. She began to launch into the story, to tell him everything that had happened with Simon and Eliza, but he shook his head and sat forward and she stopped speaking.

The rich fabric of his suit rustled and seemed louder in the confined space than it should have been. His scent wafted over to her. It was the same cologne he usually wore, a lightly spiced scent that she hadn't yet been able to place. She only knew that she quite liked it. Something about it swooshed through the butterflies in her stomach. The carriage light that hung outside the window caressed his face with soft amber color. Her breath caught at how beautiful she found him, and she forced her gaze to the empty space beside him. He wasn't even *that* handsome, not objectively when compared to someone like Devonworth, who was golden and perfect.

Lord David had a sensual quality that weighted the air around him, and he managed to take it everywhere he went. The eyes that looked at her across a formal dining room table would be the same eyes that looked down at her in bed. She'd never tested this theory, of course, but it was plain to see his effect on women. Being near him was a sensory experience for her. She shifted and pressed her thighs together. No doubt her absurd reaction to him now was because of what she was willing to offer him should he accept.

"Before we go further, I'd like to know what I shall receive in return should I agree to this proposition."

"Don't you want to hear what I'd like you to do first?" He was a curious man.

"Later. First, what will be my reward?"

Her lips parted, but she couldn't speak. Her mouth had become the Sahara. She glanced away again. Twenty other options played out in her head, but she'd already examined and discarded them all on the long train ride. He was her only hope. Picking at her skirt so she wouldn't have to look him in the eyes, she said, "Me."

The air was still and silent, broken only by his harsh exhalation of air. "Say more."

She couldn't look at him. Her eyes found the black velvet tie that held back the curtain. "A night with me."

"One entire night?"

She nodded.

"One entire night in bed with you?"

He was making a meal of this. "Yes, but only the one," she clarified.

"Forgive me, but I want to be very precise about this. One night to fuck you?"

That word lit a fire inside her. It wasn't entirely unpleasant, which was why the blaze tore through her so quickly. Her gaze shot back to his. "I *knew* that you would make this vulgar."

He wasn't smiling or smirking or anything near what she'd thought she would see on his face. Instead, he was very serious. His gaze held hers with a steadfast intensity.

"But that *is* what you intend?"

"Yes." The word was a hiss as she tried to ignore what his eyes were doing to her.

He sat back, pondering her all the while, the shadows reclaiming him. "Go on, then, Miss Dove. Tell me more."

THIRTY-THREE

ELIZA PACED THE DEVONWORTH DRAWING ROOM
the next morning at precisely ten o'clock. She was not
looking forward to this meeting with Mr. Hathaway at all.
She couldn't imagine a scenario where he would agree to allow
her to receive her inheritance while also marrying Simon, and
there was no scenario where she would not agree to marry Simon. She couldn't decide if she was simply being pragmatic or
cowardly in thinking that her best course of action would be
to head for San Francisco and leave him to rot. Jenny, however, had insisted, so here they were waiting for him.

"Please calm yourself, Eliza. It will be fine. You'll see."
Jenny seemed entirely too relaxed from her place on the sofa
flipping through this week's issue of the *Young Ladies' Journal*. She seemed more interested in the fashion plate she was
perusing than on their imminent meeting.

Eliza didn't want to snap at her sister, so she didn't say anything and continued to stalk the hearth.

A moment later, the doorbell rang and her heart dropped

into her stomach. She did not like this man. Her only real childhood memory of him was being lined up before him in her Sunday best and feeling like she was worse than nothing to him. Her opinion of him had not improved during Cora's wedding and the few dinners and balls Eliza had spent in his company.

The door opened and closed. Male voices filtered in from the entryway as Edgecomb took what had to be Mr. Hathaway's hat and gloves. Then they were standing at the threshold of the drawing room. Her blood roared in her ears, temporarily silencing the butler's announcement.

Charles Hathaway was a well-dressed man only a few years older than her mother. He was still handsome with silver-winged dark hair and Cora's blue-gray eyes. The lines on his face somehow only enhanced his innate elegance rather than making him rough or common. In truth, he was wholly forgettable, his entire demeanor made to be pleasing but not stand out.

He looked at her, since she was the one standing. "Eliza. Good morning." Then he shifted to Jenny, who regarded him coolly from her seat. "Jenny. Good to see you both again."

Eliza couldn't tell from his tone whether he had heard anything of what she had been up to lately. Violet had assured her last night that no one outside of their small circle knew of her flight to Scotland, but one could never be too certain.

"Good morning." Eliza gathered her courage to say that she wasn't marrying Mainwaring under any circumstances. She had decided that she would start with that. But at that very second, another figure appeared in the threshold beside her father.

Mainwaring.

His light brown hair was flawlessly in place, and his eyes crinkled at the corner as he smiled at her. He appeared refreshed from his travels and not as if he'd been drinking and whoring his way across Europe for the past few months.

"Mainwaring?" She couldn't quite believe he was here. Even Jenny had come to her feet at his appearance.

"You're a sight for tired eyes, Eliza. I missed you dreadfully." He reached her in three long strides and took hold of her hands. Pulling her toward him, he kissed her on the cheek.

She was too stunned to respond right away. She could only look up at him wordlessly as Mr. Hathaway made his way into the room.

"What are you doing here?" Jenny asked for her. Her sister's voice was sharp with inquisition.

"When you asked for my presence this morning to speak with you and Eliza, I assumed that it might have something to do with her betrothal. I thought it best to bring Lord Mainwaring along."

"Besides," Mainwaring added, "I wanted to see you. I came immediately after I arrived and was told you weren't at home. I'm glad you came back."

He was smiling as someone might when reuniting with their beloved after a long absence. He was so convincing that Eliza had to suppress a stab of guilt. This man had not missed her in his gallivanting across the countryside from brothel to brothel. He had not missed her at all. He was putting on a show for Mr. Hathaway, who very conveniently held the purse strings of this arrangement.

Eliza regained her senses and deftly pulled her hands away from him. "I'm glad you're here. You should hear this, as well." She absently rubbed her palms on her skirts. It didn't make sense, but she didn't want his touch to erase Simon's. Gesturing toward the seating area, she said, "Please, let us sit down."

A furrow appeared between Mainwaring's brows, and he

exchanged a questioning look with Mr. Hathaway as he did as she indicated. Eliza sat next to Jenny and the men took the chairs facing the sofa.

Mr. Hathaway opened his mouth to speak, but Eliza charged ahead. "We've asked you here so that I could tell you in person that I will not be honoring the betrothal agreement. I won't be marrying Lord Mainwaring." She had spoken to her father, but the man himself was there, so she should tell him to his face. "Lord Mainwaring, I am sorry, but I can't marry you."

"What? Why? This is preposterous." Mainwaring gripped the arms of his chair and looked from her to Mr. Hathaway for confirmation.

"Out of the question," Mr. Hathaway said immediately after. "You cannot break the agreement."

Eliza tried to hold her temper. Her announcement had no doubt been shocking, and they were entitled to their reaction. She decided to answer Mainwaring's question. "I find that I do not love you."

"But I love you very much, Eliza."

She hated how he had resorted to her first name. It implied an intimacy that didn't exist. "I do not think that you do."

"But I do." He sat forward in his chair, his expression earnest and fierce at the same time.

"You do not know me any more than I know you. You do not love me." He started to protest and she held up her hand to stop him. "If you did love me, then I sincerely hope that you wouldn't have spent your time in Europe visiting all of those . . . coffeehouses."

"Coffee . . . What do you know about . . . How do you know that?" He looked from her to Mr. Hathaway and back again.

"It's common knowledge, from what I can tell. I'm told

with some authority that there was even a bet at the Montague Club about how many of those you would visit and how many different . . . coffees . . . you might sample at your stops." Eliza savored the way he squirmed in his chair as she confronted him.

"E-Eliza . . . that is hardly a subject that someone should be discussing with you. Whoever told you that . . . they did not have your best interest . . . that is not something one talks about with a young lady."

"Did you not engage in intimate congress with *those* young women?" She tried to remember the names she had seen on the blackboard. "Are you denying there was a Lucia, a Paolina, or a Giulia?"

He blanched and he whirled to look at Mr. Hathaway beside him. "Do something."

"Eliza, please, calm yourself. There is really no need for this. Even had this happened, every young man is entitled to a few days of freedom before his wedding. You were not married," Mr. Hathaway pointed out. "Besides, I don't believe a word of it. Lord Mainwaring is a brilliant and upstanding young man. He will make you a satisfactory husband."

"I'm certain that he will make someone a . . ." She couldn't say *satisfactory* because that would be a lie. She pitied the poor woman who would be saddled with him. "A husband, but it will not be me. I am withdrawing my consent for this marriage."

"You cannot withdraw your consent. Once given it is binding," Mainwaring argued. His tone had gone from pleading to demanding.

"That is decidedly not how consent works, my lord. It can be given and taken away at will, which is what I have done. I will not marry you."

"Eliza, this will not do." There was a warning in Mr. Hathaway's voice. "He that is without sin, let him first cast a stone," he paraphrased the Bible verse. "Let us not discuss your own transgressions. Let us let bygones be bygones."

But she did want to discuss them. That was the entire point of this meeting. "You're right. I am in love with someone else, and I will marry him," she said.

Her father only shook his head. His lips were twisted in a sneer. "I won't accept anyone else. You do that and you'll lose your inheritance."

"I'm well aware of your propensity for heartlessness. I don't care. I don't want your money. I will marry him whether you agree or not. That choice isn't up to you." It felt good to say that to his face. She despised that he controlled so much of their future. Well, he wouldn't control her anymore. She was finished with him.

"This will not stand." Mainwaring rose to his feet, and for the first time Eliza wished that Devonworth was home. She did not know the viscount or what he might do. Two hundred fifty thousand dollars was an awful lot of money to lose. "You will marry me, Eliza, whether you agree or not. There is a written contract and I will not allow you to break it. I will see to the arrangements. Hathaway, I fear we must accelerate the timeline for this wedding."

"Oh, we won't be doing that, Mainwaring."

The voice came from the threshold. Lord David stood there still in his hat and gloves, walking stick at his side as if he'd only just arrived. She hadn't even heard the doorbell. The entire room stood at his entrance.

"Lord David?" Mr. Hathaway found his voice before anyone else. "I didn't hear you come in. Please don't concern yourself with this foolishness. Eliza is simply having a case of—"

"I'm afraid this foolishness does concern me." Lord David

walked casually into the room as if he was here for a social call.

Beside her, Jenny hadn't said a word and hadn't moved a muscle in the moments since Lord David had arrived. "What did you do?" Eliza whispered.

Jenny's face had a look of unrepentant guilt. "I am fixing things for you," she whispered.

"What does that mean?"

"Shh. Watch." Jenny pointedly turned back to the men, and Eliza had no choice but to follow suit. She feared the situation had quickly moved out of her control.

Lord David looked her over before his gaze settled on Jenny. Something passed between them, but Eliza had no idea what it was. Some sort of shared knowledge. Jenny nodded once, and that seemed to release him. He turned to Mr. Hathaway and said, "I've come to make you an offer of marriage for Miss Dove. Contingent on the fact that Miss Eliza be allowed to marry whomever she chooses while given full control of her inheritance."

Mr. Hathaway couldn't have looked more surprised. His mouth dropped open comically, and he even took a step backward. Mainwaring's face went from white to red. "Preposterous!"

Everyone ignored his outburst.

"But Jenny has refused to marry. She insists on a career in opera," Mr. Hathaway said.

"She'll marry me."

Lord David appeared so certain in that statement that Eliza turned to her sister. "Jenny, is this true? Have you agreed to marry this man?"

"Indeed, I have." Jenny's voice was strong and unwavering. "On the condition that you allow Eliza to marry the man of her choice and honor the inheritance agreement, I will marry Lord David. You won't find a better offer than that. He'll be a duke one day. His brother has already declared him to be his heir." She took a deep breath as the import of that settled over the room. "Think about it, Mr. Hathaway. Having the ears of Strathmore and Lord David could prove useful to you, your daughter Agnes, and your son George as they reach maturity." She referred to his legitimate children with his Society wife. The one he had left their mother to wed. "I'd go so far as to say a duke in the family could prove *vastly* more useful to you than a mere penniless viscount." It was no secret that Mainwaring hoped to marry Eliza for the settlement. Lord David, however, came from one of the wealthiest families in the kingdom.

"How dare you, girl?" Mainwaring stepped toward Jenny, but Lord David's golden-encrusted walking stick came up to stop him, settling heavily across his chest.

Eliza remembered the violence he was capable of and how he'd grabbed that man who had insulted Jenny by the throat. That warning was lurking beneath the surface now.

"You will not speak to her in that way. In fact, you should leave. This is a family matter," Lord David said.

All eyes in the room turned to Mr. Hathaway. "Yes, please leave us, Lord Mainwaring. I'm afraid the betrothal is off." Their father knew when a better offer had presented itself.

"I will not. That contract is binding—"

Mainwaring broke off and took a few steps back when Lord David turned to face him fully. "Leave now and I'll see that you receive some compensation for your trouble."

Mainwaring's jaw tightened, but he was stuck and they all knew it. The fact was, even with a legal battle, no one could force Eliza to marry him. He might have lost out on a quarter of a million dollars and an annual income, but at least some compensation was better than none.

Still, he straightened his coat and said to Lord David, "You'll be hearing from my solicitor."

"I expect I will." Lord David was completely unruffled by the idea.

Mainwaring scoffed and stormed from the room.

"I cannot let you do this, Jenny," Eliza said. She grabbed her sister's hand. "You didn't want to marry. You can't sacrifice yourself for me. I won't allow it."

"It's too late. It's done. Besides, Lord David has assured me that he won't prohibit me from singing and performing."

"That's right," Lord David said. "I only wish to wed her, not keep her captive. She can live her life."

"And you will live yours." There was a challenge in Jenny's eyes as she said that.

Lord David inclined his head in acknowledgment before turning his attention back to Mr. Hathaway. "Shall we negotiate terms?"

Mr. Hathaway agreed and they all sat.

Energy buzzed through Eliza, but she forced herself to sit and not to fidget. She could hardly believe the turn of events. She would get to marry Simon and he would get the money he needed to pay Brody back. It would have been perfect had Jenny not been forced to marry.

As their father spoke, Lord David's gaze traveled back to Jenny from time to time. It was soft in a way it wasn't when he looked at anyone else, and undeniably hungry. Jenny did a good job of not looking at him again, her attention riveted to Mr. Hathaway instead. Eliza hoped that this marriage would be a good thing for her sister.

THIRTY-FOUR

Liverpool, England
Two days later

THE COMPTON HOTEL IN LIVERPOOL WAS FIVE
floors of luxurious rooms and suites that had recently
been rebuilt to accommodate the many Americans who had
begun traveling to England. The rooms were as well-appointed
as any at Montague Club, and the expansive first floor held an
array of shops and restaurants ensuring that guests would find
everything to satisfy whatever they might need.

This is not where Simon had imagined staying as they
waited to board the ocean liner to America. Eliza had wired
him the appointed time and place, and he'd arrived only a few
minutes earlier. He'd left the train station to find a veritable
castle of a hotel. After giving his name at the front desk, the
clerk had given him a room number and he'd come upstairs.

The moment he'd knocked, Eliza had opened the door and
practically jumped into his arms. He'd managed to barely get
them both inside, shove the door closed with his foot, and set
his portmanteau on the floor.

"I missed you." She kissed him and then hugged him tight before kissing him again.

He'd missed her so much that he'd ached with it. "It wasn't until you opened the door that I understood I feared that I might never see you again, or that I'd wake up one morning and realize you hadn't been real at all."

A curl had come loose from a pin and fallen down over her cheek. He rubbed the silky length between his thumb and forefinger before pushing it back from her face. He'd missed every part of her, from her deep brown eyes to the soft husk of her voice. He kissed her softly, reverently, still not believing that he'd be able to keep on kissing her for the rest of his life.

"I'm real, Simon. This is real," she whispered against his lips.

"How is Daisy?" he asked when he was finally assured that Eliza was here and whole. "Is she here?"

It was only then that he looked up and noticed this was no mere hotel room: it was a suite, and it was as grand as the rest of the hotel had indicated it would be. They were standing in a marble entryway with arched doors leading off in different directions. Each doorway was framed by marble pillars, and the doors were carved from a rich-looking wood. A gas chandelier hung above them, sparkling with crystals.

"Yes, she's here and well and excited to see you, but first there's something you need to know." She smiled at him, but there was uncertainty in her eyes.

A terrible heaviness settled over him. She was real and he still wouldn't have her. "Is it about our marriage? Did the license not come through?"

"We'll be married," she hurried to say.

His relief was very nearly palpable.

Touching her, because he couldn't stop feeling her, he used

his thumb to free that plump lip. "Then does it have anything to do with this hotel?" He'd thought Dunn had made the hotel arrangements, but he couldn't afford this.

She nodded. "A little. Come with me."

She took his hand and led him into one of the rooms off the foyer. It was a bedroom decorated in shades of rose and touches of blue. The boots she'd worn the night he'd undressed her were lying forgotten by a winged chair, and her scent already floated in the air. This was her room. Her bed. He went half-rigid just thinking of sharing it with her.

He pulled her to him instinctively, and she made a soft sound in her throat as she felt his growing desire for her against her stomach. Her eyes began to dilate as she looked up at him, but she said firmly, "Not now, but later. I promise. We really do need to talk."

It was true, and he still needed to see Daisy. He'd never gone this long without seeing her. He missed her. Still, he kissed Eliza and let his hands roam down to her bottom. She kissed him back, but he reluctantly pulled himself away.

"Did Leigh or Rothschild pay for this suite?"

She hesitated for a fraction of a second, enough to make his suspicion rise again. "Neither. It's a wedding present . . . from my father."

"Hathaway?" he asked.

She nodded.

"Does he still believe you're marrying Mainwaring?"

"No, he knows you're the bridegroom. Well, I don't actually know if he knows who you are, but he knows I'm marrying the man I love."

"I don't understand." Simon had assumed that he'd be running from her father as much as from Brody. The man wouldn't take kindly to the fact that Simon was eloping with Eliza and dashing his chance for an aristocratic husband for her. Connections meant everything to the wealthy.

"Jenny arranged to marry Lord David Felding on the condition that I be allowed to marry the man of my choosing."

It took a moment for the words to sink through his almost instinctive refusal to accept them. "But I thought you mentioned she hadn't planned to marry under Hathaway's condition?"

"She hadn't. She sacrificed herself so that we could marry."

"But why?"

"Well, there's more. You see, part of her condition was that I still be able to inherit my share. So, you'll receive my dowry upon our marriage."

"Your dowry?" he repeated stupidly as his legs sank out from under him and he sat on the end of the bed. He heard what she said, but it didn't make sense.

She followed him down to sit beside him. "Simon, my father has agreed to give us the two hundred fifty thousand dollars. There are also some investments. I don't know the particulars, but they earn an income of about twenty thousand dollars a year. You'll be able to pay off your debt to Brody."

"No . . . I . . . How?"

"Mr. Hathaway decided that he liked the idea of a duke for a son-in-law—not that there's a legal relation—more than having Lord Mainwaring for a son-in-law. You have to admit, it does work out in his favor once Lord David inherits, but even before then he has his brother's ear. Strathmore is a formidable ally to have on his side."

Simon rose, and tossed his hat on the bed so that he could rake his fingers through his hair as he paced. This was very much not what he'd expected. It was overwhelming and unbelievable. The entire course of their future had changed in only a few short sentences.

"Simon, what's wrong?"

He couldn't even articulate it. He walked to the window, taking in the busy street below. "I don't know . . . That amount of money . . ."

She touched his back and he jerked in surprise because he hadn't been aware of her approaching. He turned to see her staring up at him in concern.

"I don't know how to . . ." What? He didn't even know how to say it.

"Nothing has to change. We pay Brody enough to placate him, and the rest we put in the bank. You can continue to work at Montague Club if you like and I can attend college. We can get Daisy a nurse and decorate her room and send her to school or hire tutors. Buy her pretty dresses and toys. It simply means that we can do what we planned to do and it will be a little easier."

"Do you still want me to be employed? To not be a gentleman and—"

"Is that what you're worried about?" The smile he loved so much was back on her face. "I want the life we talked about. I don't want the life I would've had with Mainwaring. I don't want to spend my days on social visits and my evenings attending balls, though one or two a year might be nice when August, Violet, or Cora have them. That's all I want. I want to be with you and one day buy our own little house in Blooms-bury and raise Daisy and our children. Perhaps I'll become a reporter, or a professor, or I'll work with the London Suffrage Society to pass legislation."

He slipped his arms around her waist as he felt the weight lifting from his chest. "You can be whatever you want to be. You know that I'll support you in that?"

"I know." She laid her head on his chest. He placed a kiss

to her temple, breathed in her sweet scent, and thanked God that she had come into his life.

"I still believe we should board the liner tomorrow," he said, serious again.

She looked up at him, her pretty brow furrowed.

"I don't trust Brody. I don't trust him not to take the money and try to come after me anyway." He was so angry that Simon had double-crossed him, at least in his view.

"How long would we need to stay gone?" she asked.

He shrugged. "An extended holiday, a few months. Until we've given him time to calm down."

"That sounds like a marvelous idea. Daisy will enjoy seeing the world."

He hadn't even had to ask her if Daisy could come with him. He loved her so much it hurt.

"Let's go see her," he said.

Eliza rose up on her toes and gave him a quick kiss, then took his hand and led him toward the door. "You should know that everyone is here."

"Everyone?"

"Lord Leigh and Violet, Rothschild and August, Cora and Devonworth—who just got back from Rome but came straightaway—and then Lord David, since he's all but family now, and Mr. Hathaway, too. Mr. Dunn, of course, and Jenny, my mother, and Heni."

"As long as one of them brought the marriage license, then I'm happy."

She squeezed his hand. "They did, indeed, and we'll be married very soon, Mr. Cavell."

He opened the door. "After you, Mrs. Cavell."

She giggled and he watched her walk away from him, certain that he would be happy forever.

THIRTY-FIVE

"WHICH DO YOU THINK DAISY WILL LIKE? THE white or the pink? Which would be the most useful?" Eliza held up two different pairs of tights. She was in the hosiery shop later that afternoon on the ground floor of the hotel picking out last-minute items that they would need on their trip. Jenny had come along with her because out of the three of them, she enjoyed shopping the most.

Cora and their mother had gone off to find orange blossoms because Fanny had insisted every bride needed to wear them on her wedding day. Eliza could hardly believe that they would be married tomorrow.

Lord David and Rothschild were at the coffee shop on the other side of the hotel's ground floor, while the other ladies were upstairs entertaining Heni and Daisy. They'd developed a sweet bond with them in the days they had stayed with Violet. Eliza and Jenny would go back and join them as soon as they were finished.

Jenny grinned at her with a smile that was both loving and

exasperated. "You have money now, dear. You can buy both. I'm sure she will like them."

Eliza stared at her, dimly coming to realize that she was right. Simon and Mr. Hathaway were at the bank now, along with the solicitor her father had brought to make the necessary arrangements for her inheritance. Lord Leigh had gone along for good measure to make certain that everything was arranged in Simon's favor. Dunn had gone with them to make sure Brody didn't pop out of the woodwork along the way. They were still there now, but all she needed to do was charge it to their suite.

"Then I suppose I'll take both." A slow smile spread over Eliza's face. Her entire life, her small family had been forced to pinch their pennies due to Mr. Dove's dying and leaving them almost nothing and Mr. Hathaway's refusing to fund more than the most minimal allowance. He'd even forbidden her mother from acting, believing that it might somehow reflect badly on them, and by extension, him. It would be a novel experience to not worry about money anymore.

She finished selecting her items and walked to the shop's counter. On the way, Jenny glanced out and noticed the shop across the wide corridor. "I'm going to pop into the haberdashery while you arrange payment. I want to see if they have any turquoise thread that will match my cape. I ripped the seam last night."

Jenny hurried off, and Eliza took a moment to arrange the items be charged to her room. Once the shopgirl had wrapped the tights in tissue paper, she made her way out. She drew up short and dropped her purchase when someone roughly grabbed her arm and pulled her in front of him. Something hard dug into her ribs, and she thought it might be the end of a pistol.

"Keep walking and don't ye dare slow down."

She knew that voice. It was that man who had watched her that night in Whitechapel, the one who had been with Brody. She thought she had also seen him on the riser at the fight. His name was Beck.

"This is a mistake. Simon has the money and he intends to pay Brody," she said, keeping herself calm. They were in the middle of a hotel. He wouldn't do anything to her here.

"Is that right? That why ye both plan to run away across the sea?"

He didn't believe her and nudged the gun so hard into her ribs that she knew he would bruise her.

"Believe what you will, but I am not going with you." She tried to stop, but he cursed under his breath and tightened his hold on her arm until he was twisting it behind her back. "You won't shoot me in front of all of these people."

He laughed. The fact was that the lobby was so busy with people coming and going that no one seemed to stop to notice him strong-arming her.

"Wot makes ye certain of that? Brody plans to kill ye for the fun of it."

His face got very close to her when he said that. In a panic, she bashed the back of her head against his nose. He yelped in pain and she was able to pull loose. She needed to draw him away from Jenny in case he had seen them together, but she also needed to warn Simon, who should be coming back any moment. She ran for the front door, which was standing open because a doorman was welcoming guests.

"Summon the police," she urged as she ran past him. "That man is chasing me and he has a gun."

The doorman looked behind her, but she was already outside and onto the sidewalk. She turned left to head toward the bank on the next street over, but a black carriage pulled up at the intersection, blocking her path as she started across the road. The door opened and Brody stared down at her, his lips twisted into a smirk of victory.

S IMON, DUNN, AND LEIGH WERE HURRYING BACK TO the hotel after concluding their business at the bank. Hathaway was off meeting with his solicitor. Simon was anxious to get back because the sun was already setting and if Brody was around, he'd come out at dark. The paperwork had been signed and filed with the bank. Thankfully, Hathaway had been true to his word and the transfer of funds to an account in Simon's name would be done the moment he returned with a certificate of marriage signed by the local registrar. He kept expecting to feel different now that he had a fortune in his name, but he didn't. He felt exactly the same as he had when he'd held Eliza in his arms. Nothing was better than that. Not all the money in the world. He was simply glad that he could now provide her with the sort of life she deserved. Giving such a significant portion of the money would hurt, but it would be worth it.

Leigh and Rothschild had offered to help initiate the transfer since no one believed that Simon was safe from Brody until the transaction was finished. They would arrange a meeting with him back in London and see that it was done. They had each chastised him a bit for not coming to them earlier with Brody's threats, but they didn't understand how Brody operated. He would have found another way to keep Daisy until he decided that he and Simon were done. The fight had done that; the money was only gravy to Brody. Their words had rolled off of Simon like water from a duck's back. He had Eliza now. He was untouchable.

He started when he saw Eliza hurrying down the sidewalk. She hadn't noticed him yet. He raised an arm and called out to her, but she didn't hear or see him. She'd looked behind her, and he realized that she believed someone was chasing her.

"Brody," he said, and the other men came to attention beside him.

They all started running. At that very moment, a carriage pulled up before Eliza, blocking her progress across the street, and he *knew* that Brody was inside.

Brody would kill her. He would do it just to spite Simon. Or perhaps he'd found out that she was an American heiress and he meant to ransom her to her father. Either way, she'd end up dead and Brody wouldn't blink as he did it and it would be Simon's fault.

As they crossed the street, Simon saw Dunn pull a revolver from the waistband of his trousers as he went for the carriage driver. Simon wrenched open the door of the carriage. No one was inside but Brody, who was just leaning out the other door to grab Eliza.

Simon reacted without thinking. He grabbed Brody by the back of the collar and pulled him back into the carriage. Brody lashed out with his left hand, catching Simon across the face and sending him tumbling into the wall of the carriage. It gave Brody the split second he needed to withdraw his gun with his right hand. Simon didn't know if he meant to shoot him or Eliza, but he didn't intend to give the man time to choose.

He grabbed Brody's right hand with both of his and they fought for the gun. The next seconds were a blur in his mind as they tussled. Somehow the barrel of the revolver turned upward toward Brody's neck, and in the next instant the gun went off.

Brody stilled and Eliza screamed. It took a moment for Simon to realize she hadn't been shot. Brody fell limp against the seat. The gun fell to the floor, so Simon kicked it out onto the road. Then he hurried out the other side of the carriage and pulled Eliza into his arms. Simultaneously, he looked for the carriage driver, whom Dunn and Leigh had subdued, and the man that had followed Eliza.

Lord David and Rothschild came hurrying out the door of the hotel, dragging a man between them. The man's hat had been lost in an obvious scuffle, so it was easy to identify him. Beck, the bastard.

Simon held Eliza against him and buried his nose against her neck. Her sweet rose scent washed over him.

"It's over," he whispered. "He won't threaten us again." He'd expected to feel a whole range of emotions, but he only felt relief, profound relief that went all the way down to his bones.

"Are you hurt?" Eliza ran her hands over his chest, looking for injury.

"No." He kissed her neck and then looked down into her upturned face. "It's over, Angel."

She threw herself into his chest and he thanked God that she was safe.

THIRTY-SIX

THE LOCAL REGISTRAR HAD BEEN PERSUADED TO
come to the Doves' hotel suite to perform the ceremony.
Eliza believed that the involvement of a duke and two earls
helped to greatly influence his decision. Mr. Hathaway might
have provided a donation of some kind. She didn't know and
was content to not ask questions, because it meant that she got
to marry Simon in the safety of the hotel without venturing
outside to the curious looks of everyone who knew about what
had happened last evening.

There had been an inquisition last night after the confrontation, but it was no secret what had transpired. Many witnesses stepped forward to say that Beck had been chasing her.
Several more said that they saw Brody try to grab her from the
carriage. The fact that Brody was a well-known criminal who
had been killed with his own gun helped things be wrapped
up quicker than they might have otherwise.

She felt nothing but relief that the man who had caused Simon and Daisy so much grief would be gone from their lives

for good. They both deserved to live their lives free from his dark shadow.

It was nearing noon as Eliza stood in her bedroom as her mother and sisters helped her dress. Her mother had acquired the orange blossoms she sought the day before and tucked them into her hair. Cora had brought along her own wedding dress for Eliza to wear for the occasion, since they hadn't the time to commission a new one. It was a beautiful, pure white silk with intricate lace edging and layering that flattered her figure. Jenny fashioned a bouquet for her to carry with the leftover orange blossoms and a few lilies from the suite's drawing room. She tied them all together with ribbon.

"I am so proud of you, Eliza, and you are so beautiful." Fanny smiled at Eliza's reflection at the dressing table. She stood behind her, admiring her handiwork in styling Eliza's hair. She had left it down to fall in soft waves with it pulled up at the temples where she had tucked in the orange blossoms like a crown.

"I hope Simon thinks so," Eliza said.

"Simon will think he's marrying a fairy princess," Cora said as she joined their mother and Eliza turned to face them.

"I can hardly believe it's happening." Eliza had felt like she'd been floating on a cloud all morning. Nothing seemed real because Simon would be hers now.

"Here." Jenny handed her the bouquet and smoothed down the edge of Eliza's veil.

She had opted to wear it so that it fell down her back rather than over her face, which was tradition. Nothing else in her life had happened in a traditional way, so she saw no reason not to flout tradition when it suited her. She didn't want anything between her and Simon.

"You do look beautiful," Jenny added.

"Are you certain about this, Jenny?"

"Yes, will you stop asking me that?"

"But Brody isn't a threat anymore. We don't need the inheritance."

"You don't need it? Eliza, that is *your* inheritance." In a softer tone, she added, "Besides, I gave my word, and if I back out now, Mr. Hathaway will definitely try to stop you so that he can get Mainwaring back. It's not worth the risk. Also, David and I have come to an agreement. It will be fine; you'll see. Now don't think about it anymore, and go get married so that you can enjoy your wedding night," Jenny said.

Cora snickered at the wedding night remark. "I don't think that will be a problem for her."

Eliza rolled her eyes and said, "Then let's get this started. I can't wait any longer."

They all agreed that it was time and her sisters preceded her out the door. Fanny gave her a final kiss on the cheek with a whisper of congratulations before following them. The foyer was empty by the time Eliza had done one last check in the mirror to make certain she looked her very best. The middle door that led to the drawing room where the wedding would take place was open. She walked to the threshold and the whole room quieted. Everyone was already on their feet.

Simon stood before the windows. He'd been speaking with the registrar but fell silent the moment she appeared. His eyes almost glowed with appreciation and love when he saw her. He wore a suit she'd never seen before, but it was undoubtedly one of the more formal ones he'd had made during his time at Montague Club. It was dove-gray and fit him well. His black eye from the prizefight had nearly faded entirely. There was only a little discoloration on the fine skin underneath his eye. He was breathtaking.

He held Daisy in his arms. She had been so happy to see him yesterday that she told everyone who would listen that her papa had come home. It seemed that she had reclaimed him today. Eliza had bought her a satin dress in light blue to wear for the occasion, and Fanny had made a matching crown of orange blossoms for her hair. The child smiled when she saw Eliza and yelled out, "Auntie Liza," which had everyone chuckling.

Eliza blinked back the happy tears that sprang to her eyes and rushed over to them. Leaning up, she kissed Daisy on the cheek. "Are you ready for this wedding?" she asked her. Daisy nodded and so Eliza turned her attention to Simon. "How about you, Mr. Cavell?"

He smiled down at her, a good bit of awe in his expression. "I still can't get over the fact that ye chose me. I want to get it done before ye change yer mind."

She laughed and he leaned down to kiss her before the disapproving countenance of the registrar. The next few minutes passed quickly. They repeated the vows that the official said, but all Eliza remembered was that Simon held her hand the entire time and stared at her like a man who was in love. That was the only vow she needed.

When it was finished, Fanny erupted into applause and the room followed suit. It was the happiest moment of Eliza's life.

"I love you, Simon," she whispered after he kissed her. "I love you, too, Daisy." The girl giggled and then Simon kissed Daisy's cheek and she laughed even harder, which made everyone laugh.

Eliza could hardly believe this was her life. She was very glad that she had listened to her bad angel and followed Simon that night at Montague Club. Had her good angel won that debate, none of this would have ever happened and she would have missed out on the best man she had ever known.

Simon saw her watching him and put his arm around her, pulling her close. "I will love you for all of my life, Eliza Cavell," he whispered near her ear.

She couldn't ask for anything more than that.

EPILOGUE

Montague Club
Six months later

I CAN LISTEN NO LONGER IN SILENCE. I MUST SPEAK
*to you by such means as are within my reach. You pierce
my soul. I am half agony, half hope. Tell me—"*

"Half agony, half hope!" Simon sat up abruptly and rolled
over on top of her, sending the novel, *Persuasion*, crashing to
the floor of their bedroom. The bed frame creaked under the
quick movement. "Ye stole the line."

Eliza laughed and defended herself the only way she could;
she tickled him. He laughed but quickly dragged her hands
over her head, rendering her completely defenseless to him.

Eliza enjoyed reading every night before going to sleep.
Once, a few weeks after their wedding, Simon had asked her
to read aloud to him. She had quickly surmised that he had
never read a book before. A few well-placed questions had led
her to the conclusion that he actually wasn't very advanced at
reading. He could read inventory lists, playbills, and the occasional letter, but a longer text like a novel that required deeper
insight and vocabulary was lost to him. Not because he was

incapable of learning the skill, but because he'd never had the opportunity to acquire it. So now she read to him almost every night, and he always came to her eager to know what would happen next in whatever particular book they were reading together. For Christmas, she had given him his own book, a short adventure novel like the kind she had passed to Jones, and he read on his own on the days he didn't work at Montague Club.

"I borrowed it," she explained. "*Stealing* is such a dramatic word. Besides, it perfectly summed up my feelings."

He shook his head. "Wot do ye reckon to be a fitting punishment for thievery, Mrs. Cavell?"

She smiled up at his beloved face. "I'm not certain, but if it has anything to do with that thing in your drawers pressing against my thigh, then I'm a glutton for punishment."

He started tickling her before she could finish, and her words ended in a half scream, half laugh.

"No, wait. Please! I have something very serious to tell you."

He released her and rolled off her but only barely. "If this is a trick . . ." he teased.

"It's not a trick." She sat up and noticed how his eyes lingered on the way her nightdress pulled tight against her bosom. She didn't think she would ever get tired of the way he looked at her.

It was well after midnight and he'd only returned from his shift at the club a quarter hour ago. Just long enough to strip down to his drawers and crawl into bed with her. She had changed from reading a text she had been assigned at college on Roman history to *Persuasion* by Jane Austen, the book they were currently reading together.

Camille and Jacob had given them a suite in the house attached to Montague Club. Since they spent most of their time in Paris now, the arrangement worked well. It had three bed-rooms, a drawing room, a parlor, and a study. Daisy had one of the rooms. A nanny came during the day to help take care of Daisy when Eliza had her studies and Simon his work. One day they would find their own home, but this suited them now.

Heni had decided that she wanted to attend a highly rec-ommended girls' school in the country, and she came home to her own room to live with them on holidays and breaks. Thanks to Eliza's inheritance, they had been able to fund sev-eral scholarships to the school for girls in Whitechapel. She hoped to fund many more in the years to come. She had also begun to work with August, Violet, and her sisters to open a trade school for the older children there who otherwise would be forced to become laborers.

She moved to the little writing desk she kept in their spa-cious bedroom and rifled through the books there until she found the leather-bound portfolio she sought. When she turned back to him, he was lying against the pillows, one arm behind his head, watching her in obvious appreciation. A ner-vous quiver flickered in her stomach. When August had brought the file to her earlier that day, it had seemed like such a good idea, but now she wasn't so sure.

What if he didn't want to know? What if it had been best to leave things alone?

She padded over to the bed and sat down beside him.

"Since August is active on the board of the London Home for Young Women and the orphanage attached to it, I asked if she might use her contacts to look into the old foundling home's records."

He stilled and his gaze dropped to the folder in her hand.

"It took some time, but she was finally able to locate where their records had been stored."

"What did they find?" he asked, his voice hoarse.

"I haven't looked inside because I thought you might not want me to, or that you might not want to know yourself. But it's here if you decide that you do."

He looked at the folder she had placed on the bed for a long time before he picked it up. Then he moved with purpose and efficiency, determined to see the task through. She had seen him that way at work. Something she got to do frequently now that she had unfettered access to the club.

He pulled out a few handwritten scraps of paper. His name was on top of one and Mary's on the other. "It says we were found in December 1855. They believe I was four months old and Mary a year and a half when we were left."

"That means you're twenty-three years old."

He nodded.

"Perhaps you were born in August, then?"

"That would be a good guess." He scanned the pages and said, "There doesn't seem to be much of anything else. Care to look?"

She took the papers from him and he was right. The people who had found them had given statements; there was no other identifying information, but at least he knew his age.

Setting the papers and folder aside, she said, "Shall we celebrate your birthday on our wedding anniversary, or would you like your own day?"

He smiled and pulled her onto his lap. "You've found a way to make the best day of my life even better."

"You are entirely too charming for words, Mr. Cavell."

She kissed him until they both had to come up for air and he said, "Now about that punishment . . ."

"You've been threatening to turn me over your knee for ages. You're just looking for an excuse."

"Looks as if I've found it," he growled playfully. "Now still yourself so we can be done with it. I want to know the rest of what Captain Wentworth wrote to Anne."

She squealed and tried to get away, but it was too late. She was caught and she loved every minute of it.

AUTHOR'S NOTE

Thank you for reading Eliza and Simon's story. I would like to share with you a little bit of the research that went into creating this story. I find it all very fascinating, but feel free to skip this if you don't.

Although I delved into the world of prizefighting in *The Heiress Gets a Duke*, I wasn't able to explore the culture of bare-knuckle brawling as deeply as I wanted because the hero in that book was a duke. He participated in it and even made a name for himself, but he lived on the outside of that world. I was excited to return to that world with Simon, a man who had grown up in Whitechapel and earned his livelihood for a time with his fists.

It is important to note that much of the prizefighting culture in this book is fictionalized. At the time of this book, there were two different schools/rules for bare-knuckle brawling. These were London Prize Ring Rules and Queensbury Rules. The Georgian and Regency eras were the height of bare-knuckle brawling popularity in England, but toward the end of the Regency era it was seen as too uncivilized and dangerous and fell out of favor with the upper and middle classes. The London Prize Ring Rules were developed in the early Victorian era in England and were a codified version of the unwritten rules that had been in place for about a hundred years. It was a first attempt to "civilize" the sport. This was followed by the Queensbury Rules, which went a step further by requiring padded gloves, set rules for timed rounds, and made wrestling illegal. The prizefighting in this book is inspired by the earlier set of rules, which set only the most basic parameters for participant safety.

Coffeehouses were a huge part of London life in the seventeenth and eighteenth centuries. They were a place for people to gather to discuss all manner of topics, much like we think of the public house. Individual coffeehouses were generally associated with different social classes, professions, and political leanings, so you would know where to go to find like-minded people. It is true that their popularity decreased with the rise in popularity of tea in the nineteenth century, but they still existed and tended to cater to the working classes.

On the subject of coffeehouses, in the book Mainwaring and his friends are said to be visiting coffeehouses, a code word for brothels. This is true. *Coffeehouse* was sometimes used as a more polite way to refer to a brothel. This probably goes back to the fact that occasionally a coffeehouse would do a fair brothel business on the side. It was open in the very early morning hours to coincide with the opening of markets when workers would be looking for a caffeine fix. But this might also be the same time that young men were wandering home after a night out. It was a way to serve both sets of clientele.

One of the most famous of these was Tom King's Coffee House in Covent Garden back in the eighteenth century. It was run by husband and wife Tom and Moll King. Their coffeehouse was notorious for aiding and abetting the prostitution in the area. While the couple was brought up on charges of running a brothel, they escaped prosecution due to lack of evidence. There were no rooms or beds in their establishment where the actual prostitution might take place. Instead, their establishment served as a meeting place for prostitutes and their clients. Once an agreement was reached, the prostitute and client would then relocate to another location to finish the transaction.

I was excited to dive into the rich history of the Whitechapel area and try to bring it to life. The scenes that are set there feature the landscape and real buildings that were present when Eliza and Simon were walking the streets on their night out. For example, the church of St. Mary Matfelon was standing when Simon points it out to Eliza. It had recently reopened in 1877 after the previous church had been lost to fire. Sadly, that version was mostly destroyed by fire a few years later in 1880 and was rebuilt again. That church was destroyed during the blitz in World War II. This time the destruction was cleared, and the space was turned into a garden.

Wilton's Music Hall was a real place on Graces Alley. Part of the building itself actually existed way back in the seventeenth century. It was expanded when John Wilton built a theater adding on to the original structure in 1859. It's an example of a pub hall where working men and women would come for food, drink, and entertainment after their shifts ended. Wilton wanted to bring the West End quality of entertainment to the working class of the East End. To that end, well-known entertainers were often invited to perform, including George Leybourne. The original music hall was destroyed by fire in 1877 and was undergoing reconstruction during the time of this story, but I couldn't resist writing about such an interesting place.

George Leybourne was a world-famous music hall entertainer. Many say he was the first successful music hall performer. His song "Champagne Charlie," which debuted in

1866, was as well-known in the United States as it was in Britain, with many other singers performing it from time to time. Another of his songs, "If Ever I Cease to Love," Simon sings in the book. It is interesting to note that some lines from this song were considered scandalous. However, it became a Mardi Gras anthem in New Orleans in 1872 and still can be heard there to this day.

I would be remiss in not mentioning how difficult it was for London's East Enders to raise children during this time. Unfortunately, Society has been judging women and how they raise their children since the beginning of time. In Victorian England, women were judged by how many babies they birthed who lived to maturity. If one died, then the mother was blamed. The popular thought of the day was that Queen Victoria had birthed and raised nine children without losing one to death, so she became a paragon of womanhood to which women should aspire. Since the Queen had not breast-fed her children, and indeed considered the practice ruinous to an intelligent woman, the proper woman should not as well. Unfortunately, many women did not have the means to hire a wet nurse. This meant that the use of makeshift formula came into widespread use. This wasn't the nutritionally balanced formula that we know today, but usually a mix of flour (or bread), milk, and water known as pap.

For a working woman in Whitechapel the situation was even worse. She probably wouldn't have had the choice to breastfeed or not, as she would have gone back to working long hours very soon after giving birth. She also might have been too malnourished herself to be able to breastfeed. The pap given to these babies was usually made with more water than milk to save on the cost. Combine that with the flour available in the East End, which was frequently modified with chalk additive because it was cheaper than wheat, and the babies there were hardly receiving any nutrition at all.

Much of the high infant and child mortality rate in the Victorian era is attributed to poor nutrition. Another reason is due to the implements used to feed the formula to the babies. Sometimes a glass pap boat was used. This was a little boat-shaped dish with a spout on one end so the formula could be poured into the baby's mouth. However, the rubber nipple and bottle were growing in popularity, and marketing of these items further pressured women to give up breastfeeding and wet nurses. Unfortunately, these were not the nipples and bottles that we know today. It took several decades for the modern bottle shape to evolve.

The original bottle was a banjo shape with a slope that made it very difficult to clean, so bacteria would settle on the bottom of the bottle. The rubber nipple was attached to a long rubber tube connected to the bottle; both were porous, so they absorbed bacteria. In fact, most rubber implements were not cleaned and were simply used for a couple of weeks and then discarded. Bacteria would seep into the infants' lungs and cause pneumonia, or into their intestines and cause diseases such as dysentery. (If you've read *The Stranger I Wed*, you know that some politicians of the time were still denying germ theory so that wealthy landowners wouldn't be forced to modernize sewers and sanitation systems. Yet, these politicians readily stressed the importance of mothers taking personal responsibility for the deaths of their infants while denying germ theory and exacerbating unsanitary living conditions.)

This is why I had Simon hire a wet nurse for Daisy, even though it was very expensive. I couldn't bear the thought of her growing up on pap and those bottles. The problem was so bad that the rubber hose and banjo–style bottle combination was eventually referred to as a "murder bottle."

Finally, Bedford College was the first college of higher education for women in England. It was founded by Elizabeth Jesser Reid, whose goal was to provide women with academic courses that went beyond the typical governess training, which was the common education for women at that time. Initially, the professors were all male, so the school hired women they called "Lady Visitors" to sit in on the classes and chaperone the female students. They also raised eyebrows by allowing women to draw live figures, instead of learning from statues. I like to imagine Eliza working her way through her academic studies there and then going on to take on the world.

ACKNOWLEDGMENTS

My eternal thanks to my editor, Sarah Blumenstock. Your insight and feedback are invaluable to me. You help me find the heart of these stories and are an all-around amazing editor. Thank you to my agent, Kevan Lyon, who is an absolute pleasure to work with. A gigantic thank-you to my team at Berkley, who work so hard to make my books shine. (And, especially, my long-suffering copyeditor, who has to catch all of my mistakes!) Thank you to my sister Gertrudes: Marielle and Vik. You help me brainstorm and always listen as I whine about my stories. To all of my writer friends who offer me guidance and unlimited support, I could not do this without you.

Finally, thank you to my readers who keep coming back to read my stories. I love how you love my characters as much as I do.

Turn the page for a look at Cora's story in

THE STRANGER I WED

Available now from Berkley Romance!

Oxfordshire, England
Spring 1878

TITLE-HUNTING WAS NOT FOR THE FAINT OF HEART. The occupation required a great deal of analysis, focus, and attention to detail, three qualities Cora Dove had no choice but to perfect. One had to be strategic when choosing the ideal candidate for a husband. Everyone knew that the perfect groom for a title hunter was a fortune hunter. However, it simply wasn't that easy. Too impoverished and the wealth gained from the marriage would drain away like water through a sieve.

Cora was determined that the man she married not be a gambler, at least not to excess. The likelihood of finding an aristocrat who did not gamble at all would be akin to finding a fish that did not swim. There were other considerations, too. In fact, she had made a list. Too young and he'd likely be brash and unruly. Too old and he could hold outdated ideas about a wife's role. Too temperamental or too wicked in his pursuits and he would be difficult to manage. Too attractive and heartache would inevitably ensue—this one had been the last to go on the list. Cora quite liked good-looking men and wouldn't have minded marrying one. Her sister Jenny, however, who knew more than she about the qualities of handsome men, had been insistent, so the condition had gone on the list. Only a fool would aim for the highest title and leave it at that when there were so many other considerations.

Cora was no fool. Not anymore. She had stepped off the steamer ship from New York with her mother and Eliza last week with her mission at the forefront of her mind. Find a titled husband and marry him by summer. Thankfully, she would not face the task alone. Camille, Dowager Duchess of Hereford, had agreed to act as a sort of agent to help the sisters find titled husbands.

"Camille, pardon my disbelief, but there can't possibly be suitors here," Eliza, Cora's youngest sister, remarked, her brow furrowed in distinct displeasure.

The three of them descended the steps of the train depot, umbrellas in hand to combat the spring drizzle. The train stretched out behind them on the track, belching steam into the cool air. They were in a small village—Cora had already forgotten the name—not far from Camille's country estate in Oxfordshire. The town was little more than a stop along the railroad, but it was quaint and picturesque, as Cora was finding most English villages to be. They possessed a charm lent to them by virtue of age that many of the industrial mill towns that had sprung up back home didn't have. The buildings, made of either stone or wattle and daub, had been standing for centuries longer than their brownstone back in New York. There was a security in that permanence that she found comforting.

"I quite like it," Cora said.

"As do I," Camille voiced her agreement.

Cora and her sisters had met Camille many years ago when Mr. Hathaway and Fanny were still an item, though their relationship had been in its death throes. Camille's father and Mr. Hathaway had finished some sort of business deal together, and they had been invited to spend a week with the Bridwells at their summer home. It had been an awkward week, and Cora now realized it was because Mrs. Bridwell hadn't approved of their presence there, even though Mr. Bridwell hadn't been above putting his company's profits ahead of what was socially acceptable. Cora and Camille had spent most of the time together outdoors swimming and playing on the rope swings. Thankfully, Camille remembered her and had been a wonderful source of support when Cora had contacted her with the marriage plan.

The duchess wasn't a proponent of the cash-for-class marriages that were becoming so popular between American heiresses and impoverished noblemen. Her own parents had all but auctioned her off to the highest title, and the marriage had been deeply unhappy until the much older duke had died and set her free. Now she was with Jacob Thorne, a man she loved. It had taken several letters and a few telegrams before Cora had convinced Camille that this marriage was what she wanted and that she was not being coerced by her mother. It was her negligent sire who had made this sort of marriage necessary, but Cora preferred not to dwell on that.

Instead, she devoted every waking moment to finding the perfect husband. She had a journal specifically for the task that she had diligently filled with notes about each man Camille proposed to her. She knew their ages, their immediate family members, and how they spent their days. Perhaps more importantly, she knew how their family had lost their own fortunes. That crucial bit of information could be the difference between a comfortable future and one spent scraping pennies.

Unlike the other American heiresses who came from new money families with industrial interests that kept their pockets deep, Cora and her sisters were illegitimate. They weren't marrying for mere social status, though that would be a boon; they were marrying for the very survival of their small family.

"Then you can marry any gentleman who might reside here. I'll choose one who lives in London." Eliza nodded her head in finality and Cora hid her grin. If only it were that easy of a choice.

"I understand the conditions are not ideal," Camille said, leading them around the muck and mud of the road to the higher-packed earth along the edge. They didn't seem to be heading toward the center of town but in the other direction along a narrow lane that followed the tracks before turning away. "But being able to observe these men outside of normal social conditions will give you rare insight. Since they don't know you yet and don't know that you're watching, they'll be more inclined to be themselves. Once at the house party, they'll all be on their best behavior, and you'll only see what they allow you to see."

That was certainly true. Of the ten men Camille had invited to the upcoming house party at Stonebridge Cottage, they had been able to observe five without them being aware. First, they had gone to the Lakes, where they had discreetly assessed two of their suitors who were participating in an angler tournament. They were two of the most boring individuals Cora had ever encountered. Since boredom hadn't made it onto her list, they had passed the test. Then, they had gone to a lecture at the British Museum to locate a third who had been a bit argumentative with the lecturer. She had drawn a line through his name. She wouldn't countenance a rude husband. From there, they had quietly observed two others at Hyde Park. Both were a bit snobbish in their bearing, so Cora had put a question mark by their names. Today was their last jaunt before the house party began early next week. They were here to watch a football game.

"I'm afraid the match has already begun, but we'll be able to see enough to judge their sportsmanship. I know that's not on your list, but you can learn a lot from how a man treats his teammates and adversaries," Camille continued. "Perhaps we can pop over to the public house and watch them after, though that might be pushing things."

It wouldn't do to have anyone recognize the duchess. Once they heard the sisters' American accents, their disguises of plain clothes would be quite useless to hide their identities from their prospective suitors. All objectivity would be gone, and they would lose their chance to observe them unaware.

"Perhaps we can watch for a time," Cora said.

They rounded a corner after a row of tiny houses onto a narrow dirt lane that led to a field. It did appear the game was already in progress with roughly two dozen men on the pitch. Half wore green shirtsleeves while the other half wore yellow. Both wore trousers or pantaloons that would never be white again with all the mud, along with high socks and leather boots, and their heads were bare. They chased a round leather ball across the field in a match that was much more physical than she had anticipated.

"Careful of your step, dear," Camille said, indicating a particularly deep puddle, and Cora lithely stepped around it.

When she had righted herself, the duchess and Eliza were continuing on their way to the left where a robust crowd had
gathered to cheer on the players.

Cora stood transfixed at the sheer physicality of the drama
playing out on the field. One man hurried to kick the ball,
grunting when another one ran into him, nearly sending him
careening on the soaked ground. The ball had only been
glanced, which sent it several yards toward the far side. Another man, his golden hair damp with sweat and rain and
falling about his face, cursed and then let out a victorious yell
as he ran through several opponents and managed to make
good contact with the ball, kicking it in an arc, sending it farther downfield toward the goal. The players turned as one and
hurried in that direction. If there was any sort of coordination
among them, Cora couldn't see it. They all seemed madcap in
their zeal to obtain the ball.

For a moment, she was struck by the sheer size and athlet-
icism of the men. Without a coat to hide them, their shoulders
appeared extra wide, the muscles working under the thin material of their shirts as they ran, the rain melding the fabric to
them. Their chests seemed thick and strapped with sinew. It
suddenly became apparent why good Society insisted on a
man wearing his coat at all times. It might prove too distracting otherwise. Although, most Society men she had met had a
bit of soft about them. Not like these men.

She smiled to herself and began to make her way over to
where Camille and Eliza had joined the spectators. However,
she couldn't stop herself from looking back at the one who had
kicked the ball. He was tall and muscled, his jaw square and
firm as his eyes narrowed, watching to see which way the ball
would go when it finally broke free of the group. He loped
easily toward his teammates, his long legs eating up the dis-

tance without making him seem out of breath. It was probably too much to hope that he would be one of her suitors, though the fact that he was so handsome meant he violated a rule on her list and she shouldn't consider him anyway.

As she stared at him, the ball suddenly broke free of the chaos on the field, hurtling in her direction. A player roughly her own size came rushing toward her, his eyes crazed with ferocity as he screamed with the triumph of a predator about to seize its prey. She barely got a look at him before the man she had been admiring yelled, "Briggs!" drawing her attention back to him. He'd picked up speed, running full bore in their direction, ostensibly to intercept his teammate from flattening her.

She sidestepped the ball, somehow managing to miss Briggs but stepping into the path of the golden-haired man. He tried to stop, but the change in momentum sent him skidding over a patch of mud and directly into her. Her breath rushed out of her at the initial contact, flinging her umbrella and journal in the air, and her own feet caught the mud and they tumbled to the ground together. He twisted, catching the brunt of the fall, but they rolled several more times before coming to a stop in the soggy grass. The players were still following the ball, and as they lumbered closer, sounding like a herd of cattle, she closed her eyes, expecting them to fall over her and the man. The anticipated disaster never happened as they continued running down the field. She opened her eyes to see his staring down at her. They were green like emeralds and intense with concern. She had never seen a color like them on anything but a cat.

"Are you hurt?" he asked.

She took in a breath, surprised to find that nothing was sore. "I don't think so." Her voice came out sounding winded.

He leaned over her as he ran a hand over her rib cage and

up over her breast. She gasped as he pressed, no doubt looking for injury, but her nipple tightened beneath his touch just the same, and her blood warmed in a way that was unseemly. She sucked in a hard breath. "Excuse me!"

"You are hurt."

"No!" She wrenched his hand away.

His brow furrowed, flummoxed by her outrage. "No?"

Perhaps he hadn't realized that he had all but fondled her breast with his pawing. She took in another breath and managed to speak in a calmer tone. "I am uninjured." She attempted to sit up as embarrassment began to creep in, but she was stuck beneath the weight of his thigh over hers—his very large, very solid thigh. In fact, his entire body seemed very large and very solid above her. She ought to feel more put out, but suddenly, she didn't quite mind lying here like this beneath him.

"Let me help you up," he said just as she was becoming accustomed to his attentions. Removing himself from her, he offered her his hand.

She took it, still too aware of him in a physical sense. Her heart pounded as heat suffused her cheeks. At his full height, he stood nearly a head taller than her. His torso might well have been double the width of hers. Aside from a few dances, she had never been this close to a man before, and certainly not one so attractive.

"You might watch where you're going next time." She was struggling to catch her breath as if she were the one who had run across the field. Her hand shook when she took it back, so she wiped at the blades of grass stuck to her bodice to hide the tremble. His hands followed, helping her wipe the debris away and sending her nerve endings teetering wildly.

Before she could gather herself to protest—which may have

taken a while, considering a very real part of her was enjoying the attention—he said, "You might have stayed off the pitch."

His words cut through the havoc within her. "I wasn't on the pitch. I was off to the side. Your friend, Briggs, was outside of the boundary."

"You play association football, do you?" His gaze narrowed in obvious irritation.

"No, but every game has a boundary line. I was outside of yours." She turned to indicate that fact, but there didn't actually seem to be a line designating any boundary.

His brow rose dubiously.

"Are you blaming me for the fact that you ran me over?" she asked.

His lips tightened in what might have been a suppressed grin. "No, of course not."

"Good." She wiped at her skirt.

He walked the few steps necessary to pick up her journal and umbrella, handing them back to her. After she took them, he scraped his hair out of his face, sending rivulets of water running down his cheeks. She couldn't help but watch one make its way to his mouth, where it slid smoothly over his bottom lip.

"Perhaps the next time you see the ball and an entire team of men coming toward you, you might consider removing yourself from the field of play."

There was a spark of humor in his eyes that somehow softened his words. The result was that she felt mildly annoyed but greatly intrigued. "Perhaps you might consider keeping your ball and your men on the pitch."

He smiled, but only for a second before someone called out, "Dev!" and his head swiveled in that direction.

He sobered a bit, the spark of mirth dying out as he glanced toward Camille and Eliza, who were hurrying toward them, before asking, "You're an American, are you?"

Damn. She'd forgotten all about not talking to anyone. "Yes, I'm visiting friends."

He seemed to size up Camille and then glanced at Cora once more. With a tip of his head, he ran back out onto the field to join the fray.

"Cora!" Eliza ran up and held her umbrella over them both to block the sprinkle of rain.

"That looked horrific. Are you hurt?" Camille wiped at the grass and mud on Cora's skirt with a handkerchief, nearly losing her hat and veil in the process.

"Not unless you count my bruised pride." Cora smiled and led them away from the field.

"He might have broken your ribs," Eliza said, somewhat indignant on her behalf.

"But he didn't."

"Thank goodness for that," Camille added, standing to her full height, her attention back on the game still in play. "He hasn't yet confirmed his attendance at the house party. If he broke your rib, I suspect he wouldn't come at all."

Cora whipped around to look at her friend before finding the man called Dev among the players. He whooped and raised his hands above his head in triumph as his teammate scored a goal. "Dev," she whispered. Then louder, "Devonworth?"

"Yes, that was the Earl of Devonworth," Camille confirmed for her.

That name was in her journal. She had written down his family members, his family history, and the fact that he was passionate about his seat in Parliament. She had thought he might be an ideal candidate for husband because he met all the requirements. Except now she knew he was handsome. Too handsome, really. He completely violated the last rule.

For the first time, Cora understood why Jenny had insisted on that rule. It would be terribly difficult to divorce a man so tempting.

Harper St. George grew up in the rural backwoods of Alabama and the northwest Florida coast, where her love of history began. She now makes her home in the Atlanta area writing historical fiction romance set in various time periods, from the Viking Era to the Gilded Age. Her novels have been translated into ten languages.

VISIT THE AUTHOR ONLINE

HarperStGeorge
HarperStGeorge
HarperStGeorge.com